A s... appeared on V.... ...
And it was growing fast.

Foam gushed out through Victor's clenched teeth and his body shook. "Do it, Alex," he rasped, choking and gagging. "Do it!"

Alex released the safety and pointed his weapon at the dying man. Just as he was about to fire, Victor's gray hand suddenly shot out and grabbed Jo's shoulder. He pulled the surprised woman on top of him as Jo screamed in horror.

They were too late. The colloid had taken over.

And suddenly Jo wasn't screaming any-more . . .

Other Avon Books by
Tim Sullivan

DESTINY'S END

THE PARASITE WAR

TIM SULLIVAN

AVON BOOKS ◆ NEW YORK

THE PARASITE WAR is an original publication of Avon Books.
This work has never before appeared in book form. This work is a
novel. Any similarity to actual persons or events is purely coincidental.

AVON BOOKS
A division of
The Hearst Corporation
105 Madison Avenue
New York, New York 10016

Copyright © 1989 by Timothy R. Sullivan
Front cover illustration by Doug Beekman
Published by arrangement with the author
Library of Congress Catalog Card Number: 89-91347
ISBN: 0-380-75550-5

First Avon Books Printing: December 1989

AVON TRADEMARK REG. U.S. PAT. OFF. AND IN OTHER COUNTRIES, MARCA
REGISTRADA, HECHO EN U.S.A.

Printed in the U.S.A.

RA 10 9 8 7 6 5 4 3 2 1

For Wendy

ACKNOWLEDGMENTS

To Valerie Smith, Michael Swanwick, Terry Bisson for naming the other baby, Gardner Dozois for naming this baby; and special thanks to Greg Frost for his valuable help in weapons research. The author would also like to acknowledge the influence of certain works by Robert A. Heinlein, Philip K. Dick, Jack Finney, and Hal Clement.

Ah! wherefore with infection should he live,
And with his presence grace impiety,
That sin by him advantage should achieve
And lace itself with his society?
Why should false painting imitate his cheek
And steal dead seeing of his living hue?
Why should poor beauty indirectly seek
Roses of shadow, since his rose is true? . . .

—WILLIAM SHAKESPEARE
(from Sonnet LXXVII)

Chapter One

CHAPTER ONE

The room was dark. Just enough moonlight slanted through the broken windows for Alex Ward to make out the debris littering the floor, chunks of ceiling plaster lying in heaps amid the wrecked office furniture. He had gone from one floor to the next, until he had ascended almost to the top of this abandoned insurance building. He was looking for something—anything—that he could sell in the sewer, but the lower floors had been picked clean. His best chances were up high in these old executive suits, where he might find a bottle of liquor behind a wall painting, or a gold pen and pencil set, something he could trade for food or ammunition.

Besides, there weren't likely to be any colloids up here. He couldn't afford to waste ammunition, so it was best to hunt where attacks were infrequent . . . infrequent, but not unheard of. Alex fondled the barrel of his Ingram 9mm to reassure himself.

He overturned some plaster lumps with his boot. Underneath them was something with a shiny edge that might have been glass or metal. He reached down and gently pried it loose. Dusting it off, he held it up to the moonlight.

It was a photograph in a gilt frame, showing a man and two young children smiling through the cracked glass. They were probably the husband and kids of the executive who used to inhabit this office. Most likely all four were dead by now. If they weren't, they wished they were . . . that much was certain.

Alex sighed and stuffed the picture under his shirt, figuring the frame would be worth something.

He walked slowly, stepping around a yard-wide hole in the floor, and entered the adjoining room. The windows, ten feet high from floor to ceiling, had long ago been smashed, and a cool breeze stirred the dust on the floor, piling it against the wainscoting.

Hundreds of feet below, the dead city streets were a blackened labyrinth, littered with insectile wrecked cars. Few buildings stood intact. The crumbled ruin of Independence Hall aroused memories of Philadelphia as it had been, before the colloids came. The old city had been vibrant then, but now those days seemed as distant as a dream.

Something flapped out of the shadows, flying straight at his face from the floor above. Its unearthly shriek echoed in the enclosed space as Alex crouched and flailed at it with the Ingram. It sailed past his head, stirring the short hairs on the back of his neck, and smacked onto the wall beside him. It clung there, pulsing in the moonlight, a four-foot-long, shapeless thing.

It would be on him again in a second if he didn't kill it. Alex fired a burst and the thing exploded in wet, stinking chunks. Hot liquid splattered onto his clothes and skin, as bits of the nonshape fell quivering to the floor.

Before he could take a breath, something snaked around his right ankle.

"Jesus!" He jerked his foot away before the pseudopod could get a purchase on him. Hopping backwards, he turned and nearly stepped into a viscous hump, its snake-like pseudopods whipping as it advanced. Behind it was a dripping coil that writhed like a worm in pain.

Time to go.

The Ingram's flash strobe-lit the room, its roar deafening as spray from the two monsters soaked his ragged clothing and burnt his skin. The acrid smell of burnt gunpowder mingled with the colloids' stench. Before the pieces of the three things could regroup, he sprinted toward the door, skidding on the slime and nearly falling. Heart pounding, he managed to stay on his feet and get into the outer office, where he was confronted with more colloids than he had ever hoped to see in one place. Leaping, squirming, burbling, chittering, gurgling, screaming—they came at him.

He fired, muscles straining against the recoil, and backed away as the colloids were torn to pustular shreds by 9mm slugs. The monsters wailed hideously, pieces of them spinning through the dusty air and slapping against the walls and floor. More of them closed in on him through the outer door, and the quaking remains of those he'd shot were starting to come after him, too. He couldn't kill them, could hardly slow them down. There was only one way out.

Behind him was the hole in the floor. It was ten or twelve feet to the lower level, and there was no telling what was down there, but he had no choice. He jumped.

He landed on his feet and fell to his knees, rolling over in plaster, wood, and masonry. He struck a jagged board, and a nail protruding from it ripped his clothing, tearing the skin on his back. Somehow he held onto the Ingram and managed to stand. His shin struck a fallen I-beam and he groaned, but he was still able to walk.

Looking up, he saw a bloated thing pulsing on the edge of the jagged hole. He kept the Ingram trained on it as he backed out of the room. No use wasting ammo if it stayed where it was.

There was nothing moving in the corridor. He had to get to the stairwell before the colloids did. Their hesitation wouldn't last long. He had allowed them to follow him upstairs and corner him, and it was only by dint of sheer manic energy that he had escaped.

The dark maw of an open elevator door was between him and the stairwell. Alex winced as he pressed his wounded back against the wall and slid by, facing the elevator. A colloid oozed out and slithered toward him. He fired, fingers and forearms aching, and sprinted for the stairwell, adrenaline pumping as caustic spray and his own hot blood soaked into his shirt. He took several stairs at a time, leaping down to each landing with the Ingram's barrel out in front of him, in case more colloids were waiting. His footsteps echoed in the stairwell. As he glanced over his shoulder to see if they were coming after him, he nearly stepped on a flowing mass of living tissue. The thing had crawled out from its roost behind the stairs, and he had surprised it as much as it had surprised him. Sensing his presence, it recoiled like an amoeba stung by electricity. Alex pointed the Ingram at it as the colloid pooled on the landing. He squeezed the trigger. The firing pin clicked on an empty chamber.

He was out of ammunition.

The colloid began to rush toward him, a coughing, gelatinous stream of gray tissue. It moved faster than it had any right to, but not fast enough to catch Alex. Grasping the handrail, he vaulted onto the stairs below, unable to keep his footing. He slammed down onto the next landing painfully. Dazed, he looked up to see the colloid descending the stairs like a sickly, slow-motion waterfall.

It would be on him in a second if he didn't move. Behind it were four or five more colloids, and he heard the liquid sounds of still others, just above. Alex somehow made it to his feet and bolted, taking the stairs three at a time.

It took a lifetime to get to the bottom and out into the night air. He hobbled down Market Street until he found a grating. Lifting it, he dropped it onto the cracked pavement with a clang. He climbed down into the filthy sewer water, grateful to have the burning spray washed from his body, and made his way west, away from the building where he had been attacked. By now, the street above was swarming with colloids. It was pitch dark down in the sewer, but it was the only place the colloids wouldn't go. They avoided any place where there was a lot of water.

Half an hour later, still wading waist-deep, caked blood gluing his shirt to his back, Alex stopped to catch his breath. He climbed up on a ledge and sat gasping. When he had recovered, and was convinced that he would not bleed to death, he took the framed photograph out and looked at it again. It was dawn by now, and enough light filtered through from the grating above for him to see.

Sweat dripped from the end of his nose onto the cracked glass covering the picture, as he permitted himself a moment of longing for the days when families like this one had existed. He'd had his own wife and kid, Sharon and Billy. It hurt to think about them.

Alex tucked the photograph into his tattered shirt. He got up and resumed moving, remembering that sentiment served no purpose in the scheme of things. These people in the photograph, even the children, no longer existed. Some of their tissues might live on, transformed into monstrosities like those that had attacked him tonight. But it would not do to think of the colloids as being human in any way. They were his enemies, and he had to fight them.

If only it wasn't so difficult to kill them.

Splashing into the filthy water, he surged ahead, growing more and more angry as he went. It was so unfair, being able to die while your enemies could hardly be killed. You could immerse them in water and dissolve them, or completely burn them, but these things were not easy to do. No matter how many pieces you blew them into, they kept coming. They would feed, recombine, and grow, and be just as threatening in a matter of days, or even hours. All you could do was slow them down, make them a bit more manageable, but if you didn't get away from them they'd mire you down and eat you alive. He'd seen people covered with the things, colloids of all kinds, different shapes and sizes—people drowning in them.

The thought made him move faster, dirty water rolling around his churning legs. The inability to slow down, even after the crisis had passed, was symptomatic of his illness. He had been hospitalized after Sharon and Billy died, back when there still were hospitals, because he had fallen into a deep depression. Bipolar disorder was the diagnosis—meaning that he was what used to be called a manic-depressive.

"Hey!"

Alex swung the Ingram around, forgetting that he had no bullets. A woman crouched against the wet, stone curve of the sewer.

"Don't shoot," she said. "I'm not infected."

He lowered the gun barrel, hoping that she wouldn't notice his trembling hands. "I can see that."

"What is that thing, an Uzi?"

"No, an Ingram 9mm, semi-automatic." He didn't mention that he had made it fully automatic by taping pennies under the firing mechanism. It was a trick he'd learned in the old days, from a casual conversation with an off-duty cop in a bar.

The woman moved closer, the sounds of swishing water around her. She was thin, with dark eyes and matted, curly hair. Not bad looking, but filthy . . . just like him.

"Have you got ammunition for it?" she asked. Her voice was husky.

"What do you want with me?" Alex asked abruptly, not wanting to answer her question.

The woman smiled knowingly, showing that she had all her teeth. "I want to know it you've got anything to trade."

"Are you packing?" he asked.

"Just this." She reached inside her ragged coat and showed him a .32 revolver. She stuffed it back where it had been. "So, what have you got for me?"

"How do I know you have anything worth trading?" demanded Alex, glaring at her.

"Kind of hyper, aren't you?" She smiled again. "What's your name, anyway?"

He hesitated, and then said, "Alex Ward."

"Alex Ward . . . I've heard of you. *Everybody's* heard of you."

"Yeah, right." Alex did not permit himself to exhibit pride. It was dangerous to have an inflated ego.

"No, I mean it. They say *you* don't hide out down in the sewer."

"So what am I doing here now?"

"Now maybe, but not all the time, not like the rest of us."

That was because he couldn't sit still for long, not once he got manic. He didn't tell her that, either.

"So what have you got to show me, Alex?"

Not sure why he was doing it, he withdrew the photograph from his clothing and handed it to her. She looked at it for a long time, and then handed it back to him.

"You don't want it?" he asked.

"I want it, but I can't afford it." She turned away, as if to leave.

"How do you know that?" he said. "I haven't named a price."

She whirled, sloshing dirty water at him. "I've only got one thing to offer," she said angrily.

"I know."

The woman was surprised. "You'd give me the picture? Just for sex?"

"Yeah."

"Been a while, huh?"

"Maybe."

She took his tremulous hand. Hers felt warm and dry.
"Want to know my name?" she asked softly.

He nodded.

"Jo." She began to lead him through the darkness.
After a few minutes they came to a storm drain raised up
about five feet above the water line. The grating had
been sealed with concrete. There was a ledge just below
the opening, making it easy to climb up. Inside the storm
drain was a dry place with old rags and blankets piled
high to make a nest. A kerosene lantern, some canned
goods and a plastic jug of water were on a ledge in the
back.

"They built a high-rise here, so they had to re-route
the drains," Jo explained, climbing up. "Just before the
colloids came."

"How do you know that?" Alex pushed himself up and
joined her on the bed of rags.

"My husband was the architect, and I remember him
complaining about all the trouble he was having with the
city, because the building extended out over the sewer.
The contractor had to dig a new drain."

How are the mighty fallen, Alex thought. This woman
had once had it all, and now she lived in a sewer. Still,
she had a better set-up than most of the survivors down
here; and the sewer was one of the few places in the city
where there *were* any survivors. She still looked pretty
good, and sex was a commodity that was always in de-
mand. She was doing all right, considering.

"Give me the picture," Jo said

He did as she asked.

She took off her torn clothing, revealing a slender,
shapely body that immediately aroused Alex. He removed
his clothes and she gently touched the raw scar on his
back.

"Now I'll give you what you need," she said.

Embracing, they began to kiss. Jo showed more interest than she had to, Alex thought, becoming wildly excited. In the dripping darkness they made long, feral love until he was spent, and he was able to sleep fitfully at last.

CHAPTER TWO

Alex had planned to slip away, but he couldn't pull his arm out from underneath Jo's head without nudging her. She blinked and opened her eyes to the dim light. "Good morning," she said, seeming to be wide awake already.

"Afternoon is more like it."

"Yeah. This morning was nice though, Alex."

He scratched at his beard. "It helped get me out of a bad state of mind. Last night I was jumped by more colloids than I've ever seen before."

"Well, they won't come down here." She stretched, and said, "How's that cut on your back?"

"It's healing." Alex listened to the susurrant gurglings from below. The sewer water was murky, but there were few pollutants in it anymore. It had been three years since a toilet had been flushed or a factory had dumped toxins in the rivers, so there was little chance of catching diseases. Other problems were imminent, though.

"It's September now," he said. "In a few weeks it'll be too cold to stay down here."

"It gets rough in the winter, but where else can you go?"

"Out of the city."

"And starve."

"People lived off the land for thousands of years. Besides, there aren't as many colloids out in the country."

"Farmer Alex, how do you know what it's like out in the country?" Jo asked.

He tried not to be annoyed at her sarcasm. "It stands to reason. Where there are fewer people, there have to be fewer colloids, too."

"What about animals?"

"Uh-uh. Humans are the food of choice." He felt Jo's

9

warm body shudder against him. After all this time, she still didn't like to think about it. Who did? Still, it was a fact of life. Colloids ate people.

"I've got to get some kerosene. You want to go to Suburban Station with me?" Jo asked.

"What for?"

"Well, for one thing, you said you were in a fire fight last night. You must need more bullets."

She was sharp. "Yeah, I need some ammo," he admitted, "but now I don't have anything left to trade."

"You gave me all your valuables, did you? I should be flattered." He liked the throaty way she said that. "Look, come with me, and I'll get you some bullets."

"You'd do that?" He didn't have many rounds left.

"Why not? I could use a partner."

"Like a pimp, you mean?" Alex asked sourly.

"No, a partner. I can do other things besides selling my body, you know."

He felt like a jerk. "Sorry. I didn't mean to insult you."

"Forget it." She sat up, pulled on a tattered jersey and stuffed a few items into a navy blue backpack. "You want to come?"

He shrugged. "Why not?"

As soon as they were both dressed, they ate half a can of beans and headed east. Jo took the lantern, since their route frequently led them through total darkness. Along the way they talked a little about the old days. Alex learned that Jo had been a social worker, and she seemed amused when he told her that he had worked in the city planner's office. Their destination, half an hour away through a series of interconnected passageways, was the Suburban Station Concourse underlying much of Philadelphia's Center City. Abandoned shops and restaurants lined the subterranean corridors, leading to the decaying commuter train station. The silent tunnels provided quick escape routes should colloids interrupt the bartering in this makeshift marketplace.

Alex and Jo walked up the broken concrete steps of the subway and saw a few people, most of them hiding in the shadows of the wrecked shops. All of them were armed.

"How's business, Jo?" a grizzled, gray-haired black man asked as they approached him. He sat with his back against the wall, resting his one arm on a stack of boxes. Alex had seen him before, but had never done business with him.

"Not bad, Victor. Got a sucker right here." She smiled at the one-armed man.

Alex looked carefully at her. Was she joking? Or was she so sure of herself that she dared to mock him?

"That man don't look like no sucker to me," Victor said, pointing his stump at Alex. "That's Alex Ward . . . and he's *bad*."

"He won't be bad for long, not unless you can sell me some bullets for that popgun he's got with him."

"Ingram nine? We might be able to do business."

It had never occurred to Alex that this guy would sell ammo. He was still learning, it seemed.

"I don't mind selling bullets to heroes," said Victor, "but I got to eat, too."

"You'll be able to get some food with this." Jo took out the picture and handed it to Victor.

"Pretty," he said.

"More than pretty," Jo replied. "That's real gold."

"Yeah, but it ain't got the value it once had."

"People still want it."

"Not when they got colloids crawling up they ass, they don't."

"Victor, don't give me that crap. You can get a lot of food with this, and a lot of ammo. You know that people want gold as much as they ever did."

Victor smiled, a beautiful, friendly smile. "Can't bullshit you Society Hill mamas about gold, I guess."

Jo stood with hands on hips, waiting to hear his offer. Alex tried to keep from laughing.

"I can give you two boxes."

"Two boxes! That won't last five minutes in a fire fight."

"If you can get it someplace else . . . "

Grudgingly, Jo shook her head and handed the photograph to Victor. They had all known that she would give in from the start. Nobody manufactured ammunition anymore, so its value went up steadily. It was, quite literally, as good as gold. Better, in fact.

"I meet you back here in a couple hours with the ammo," Victor said.

"Right now I need some kerosene," Jo said.

"Got that right here," Victor replied, moving the boxes around until he found one containing six stoppered glass bottles. He handed a bottle to her, and she stuffed it into her backpack along with the lantern.

"Are you gonna let him keep the picture without any collateral?" Alex said, feeling duty bound to comment on the apparent tenuousness of the deal.

Victor raised his eyebrows, but said nothing.

"You can trust him," said Jo. "Don't worry."

Victor stood up and stretched. "Be cool, hear?" He walked away, his footsteps echoing through the nearly empty Concourse.

"Want to take a look up top?" Alex said a few minutes later. He had never been good at waiting patiently.

"Now?" Jo looked a little nervous.

"No time like the present." Some action would do him good, and he wanted to see how Jo would handle herself up on the street. She had selected him for a partner, but he didn't know for sure if she was good enough to work with him. Besides, he might as well use up the last of his ammo.

She looked at him earnestly. "Okay."

They came up the stairs at Penn Center, across the street from City Hall. The giant clothespin statue lay broken on its side, part of it extending into the street. The colonnades of City Hall still stood, but the tower and the statue of William Penn had been destroyed by rocket fire during the war, in a vain attempt to wipe out the colloids before it was too late.

"I used to work on the fourth floor over there," Alex said.

"Oh, yeah?"

"What happened to your husband, the architect?" Alex asked as they were crossing the street.

"He woke up one morning with a growth on his chest," Jo said with controlled emotion. "He made an appointment with a dermatologist. They said they could squeeze him in next week. That was on Friday. He came home from his golf game early on Saturday. By midnight on Sunday, the colloid covered his chest. It ate him alive."

Alex felt a constriction in his throat. "That's pretty much what happened to my wife and kid."

They walked silently through the abandoned plaza,

watching for movement. The sun was warm, Indian summer weather. A breeze moved dust lazily across the cracked pavement of 15th Street.

"Been in City Hall lately?" Alex asked.

Jo seemed a little annoyed at his bravado. "Not in the past three years," she said, referring to the time since the colloids had taken over. "I like it better in the sewer."

"Some people said that *before* the war."

"I would have thought we'd see a colloid or two by now," Jo said.

"Why? There's not much food for them around here, not above ground. This neighborhood's been deserted for a long time."

They entered through an arch and moved cautiously into the passageway at the south entrance to City Hall, opposite Broad Street. Limestone boulders stood embedded in detritus, the remains of the fallen tower. They climbed over these to reach the open square at the building's heart. On the east side, Alex noticed a metal door that had always been locked before; he had failed to force it open on more than one occasion.

Nevertheless, it was ajar now.

"Somebody's been in there," he said softly. "Looks like they bent the door when they smashed the lock, and now they can't get it completely shut."

They approached the door, finding that it opened easily. When they saw what was in the dark storeroom beyond, they wished that they had left it alone.

A man lay on the floor, gasping and shuddering. A colloid sucked at him, clinging to his torso from crotch to throat. A pseudopod stretched across the right side of his face, and through the clear, pulsing gel, the corroding muscles of his jaw worked visibly.

The colloid, sensing their presence, oozed off the dying man in a pink gout, slurping toward a rusted vent.

"Burn it!" the dying man cried.

"Jo, the kerosene!" Alex fired a burst in front of the colloid to slow it down, as Jo yanked the jar out of her backpack and tossed it to him. Cradling the Ingram in the crook of his left arm, Alex unstopped the bottle and splashed it onto the colloid. The colloid heaved and flattened against the wall.

Alex reached inside his shirt and withdrew a tiny box. He smiled as he felt its dryness. Opening it and pulling out a match, he snapped his thumbnail against the matchhead. The light of the match flared in the dim light, revealing tools and cable spools. The acrid smell of sulphur stung his nostrils.

While it still burned, Alex tossed the match at the colloid. A shrill, unearthly scream filled the cramped space as the crawling thing went up in flames, writhing and blackening, shivering and shrinking into a charred, black heap. Its scream faded as it was consumed, until it was silent. An almost intolerable stench filled the storeroom. Black snowflakes fell around Jo and Alex as they tried to comfort the dying man.

"Didn't think they'd be downtown anymore," the man said, his words distorted through mutilated lips. It was hard to look at him, despite all the colloid hosts Alex had seen. "Thought they were gone."

"So did we, man," Alex said. "There's always one around, though, God damn it."

Jo stroked the man's head, where it had not been eaten away by the colloid.

"Fire," the dying man said. "The only way to deal with them."

Alex nodded. "Yeah."

The dying man sighed. His ribs showed through translucent flesh. Veins and arteries pulsed sluggishly. His liver was clearly visible.

"Kill me," he said.

Alex did not hesitate. "Jo, you don't have to watch. Go on outside."

She looked straight at him. A tear glistened in the corner of one eye. "We're partners," she said. "I'll stay."

He nodded, gently pulling her away from the dying man. He stood over the shuddering, prostrate form and said, "I'm sorry."

"Me, too," said the dying man.

Alex shot him three times in the heart.

CHAPTER THREE

It didn't take long to get back to Suburban Station, and Victor was waiting as he had promised.

"Everything cool?" he asked, seeing in their faces that something had happened.

"We ran into a colloid having lunch," Alex said.

Victor nodded. "How far gone?"

"Half way. It died of indigestion, though."

Smiling, Victor said, "Heartburn?"

"Right. Your kerosene came in handy."

"Too bad it's in short supply." Victor withdrew two boxes of ammunition from a sack. "But not as short as these."

It was better than nothing, Alex thought grimly as he accepted the bullets. He would have to scour the underground for more ammunition . . . after he secured something to buy it with. Life could be a bitch.

"Tell you the truth, man," Victor said. "It's the best I could do."

"Sure, Victor," Jo said. "You aren't hoarding anything, are you?"

"Babe, would I hold out on you?" Victor smiled broadly.

Jo grinned, too. "Someday, I'll find out where your stash is. You'll go there to get a few goodies and find yourself cleaned out."

"Shee-it." Victor leaned back against the wall and wiped his brow with a red handkerchief. "The way things are going, it probably don't much matter."

Concerned, Jo reached out and placed her palm on his forehead. "You've got a temperature, Vic. Better find some place to lie down."

"Yeah. Felt a little misery this morning, but I thought it would go away."

"Do you think it might be a colloid?" Alex asked.

15

"Please don't say that," Jo said.

"It's all right," Victor told her. "That's a question has to be asked when anybody gets sick." He looked at Alex. "Truth is, man, I don't know. Might just be a regular virus. Might be one of them slimy muffugs. I can't tell."

"Better get moving," Alex said. "You'll be easy prey if you get too weak."

"I got a ways to go to my crib." Victor's eyes were very red. He was clearly feeling worse every minute.

"Maybe we better take you back to my place," said Jo. "Keep an eye on you."

"You don't mind?"

"Come on, man." Alex gave him a hand, grasping Victor's one arm.

"You know," Victor said as they went underground. "We be lucky to live here. Some of the other cities—L.A., Miami—got no tunnels underneath. No place to hide from them creepy-crawlies."

"That's right," said Alex, wondering if delirium was setting in.

"Way I figure it, most everybody's dead in those places. Maybe we're like rats living in the sewers, but at least we're living."

"Yes, at least we're living," Jo repeated.

They made their way along the rusted tracks until Jo pointed to the shaft above, which was practically invisible even in the lantern light. They climbed up, Victor having some difficulty, and crept through to the sewer on the other side. The entire city, on both sides of the Schuylkill River, had been built over a system of passageways, steam vents, gas lines, and tunnels, something of a subterranean city in itself. Most of those who had lived aboveground knew little about this dark labyrinth before the colloids came, but the less fortunate street people had been well acquainted with Philadelphia's underworld. Maybe that was why so many of them were still alive.

"Man, it's getting worse," Victor said, gasping. "I don't like to whine, but I'm really feeling sick. I don't know if I can make it much longer."

"We'll be there soon," Jo said.

"All right."

Five minutes later, they were helping Victor up into

her—their—nest. Victor lay back, breathing heavily, sweat droplets like pearls on his forehead.

"Hanging in there, man?" Alex asked.

"Still alive," Victor said, but his voice was weak and tremulous.

Alex sensed that a bad end was coming for Jo's friend. He could not be certain, but it looked as if Victor might be infected by a colloid.

Closing his eyes, Victor tried to sleep. After only a few minutes, however, he lurched toward the vent opening. He hung his head over the edge and vomited into the slowly moving water below.

"Don't worry," he said, gasping and falling back on the piled rags. "It's biodegradable."

Alex and Jo tried to smile, understanding just what a brave man he was. The odds were that he was being eaten from the inside out by an alien organism, and here he was making jokes at his own expense.

"Know how I lost this?" Victor asked, raising the stump of his right arm. "One of them bastards infected me two years ago. I cut that muffug off myself, man."

Jo was weeping now, softly.

"Always knew they was gonna get me again, sooner or later."

"You can't be sure," Jo said, sniffing and wiping her eyes with the back of her hand.

"I'm sure." Victor looked right at her. "This time it's deep inside me, though. In my guts. No way to cut it out."

"Jesus," said Alex.

"I want you to do something for me."

"Name it."

"Kill me."

Shit, Alex thought. Two in one fucking day. And though he hardly knew this man, it pained him to have to do it. This wretched world needed more men with Victor's balls. "It'll be clean," said Alex.

"Thanks."

Alex nodded, and Victor closed his eyes. When it became apparent that he had lost consciousness, Jo said, "How can we be certain? There's so much disease in the world, and no medicine to stop the contagion. It could be anything."

"Jo, he didn't get this from eating green apples. He's got a colloid inside him. Do you think he would say what he did if he wasn't positive?"

"He's delirious. He said himself that he lost his arm to a colloid. Maybe he's just got a fever and thinks he's infected."

Alex had to admit that it was possible. "We'll wait a little while longer, then. But you know how quick it can be past the initial stage. We'll have to keep a vigil."

"Don't worry. I'll stay with him."

"We both will, Jo. Like you said, we're in it together."

She managed a wan smile. Shaking a few drops of clean water from a canteen onto a rag, she gently wiped Victor's face.

"He's so hot."

Alex said nothing. Leaning against the wall, he waited for the inevitable. The Ingram was in his lap.

Alex heard people talking, a man and a woman. They seemed to be far away, at the bottom of a well. He was in the psycho ward, sure as shit stinks. Thirteen Thompson, as it was so esoterically called. The thirteenth floor of the Thompson Wing of Jefferson University Hospital. The nut house. He couldn't get into the veterans' hospital because this wasn't service related. That was why he was here. But no, he wasn't in any hospital. He must have been dozing, heard the nurses out in the hall, or something. A man and a woman. No, there was water dripping.

Opening his eyes, he remembered where he was. In a sewer, cramped in a ventilator shaft with an ex-Society Hill princess and a dying man.

Victor was talking. He seemed lucid, though he looked terrible. His eyes were red and rheumic, and his skin was ashen. He was sweating, though it was chilly in the sewer tonight.

"Jo," Victor was saying in a gasping voice, "I want you and Alex to have my stash."

"You're going to be all right," Jo said. "Don't start writing your last will and testament just yet, all right?"

"I'm telling you, babe. This is it."

"Victor . . ."

"Once it starts crawling up my spine, what you see won't be me anymore. My body's gonna belong to some monster from Jesus only knows where. I might attack you then. So you gotta make sure Alex kills me before that."

Jo could no longer convincingly pretend that she didn't think it was going to happen. "Oh, Victor, I'm so sorry."

"You got nothin' to be sorry for, Jo. You be a good friend."

She was crying openly now, the tears like jewels in the lantern light. "I'm sorry. I guess I should be used to this by now."

"You never get used to this shit," Victor said. "But listen, babe. Let me tell you where my stash is at. First thing is, reach inside my coat and pull out that big ol' forty four."

Jo did so, withdrawing an enormous pistol.

"You'll find bullets in my pockets," Victor said, wheezing. "Now, listen to what I tell you."

Victor grimaced and sat part way up, suffering a spasm. He fell back on the pile of rags and groaned. "You got to get across the river to West Philly."

"Where in West Philly?" Alex said, leaning forward. When Victor had told them that his place was too far for a sick man to go, he wasn't kidding.

"Basement off Lancaster, house got leveled during the war. But there's a way to get into the basement. I put some planks over the steps and covered it with trash. Whole neighborhood's all wrecked, and nobody goes there much anymore. So there ain't many colloids around there, either."

"What street is it?"

"Ishan." Victor choked.

"Ishan? I don't know that street. Are you sure that's the right . . . ?"

Victor's mouth opened wide, spittle flecking his lips. He coughed spasmodically and gagged. He was unable to breathe, rasping and choking. A lump appeared on his throat.

At first Alex couldn't tell if it was Victor's Adam's apple, but then he saw that it was too low on the throat. And it was swelling, fast enough for him to see it balloon and threaten to break the skin.

"Good God!" Jo cried.

The death rattle sounded in Victor's throat. Foam gushed out through his clenched teeth and his body shook alarmingly. "Do it!" he rasped. "Do it, Alex!"

Alex took the safety off his weapon and pointed it at the dying man. But just as he was about to fire, Victor's gray hand shot out and grasped Jo's shoulder. He pulled her on top of him, as she screamed in horror. The colloid had taken over.

"Jo, get away from him!" Alex shouted. But she couldn't. And he couldn't get a shot off without running the risk of hitting her. Alex bolted toward the struggling figures.

Jo wasn't screaming anymore. She reached down to her boot and pulled out something that clicked and gleamed in the dim light. It was a switchblade. With one quick and graceful motion, she cut Victor's throat.

The gray hand relaxed its grip on her shoulder and fell away. Victor gurgled, the foam turning pink, and then crimson flowed so dark that it looked black in the lamplight. Blood hissed from the deep cut across the carotid artery as Victor's body shuddered and was still.

Jo shrank back away from the corpse. "Will the colloid come out?" she asked. "Can it infect us now?"

"Probably not. It's suffering from shock now, with its hooks so deep into his nervous system."

Alex pushed the body with his foot, until it teetered on the edge of the shaft. He kicked it hard, and it went over the ledge, splashing below.

"Don't you think we should have burned it?" Jo asked, her eyes wide with fear.

"No, it will probably dissolve. They don't like water very much, unless it's inside a living organism."

"Yeah, right. Alex, hold me."

He put his arm around her, feeling her trembling body. His heart was pounding, too. He had almost lost her, so soon after finding her.

In spite of the need to preserve kerosene, they left the lantern burning even while they were asleep that night.

CHAPTER FOUR

"How the hell do we find Ishan Street, or Ishan Place, or Ishan Court, or whatever it is?" Alex said. They were moving slowly through a trolley tunnel, following the tracks. This route would take them under the Schuylkill River to West Philadelphia. They were on an upward incline now, which meant that they would soon see daylight.

"I don't know, Alex. We'll just have to look."

"But where? Lancaster's a long, long street. It goes on for miles."

"True, but don't you think it's worth putting some time into? Think of what we might get out of this."

"I don't know. When he traded bullets for the picture frame, Victor claimed he didn't have much left."

"He always said things like that. It was just the way he did business." There was a trace of sadness in her voice, but she would be all right.

A faint light filtered down through the tunnel mouth ahead. The rubble deepened as they came closer to the surface, until they had to pick their way, with difficulty, through trash that was sometimes hip deep.

They finally climbed out into the sunlight. The remains of West Philadelphia stretched out before them. A few blocks to the south were the blackened stones that had been the University of Pennsylvania, built in the Age of Enlightenment and destroyed in a fruitless effort to purge the city of colloids, three years earlier. To the north was ghetto, where the rats now held dominion over all.

"It's been a long time since I've been to West Philly," Alex said.

"No wonder." Jo shook her head. "And I thought Center City was in a bad way."

"Even if I knew where Ishan was in the first place, it

would still be hard to find. There aren't too many street signs left around here."

Perhaps Jo could see the hopelessness of the situation, now that they had actually come this far. They were faced with dozens of square miles of rubble. "Lancaster goes all the way out to Paoli and beyond," he said.

"True, but it stands to reason that Victor wouldn't keep his stash miles from where he did his business. I bet it's not all that far from where we're standing."

She didn't give up easily. "Well, let's get started."

They roamed through the abandoned streets and ruined row houses, few of which still stood in one piece. Looking for planks covered by trash was akin to finding the proverbial needle in a haystack. Debris was everywhere, though there was not nearly so much paper as in the old days, and the once ubiquitous fast-food containers were rarely seen anymore.

While they were going through a house that still had three walls standing, Alex thought he heard bricks clink. The Ingram's safety went off before he even thought about it, and he made a hand motion for Jo to be quiet. Backing up, and wincing as his still fresh scar rubbed against the bare bricks, he walked softly to the rear of the house.

Footsteps sounded just beyond the wall.

Alex moved out quickly, pointing his weapon ahead of him as he came into the open. Half a step and he would be back inside, covered by the wall.

"Don't move!" he shouted.

The man walking toward him showed no concern. In fact, he didn't even seem to notice Alex. He was tall and graybearded, wearing a ragged cassock and carrying a long piece of white, plastic piping like a staff. He reminded Alex of a biblical prophet. Besides the pipe, he didn't seem to be carrying any weapons.

"I thought I told you to hold still!" Alex roared.

The bearded man walked right past him, tapping with the pipe as if he were blind—which he clearly was not—and entered the three-sided house. Astonished, Alex followed him in and watched as he approached Jo.

"Daughter, I've come to you because you've been chosen," he said in a booming voice as he stopped in front of her. He raised the pipe above his head, but Alex saw that he had no intention of striking out with it. "The Good Lord has singled you out for salvation, and I am his prophet, come to anoint you."

"Terrific," Jo said, arching one eyebrow elegantly as she glanced at Alex. "I always thought I was kind of special."

"Me, too." Alex moved toward them, putting the safety on the Ingram. He looked up at the bearded man, who must have been nearly seven feet tall. "But your friend the prophet doesn't recognize my divinity, I guess."

The bearded man turned on him. "You blaspheme. This woman is not divine, she has merely been singled out for a purpose by God."

"Yeah, I guess there is a difference."

"Indeed there is, sir." The old man looked straight at him, and Alex was almost startled by the blue clarity of his eyes. They were the eyes of someone thirty years younger than this man.

"What is your name?" Jo asked him.

He turned back to her, and opened his mouth. No words came for a few seconds, as if he were struggling to remember. At last he said, "Samuel."

"My name is Jo, Samuel. And this is Alex."

"This man is a warrior," said Samuel. "The Lord has protected him from harm in this wasteland. And now he has been sent to help you, Jo."

"Help me do what?"

Samuel bowed his head. "I don't know, for I have not been given that knowledge. The Lord will make His purpose clear in His own good time."

"Yeah, I guess He will." It occurred to Alex that he might have run into this man on the streets of Center City before the war. There were so many street people, sad schizophrenics with no place to go. It was ironic that so many of them had survived, while most of those who had gotten along in the old days were gone. The meek had inherited the earth, after all—what was left of it.

"When was the last time you had something to eat, Samuel?" Alex asked. "We've got a little food we can share."

Jo looked at him with surprise.

"The Lord's work is demanding," Alex said, pulling a can of pineapple chunks from his pack and pulling the tab. "Can't do it on an empty stomach."

"Yours is a generous spirit, my son," Samuel said. "I know the Lord will take note of what you have done."

"You'd do the same for me, wouldn't you?"

But Samuel was too busy wolfing down the sweet fruit chunks to answer. He squatted by the brick wall and enjoyed himself.

"How do you suppose he survived all this time?" said Jo. "He's so old and slow moving."

"Perhaps the Lord is protecting him," Alex said.

"Right."

He laughed. "Well, what's your explanation?"

Jo shrugged, and turned to Samuel. "I don't know, but maybe he can help us find Ishan."

"Ishan?" Samuel looked up, wiping juice from his lips. "I know that sinful street."

Jo offered a quick I-told-you-so glance to Alex. "Is it far from here, Samuel?"

"No, not at all. The Lord directed my path to that street many times, before the evil befell the world. It was as if divine forces had wanted me to take note of it each time I passed it."

Alex began to wonder if the old guy really did know where it was. A schizophrenic might say anything. On the other hand, he probably knew West Philly better than they did.

"Could you lead us there?" Jo asked.

"Yes, I shall lead you, since you have been so kind as to share your food with me." Samuel rose from the broken bricks and raised his plastic staff. "Come, follow me."

Alex could hardly refrain from laughing. There was only a remote chance that Samuel knew where he was going, but even so, it would do little harm to humor Jo. After all, who knew what they might find while they went around in circles. West Philly probably wasn't picked clean yet.

As they walked, always clinging to the shadows of gutted buildings, Alex tried to get his bearings. He thought they were somewhere near 34th Street. It seemed that

Samuel actually might be leading them in the general direction of Lancaster Avenue, at the very least.

At the summit of a hill, Samuel turned and barred their way with his staff. "Satan's minions wait below," he said. "We can go no farther."

There were three people moving through the razed houses at the foot of the hill.

"Wait here," Alex said, feeling the adrenaline flow. He slipped around the protesting Samuel and crouched in what had once been an alley, now little more than a rough trench cutting through the weather-packed debris.

Taking a circuitous route, Alex silently made his way down toward the three shambling figures. He crawled through a bombed-out basement, oblivious to the sharp edges of the bricks gouging his skin through the holes in his clothing. At the bottom of a stairway, he waited. If he had guessed right, at least one of the three should be passing by in a few seconds.

Alex's calculations proved to be correct. The thing walked right past him, and from his low vantage Alex got a good look. Good enough to see blue blotches on the gaunt man's face. Infected; in an early stage, but irrevocable. The poor bastard didn't even have Victor's miserable option of hacking off a limb. It would have taken an experienced surgeon to cut it out of his face.

Before moving on, Alex waited until he could no longer hear the scuffing of the infected man's shoes. He went back the way he had come, careful not to be seen by the other two infected people. Emerging from the basement, he heard Jo scream.

Dropping any attempt at caution, Alex sprinted back up the hill, simultaneously releasing the Ingram's safety. As soon as he came into the open, he saw what had happened.

They were all around Jo and Samuel, the latter brandishing his white plastic pipe to ward them off. They were all in the early stages, still recognizably human in shape. They had suckered Alex into leaving his group.

Now they were attacking.

CHAPTER FIVE

Alex didn't dare to shoot, because the infected—ten or twelve strong—were too close to Jo and Samuel. He would have to move fast.

Now that he was out in the open, however, he realized that he had underestimated their attackers once again. More bodies lurched out of doorways and blasted cellars, coming straight for him.

He waited until three of them were close together, and fired a sweeping burst to cut them down. He had effectively cut a hole in their ranks, and he charged through with his head down, like a bull. On the hilltop, Jo's attackers hesitated at the sound of the gunshots. One of them turned awkwardly toward him, a naked woman with the telltale blue patches all over her pale skin.

Alex shot her down without hesitation.

Jo had both pistols out, and she pointed the .32 directly at the face of the nearest zombie. She fired once and pivoted to face the next assailant. The .44 blew the right arm off this one.

Clutching the pipe like a baseball bat, Samuel flailed at them. He connected with a wet, meaty smack, sending one of the infected men into a splayed somersault.

As Alex gained the top of the hill, bony hands reached for him. He used the stock of the Ingram to fend them off, and kicked the fallen attackers out of the way. He shot two more down to clear a path.

"Get moving!" he shouted, turning to cover those who were still standing. As Jo and Samuel ran, Alex shot the nearest of the infected, satisfied to see the one behind it stumble over the body. He turned around and ran after Jo and Samuel. There was no danger of this bunch catching up with them now. Even in the early stages of infection, motor response was severely debilitated.

He caught up with Samuel and Jo a few blocks away. "It's all right," he said, breathing heavily from exertion. "They're way back there."

"But if there are any others nearby they will know we're here," Samuel said. Except for a residue of sweat on his lined face, he showed no signs of the struggle.

"Yeah, we'll keep our eyes peeled." Alex gestured to the east. "Meantime, do you think there's any other way to get to Ishan?"

Samuel's brow furrowed as if an invisible engraver were at work on his forehead. "That *is* Ishan Street."

"That's what I was afraid of."

"Don't you see what this means, Alex?" Jo said, her face flushed. "The infected must be looking for Victor's stash, too."

"Not necessarily. They could just have wandered into this neighborhood."

"Freshly infected, and with a plan of attack against intruders? Come on."

"You may be right, Jo. But that means there's no chance to search for the stash. If I'm right, we can come back later and start all over again. If you're right, we might as well forget it."

Jo looked back toward Ishan Street. "We have to try."

"Then let's lie low for a while. We'll check it out in a few days. If they're still here, we'll know they're looking for Victor's stash. And if they *are* looking for it, how did they learn about it in the first place?"

"I don't know, but I'd really like to find out what he hid down there."

"Wouldn't we both?" They were walking toward the river. There was no sense in staying in West Philadelphia under the circumstances.

"What about Samuel?" Jo asked, as they reached the tunnel mouth.

Alex turned and glanced at the older man, who walked behind them solemnly. "Well, he got along all right without us before. I guess he can do it again."

"But he helped us find what we were looking for, Alex," Jo said. "We can't just leave him to fend for himself. We might not have been able to fight our way out if he hadn't been with us."

Alex had his doubts about that. It seemed to him that the Ingram had made the difference. But he had seen the old man swinging his pipe like Mike Schmidt; Samuel's support hadn't hurt them. Still, there were certain considerations to be made. They were living from moment to moment, with barely enough food for themselves, much less another person.

"Do you really think it's a good idea?" he said. "I know he said you were the Chosen One, but we've still gotta eat."

Jo glared at him, and Alex decided that it was no good to object. Reason was clearly not what would determine this decision. He shrugged, overruled. Maybe it wasn't such a bad idea. There would be strength in numbers, and Samuel probably wouldn't eat very much.

Alex turned and said, "So, Samuel, do you want to come with us?"

Samuel shook his gray head. "I cannot join you. My mission is to return to the wilderness, where I shall remain until I receive further signs from God."

Somehow, this announcement did not tempt Alex to laugh. Leaving Samuel alone seemed tantamount to a death sentence, with the infected roaming these streets. But Alex remembered what the schizophrenics had been like at the hospital. There was no arguing with them.

"Thank you for what you did," Alex said.

Sternly, Samuel nodded in acknowledgment of their gratitude. He turned and, using the pipe as a walking stick, made his way back through the endless maze of wrecked houses, whence he had come.

Alex and Jo shifted some of the trash around and entered the tunnel. There was enough light so that they didn't have to use the lantern for the first hundred feet or so, as they passed under the river.

"Do you think we'll ever see him again?" said Jo.

"I don't know."

A couple of hours later they had made their way through the steam vents and sewers, and were approaching their nest.

"There's no place like home," Jo said.

Alex laughed. He helped Jo up into the shaft and they divested themselves of their equipment and clothing. Lust came over them suddenly, perhaps as a result of the danger they had faced this afternoon. The notion that there is nothing like a proximity of death to make one appreciate life flitted briefly through Alex's mind. But soon he was preoccupied with less philosophical matters.

As Alex kissed her deeply, Jo slowly descended on him. Moving languorously at first, they locked together in a hot love embrace, rocking back and forth with increasing speed. He kneaded her soft skin as she ran her fingers through his hair with one hand and caressed his back with the other. Some time later, they climaxed together.

Deeply satisfied, Alex examined Jo's face with his fingertips. "You're beautiful," he said.

She laughed. "And you're crazy."

"That's true, but you're still beautiful."

They disentangled and slept for awhile. Something awakened Alex during the night. A splashing in the water below. Perhaps it was only a rat. Or maybe some lost soul trying to get away from the colloids.

Alex reached for the Ingram, just in case. Even in this total darkness, he knew exactly where to find it.

Nudging Jo, he whispered to her to get dressed. He heard more soft splashing, as if the intruder were trying to be stealthy. He could tell from the way Jo breathed that she heard it too. She fumbled with her clothes in the darkness, and then Alex heard her checking the chamber of the .32.

They waited. The next splash was much nearer than the previous one. Alex had no doubts now; whoever it was, was coming straight towards them. He got his hunting knife out of the pack.

He clicked off the safety, and Jo did the same. He could hear her breathing, but nothing else. His heart grew large in his chest. An eternity seemed to pass, an eternity in which nothing happened. He could almost believe that the intruder had passed them by. Almost . . . but not quite.

Something was on the ledge. An animal? A hand? Alex knew how to find out. He swept the hunting knife before him low over the ledge, blade first, in a broad arc. He heard a scream, followed by loud splashing.

And then there was silence again.

Whoever was down there knew where they were. Alex and Jo didn't know how many they were up against, and they weren't about to light the lantern to find out. If those outside were human marauders with guns, they were finished. If not, they were in pretty good shape. The shaft was not easily accessible, and only one person at a time could climb up on the ledge to get in. If these were infected people, quick movements were out of the question.

There was the sound of heavy breathing as somebody tried to climb up. Alex estimated about where the attacker's head would be and aimed a well-placed kick. His boot connected with a hard, meaty smack: there was a groan, followed by a loud splash.

Now the water below them was alive with movement. More than one was coming up this time. A deafening burst from the Ingram illuminated three blotchy faces for an instant. Half the head of the nearest was blown away as the shaft was plunged into darkness again.

"How many did you see down below?" he said.

"I don't know, but there were a lot of them down there," Jo replied.

"Maybe we better—" Fingers clutched at his ankle. He tried to strike at it with the gun butt, but succeeded only in painfully hitting himself on the foot. The hand gained a firm grip on his ankle, pulling him toward the brink. Alex didn't dare to shoot, for fear that he would blow his own leg off in the dark.

"Jo!" he shouted. "It's got me!"

His ankle was pulled hard, and he landed sharply on his ass. He tried to shake off his assailant, but he couldn't tell which way to kick. A match flared in the darkness, blinding him. A shot went off, and the hand relaxed its grip. The body it belonged to splashed into the water below.

"Shit!" Jo exclaimed as the match burned her fingers. She struck another, using it to light the lantern. She shot another attacker through the head, clearing the ledge, and placed the lantern there. Taking Alex by the elbow, she pulled him back into the recesses of the shaft. Since it sloped upward, they could see the infected milling in the waist deep water below, while they were hidden in the shadows. After that it was like shooting the famous fish in a barrel.

When the infected were all dead, Alex said, "We better gather up all we can and beat feet the hell out of here."

"Why? There aren't any more of them."

"Not right now, but there are more coming, you can count on it."

"But they don't do things that way, do they?" Jo sounded frightened.

"They didn't used to, but then, they never used to come down into the sewer, either. Maybe it's because food is getting scarce. These goddamn parasites can't live on dead bodies."

Jo was busily stuffing things into her backpack. She rolled the rest up in a blanket. Peering over the ledge, at the bodies floating in the water, she said, "Do we dare to go down there now? Won't they infect us?"

"We're safer in the water. The virus, or whatever it is, is more likely to infect us if we stay up here. In the water, the colloid form will dissolve as soon as it gets out of the body."

Alex hopped over the side. A moment later, Jo splashed down after him. With his gun barrel, he pushed the bodies out of the way and started moving out.

As soon as they were far enough away to talk, Jo said, "I just thought of something."

"What?"

"They followed us back, didn't they? They followed us, and listened to us making love, and waited until they thought we were asleep. And they did it all without making a sound."

"Yeah, that's how it looks."

"But how could they do that?"

"They must communicate in some way we don't know . . . maybe telepathy."

"But how could some virus, even if it was created for germ warfare, make people telepathic?"

"I don't know, but it would explain why we hear colloids screaming when we burn them. I always wondered how they could do it without any vocal apparatus."

"You mean that we hear it in our minds?"

"Got a better explanation?"

"No . . . but what kind of a virus could do that?"

"We don't know if it is a virus. It's something like one, that's all we know."

"Do you think the Russians made it, or our people?"

"What difference does it make? It's here now, even if it came from outer space."

CHAPTER SIX

Where would they go? That was what they discussed now, as they moved through the night. If the colloids no longer feared dissolving in water—and why should they, while there were hosts to carry them?—the sewer wasn't safe anymore. Where else in the city could humans hide?

"The only place where we've got a chance is the park," Alex said as they came up the steps of the Broad Street Subway. There was a waning moon, just past full, that lit their way.

"You mean Fairmount Park?"

"Yeah, it stretches for miles, and it's completely overgrown. We might be able to survive there for a while."

"You don't think the colloids will look for us there?"

"Even if they do, we'll have a lot of room to elude them."

Jo shrugged. "What have we got to lose?"

They had a hike of a mile or more, before they reached Fairmount Park. They stuck to alleys and narrow, back streets as much as they could, which more than doubled the time it took to reach their destination. Twice they saw the glistening hump of a colloid, one sliding down a brick wall, the other pulsating in a doorway. They managed to get by both of them without being sensed. They didn't stop until they were knee deep in weeds, the statues of the park rising ominously in the shadows. This had been a dangerous place even when the city was still alive, a place known for rapists and muggers, a far cry from the intent of its designers in the nineteenth century, who had envisioned a sylvan paradise in the heart of the city. The demise of mankind had left the park a little cleaner, at least; there was no fresh graffiti on the monuments. In the end, Alex thought grimly, the planet might be better off under the rule of the colloids. He decided not to think about it. This was no time to fall into a depressed state.

"I used to jog here," Jo said, her voice sad and distant. "Over there by Boathouse Row."

Alex turned in the direction she faced, and saw the shards of the old boathouses rising up from the river like decaying teeth. It somehow was not nostalgic to remember the rowers in their sculls, who had been a familiar sight in the old days. It hurt to think about the world the way it used to be.

"We've got to go further in, away from the river," he said.

Jo nodded, and they moved on. There were many stone structures in the park, even outbuildings that they might be able to live in.

"There must be other people hiding out around here," said Alex.

"Yeah."

"We don't want to get blown away by humans who mistake us for infected stiffs. Let's be just as careful here as we would outside the park."

"It seems as though you've planned this out," Jo said.

"Yeah, I've thought about coming here more than once. You know how the sewer can get to you."

The foliage was so thick now that they could hardly move. It was amazing how much nature had reclaimed in only three years. Alex stopped and removed a machete from his pack. He hated to dull the blade, but this seemed like the time to use it. He started hacking away at the branches until he and Jo could move forward a little faster.

"You know, this just might work out," he said. "It's like the goddamn Amazon Jungle back here."

Jo smiled, enjoying the first pleasant moment they had experienced today. The possibility of survival seemed a little more feasible now, at least. That was something.

"You know, it's funny," she said. "I've been living down in the sewer for a long time. It never occurred to me that I might come up and live on the surface again, because there were other people underground, and there was bartering going on so you could at least get a little food and some weapons. What are we gonna live on now?"

"There are brooks and ponds in this park. By now they should be fairly clean. After all, it's been three years since any waste has been pumped into the river. If we boil our water, it should get rid of any residue. As for food, well, as you pointed out before, there must be other people in this park. It won't be long before we'll run into some of them."

"Let's hope they're not too territorial."

"Yeah."

They went a little further, until they came to a stone bridge. There was a large enough ledge underneath it for them to lie down on and get some rest, and roots and underbrush kept them pretty well hidden. Feeling that things had worked out better than they could have hoped a few hours ago, they covered themselves with torn blankets and stretched out, completely exhausted. The ground was hard, and it wasn't quite warm enough for comfort, but they were both asleep within seconds.

Alex awakened, finding Jo's head nestled against his chest. He was touched by the innocent expression on her still dreaming face. Birdsong and the water running under the bridge were soothing, constant sounds. He could almost believe that the colloids had never existed. But this was not his wife lying with him. She was gone, and so was his son. And the entire world was as dangerous as Viet Nam had been in the sixties, when he had been with a Marine infantry division in Quang Tri Province.

There was another sound, faintly and pleasantly audible over the rushing brook. It was something Alex hadn't heard in a very long time. Someone was playing music!

He jostled Jo awake. "What?" she said sleepily.

"Listen."

A gradual awareness crept over her features, as she began to perceive what she was hearing.

"It's a guitar," she said, smiling. "God, that's so beautiful!"

They rose, and, without even rolling up their blankets, began to move toward the music. The simple guitar chords broke the morning stillness with a purity that instilled in them a childlike wonder. It was easy to find the music's source. They didn't speak while they stole through the weeds toward the hirsute musician, who sat on a log strumming complacently, as if the entire world were at peace.

The guitarist didn't finish the song he was playing, but began to play another one. Hitting a note that didn't please him, he went back to the beginning of the song again. The same thing happened, and he started a third time.

Alex decided to show himself while some of the magic still lingered. He didn't want to listen to a long rehearsal if he could help it.

"Hello," he said, stepping out of the bushes.

An Uzi was pointed at him so quickly that he wondered why he hadn't seen it before coming into the open. The Ingram still at his side, Alex felt naked. Fortunately, Jo was covering him from the bushes.

"Put that thing down, or I'll blow your fucking head off," she commanded the guitarist.

The musician looked surprised, holding the neck of the guitar in his left hand, the Uzi in his right. "Which do you want me to put down, the gun or the ax?" he asked in a calm voice.

Alex laughed. "Just the gun, please."

The musician stooped and carefully set the Uzi on the ground. He held the guitar to his breast as though it were his only child. "This guitar is all I got," he said without emotion.

"Take it easy. We're not after your guitar, or anything else that belongs to you," Alex replied. "Jo, come on out here."

Jo emerged from the bushes, her pistol trained on the guitarist. Walking toward the musician, Alex lifted the Uzi off the ground and, holding one weapon in either hand, said, "You can put that away now, Jo."

"Are you sure?" she asked.

"I think so. He was only trying to protect himself."

"I guess we can't hold that against him," Jo lowered the .32's barrel. "But we don't know if he's got any friends hanging around here."

"Are you shitting me?" the musician said.

Jo and Alex looked at him.

"Friends? Nobody can trust anybody these days. Just when you think you can trust somebody, they get infected and try to kill you."

They looked at each other now. "We trust each other," Jo said softly.

"Right," the musician said.

"What's your name?" Jo asked him.

"Flash," he replied. "Frank Lloyd Ash, really, but people used to call me Flash."

"F.L. Ash," said Alex. "You used to play with the Dream Architects. We saw you at the Tower Theater back in '69."

Flash smiled appreciatively. "Fuckin' A. We opened for the Moody Blues. You were there, huh, man?"

"I sure was. I liked you guys at least as much as the Moody Blues."

Modestly, Flash said, "Probably just because you knew we were local boys."

They all laughed. "How long have you been living in the park?" Jo asked.

"Couple years. I came here to get as close to nature as I could, before the end came. Only thing is, it hasn't come yet. Not for me, anyway. You know, I was a junkie before the colloids got here. Cleaned my body out since, but for what? My guts are just gonna be filled up with one of them slimy glopolas, sooner or later." Flash's face was expressionless, his brown eyes hard, as he described the seemingly inevitable fate of every human being on earth.

"You can't be so sure of that," Jo said. "There might be some survivors. *You* could survive."

"Dream on," Flash said. "So you just came into the park, huh? Where you been hiding out all this time?"

"In the sewer," Alex said.

"The fuckin' sewer! I couldn't take it down there."

"Where else is there?"

"The country," Flash said. "But it's a long hike, and there's a lot of colloids between here and there."

"That's where we're going, though."

"Let me know when you're leaving. I might go with you, if you don't mind."

"We'll think about it."

"What happened down in the sewer?" Flash asked.

"The colloids are sending their fresh victims down there lately. There are so few people left on the surface that they've got to do something for food, I guess."

"Is nothing sacred?" Flash said. "Can't even hang out in the sewer no more."

Alex laughed again. Flash's deadpan humor was almost as appealing as his guitar playing.

"You know, it's a funny thing," said Flash. "I've played this ax within a few yards of colloids, and they never seem to notice. They've come after me, sure, but they don't seem to hear my music, even when the body they've infected is still in one piece. As soon as they take over the central nervous system, the victim loses all interest in things like music. I hear they're not much for art galleries, either."

"That's all right," Alex said. "I was never much for art galleries, either."

"Well, different strokes." Flash picked up his guitar again. "Mind if I strum some?"

"Please do." Jo and Alex made themselves at home, sitting on the ground. Flash seemed to forget all about them as he played the old songs that had almost sent him to the top of the charts so long ago. His style was out of date, jazz-rock fusion from the late sixties and early seventies, not for all tastes. It was difficult to play, and was not really suited for an acoustic guitar, but it sounded marvelous to his tiny audience.

When he finished playing, they talked some more.

"Were you a musician right up until the colloids came?" Jo asked him.

"Part of the time. I did gigs around Philly, South Jersey, Wilmington. New York once in a while. The usual musician's bullshit. You know, twenty years past my prime, and knowing it's all downhill from here. But what else are you gonna do?"

"You hung in there," said Alex. "That's what's important."

Flash looked at him with clear eyes. "You sound like my old man."

They all laughed again. Flash kept them laughing for hours as they sat and talked. His streetwise witticisms were welcome after the grim struggle Alex and Jo had faced the night before. It occurred to Alex that he probably would not have laughed at these jokes three years earlier. They would doubtless have seemed stale and too sixtiesish in tone. Somehow, sitting in this clearing on a cool autumn morning, Flash seemed like the funniest man in the world.

Flash, too, seemed to be enjoying the camaraderie. He was a born entertainer, who burst into song to punctuate his gags.

"Here I come, walkin' down the street," he sang, "I'm a forty-year-old freak, just a beatin' my meat."

Jo and Alex doubled over with laughter.

It was at that very precious, vulnerable moment that they were attacked.

CHAPTER SEVEN

"Throw the guns over there," said the thin, white-haired woman. She pointed an old German Mauser at Alex.

They had no choice but to do as she said. Alex tossed the Ingram and Flash's Uzi into the bushes. He recalled bitterly that Victor's .44 had been left behind in the sewer. If only he had it under his clothing now . . .

"You, too, lady" their attacker said.

Reluctantly, Jo lobbed the .32 after the other guns.

"Now, let me see what you've got for food," the old woman said.

"There's no food here," Flash told her.

The old woman grimaced. "I don't believe you."

"Well, it's the truth. I haven't got anything here. And you can see that these people don't have anything."

The old woman stepped closer to Jo and Alex. She didn't seem to be infected at all. Just another forager, trying to survive. "It was very foolish of you to sit here, singing and shouting," she said. "I could hear you from that hill way over there." She gestured with her rifle barrel.

Flash came up behind her with something that glinted in the dappled sunlight. One blow on the back of the head, and the old woman went down with a groan.

"Sorry, mom," said Flash. He gently sat the old woman against the fallen tree. "That's the thing about the park. Plenty of company."

"She's bleeding," said Jo, kneeling to help their would-be attacker.

"Jo, she might have killed us," Alex pointed out, as he retrieved their weapons.

"I don't think that was what she had in mind," said

Flash. "I mean, she could have just shot us from the bushes."

"True."

"I hope she doesn't have a concussion," Jo said. She tore a strip from what was left of her shirt and wiped the blood from the old woman's eyes.

"She'll be okay," Flash said. "We can tote her to my place, if your old man will give me a hand."

Alex nodded assent. Together, they picked up the woman and carried her through the woods, Alex holding her ankles and Flash cupping his hands under her arms.

"Keep your eyes peeled," Alex instructed Jo. It seemed that the park was a dangerous place after all, but not because of the colloids. Because of people. In the sewer, there had been a certain sense of commiseration, if not camaraderie. Up here in the open anyone could be infected, and so no one could be trusted. Of course, the underground wouldn't be any different from now on—if there was an underground anymore. At least they could live like human beings here in the park, albeit primitively, instead of like rats creeping through the sewers.

Flash led them through a crumbling arch, and up some stone steps. By the time they had reached the top, the two men were winded. Jo offered to help out.

"It's not much farther," puffed Flash. "Alex and I can make it."

They went down the back side of the hill, where they found what appeared to be an area where logs and discarded vegetation had long ago been deposited by workmen. Untended, weeds and brambles had grown into an impenetrable thicket.

"Looks like a dead end, doesn't it?" Flash said. "But watch this." He moved a few branches, and a passageway appeared. "Just like in a fairy tale."

A few yards in was a brick cottage. There was a metal door with a combination lock, which Flash quickly opened. They took the still unconscious woman inside and laid her on a mattress on the floor.

"The caretakers used to use this place," Flash explained. "Maybe even lived here at one time."

Alex and Jo looked around. There was wooden furniture on the stone floor, most of it in pretty good shape, and several mattresses. Best of all was a fireplace.

"Pretty cozy," Alex said.

"Be it ever so humble." Flash grinned. "I got some water over here. He found a clean rag, dabbed it in a large plastic container and handed it to Jo. She used the damp cloth to clean the woman's wound.

"She's coming around," Jo said.

Indeed, the old woman's eyes were open now. Fear showed in them, but she said nothing.

"Let me get her a drink." Flash took a tin cup from a shelf and dipped into the plastic container. He gave it to Jo, who used it to moisten the old woman's lips. "Can you drink some of this?" she asked.

The old woman tried to, but it went down wrong and she choked. Jo leaned her forward and patted her on the back until the fit of coughing subsided.

"I think she needs a doctor," Jo said.

"I *am* a doctor!" the old woman shouted, hacking and coughing.

"Yeah, right," said Flash.

"I have a Ph.D. from the University of Pennsylvania, young man." She swallowed a little water.

"In what discipline . . . Doctor?" asked Alex.

"Microbiology." The old woman took another sip and sat up straight, perhaps deriving more strength from her captors' newfound respect than from the liquid nourishment. "Class of nineteen forty-eight. My name is Claire Siegel, Ph.D."

"Are you one of the people who unleashed the colloids on the rest of us?" Flash demanded. "A little government project, maybe? Something to keep the evil Russkies at bay?"

Doctor Siegel looked at Flash as if he were the most contemptible ignoramus who ever lived. "You don't really think this plague came out of a laboratory, do you?"

"Where else?" Flash shrugged.

"Maybe God is punishing the unfaithful. You're a likely looking sinner. Maybe you're next."

Alex and Jo glanced at one another, wondering if the elderly scientist were joking.

"It's as good an explanation as any," Doctor Siegel

said, seeing the look that passed between them. "What the hell did we ever learn about them? A virus that infects the nervous system oncologically, and then eats away at the tissues, suspending them in a colloidal gel, transforming them into some slimy goo that attacks any living human being it happens to run into."

"Seems like you've been out of touch for awhile," Alex said. "The colloids have developed some new tricks in recent days."

Doctor Siegel looked apprehensive. She said nothing, however.

"They can communicate telepathically, and, if they're riding a fresh host, they can control their fear of water. I'd say those survivors who didn't get out of the sewers in the past few days are probably history by now."

Doctor Siegel shook her wild, white mane. "Then the park's the last place in the city with any degree of safety."

"That won't last very long, most likely," said Alex.

"Especially with looters running around," Flash said. "If there's a threat from inside as well as outside, we don't have a chance."

"What are you driving at?" Doctor Siegel asked.

"I'm saying we ought to all stick together, mama."

"And fight off the evil oppressors, is that it?" Siegel sneered at him. "Well, sonny, these colloids are even more pervasive than capitalism, and your generation didn't do very well with your so-called rebellion back in the sixties, as I recall. Found out you liked money better than a decent world, didn't you?"

"Some of us never sold out," Flash said angrily.

"No, you turned to drugs instead. And now you're sitting here self-righteously telling the rest of us how to stand up to the colloids."

"It's worth a try," Alex said, annoyed at Doctor Siegel's pessimism. "Maybe if we team up, we'll have a better chance of survival."

"And maybe we'll end up harboring Typhoid Mary, not realizing she's among us until it's too late."

"I'm not saying we don't have to be cautious," Alex said.

"Then what *are* you saying?"

"That we've got to do something. I've lived like scum for three years, and I don't want to any longer."

"So you came up out of the sewer into the light. Admittedly a heady experience, but are you sure you're not getting carried away, Mr. . . . ?"

"Ward, Alex Ward. This is Jo, and the Young Turk you've been arguing with is called Flash."

Doctor Siegel sighed at that last. "Spare me." She got to her feet, shaky but unassisted. "Quite a rap on the head you gave me," she said to Flash.

"What would *you* have done?" Flash responded.

She shrugged. "You know, I'm getting to be pretty old. I don't know how much longer I can stand to live out on my own, so I'll try to get along with you people for awhile. I warn you, though, I'm cranky."

"Yeah, we noticed." Flash grinned at her.

It occurred to Alex that these two actually liked each other, in spite of their inauspicious introduction. It would probably not do to mention such a notion at this juncture, but it seemed that some sort of mother-son dynamic was at work here. He was touched by the possibilities.

"Well, is this place going to be headquarters?" Doctor Siegel asked.

"For now, at least, it seems like a good idea," said Alex. "What do you think, Flash? This hideout is yours by squatter's rights, after all. It seems to me that we can only live here if you say it's okay."

"It was my idea, wasn't it? Hopefully, my house will soon be too small for what I have in mind."

"Which is . . . ?" Jo asked.

"If every uninfected person in Philadelphia can get together to fight this thing, maybe we can start something."

"Maybe," Siegel said. "And then again . . . "

Jo laughed. "Every movement needs a sophist," she said. "Just to keep everything in perspective. I think we've found ours."

In spite of herself, Claire Siegel smiled for the first time since she had met them.

CHAPTER EIGHT

"Are there any veterans among us?" Flash asked.

Three more people had been added to their numbers since the day Alex and Jo had first heard Flash playing his guitar. They were three disheveled souls, two men and a woman, seated on the floor of the little stone house. One of them, a man named Riquelme, responded to Flash's question. "I was in the Army," he said in a lilting Puerto Rican accent. "But I don't want to tell anybody what to do."

"What about you, man?" Flash turned to Alex.

"Yeah, I was in Nam."

"Combat outfit?"

"Yeah."

Flash grinned broadly. "Now we're getting someplace."

"Don't be too sure of that. Remember who won the war."

"Hey, it wasn't your fault, old buddy. It was those dirty protesters back home, right?"

Alex laughed. "Right."

"We got us a military strategist here, folks," whooped Flash.

The new people showed little reaction, but Doctor Siegel sat up and took notice. "Alex, do you think you can come up with a strategy, or is this bird talking through his hat?"

"Well, there are some things about the enemy that we know. We can make battle plans based on those facts."

"Um-hm."

"The trouble is, the colloids keep mutating. And their behavior seems to be changing, too. I don't know how to predict what they're going to do next."

"Well, doesn't it seem to you that they are changing in stages?" Doctor Siegel said. "A few things were learned about them early on. For example, they seem to retain human nervous tissue after the host has been consumed, while the glial tissue vanishes into the colloidal mass."

"Huh?" said Riquelme.

"That means that the neuroglia—tissue that supports the nervous system—is disposed of, while the nerves themselves survive."

"Oh."

"For three years," Dr. Siegel continued, "things have pretty much remained the same. Now they've killed off most of the human race, and they're changing into something new. At least that's the way it looks from where I sit."

"You mean that they'll stay the way they are for a while?" Alex asked.

"I can't be sure, but I think it's a safe bet. Organisms don't evolve overnight. There has to be a pattern, but it's unfamiliar to us."

"If you're right, we've got a few years before they move on to the next phase, right?"

"Not necessarily. Just look at the physical development of a human being, for example. A brief period of infancy, a decade of childhood, six years of adolescence . . . and then forty to seventy years of adulthood."

"But adulthood can be broken down into phases, too," Jo put in. "The same twenty-year-old at fifty can be like two different people."

"True. We can say that there's young adulthood, early middle age, middle age, and senescence."

"You forgot one," said one of the new people, a gaunt, glassy-eyed man of indeterminate age. Alex had thought him to be asleep through the entire discussion.

"Which one did we forget?" Doctor Siegel asked.

"The last one—death." This was uttered in a deep, portentous tone.

Siegel shook her head at this melodramatic pronouncement. "I don't think any of us have forgotten that for a minute."

"Haven't you, though?" the hypnoidal man persisted, speaking very slowly. "Is that why you're asking us to risk our lives for some cockamamie paramilitary scheme?"

"Do you want to just give in to the colloids?" Alex

asked, surprising himself by the anger in his tone. "Just lie down and let them have the Earth?"

"Better dead then red?" was the sneering reply. "I think our ex-radical friend over here remembers that argument."

"Are you referring to me?" Flash said.

"What do you think can come of violence, except more violence?" the rabble-rouser said.

The other new people murmured in agreement.

"That's right," said the woman, who said her name was Jill. "We've been getting along all right so far. We're still alive."

"But for how long?" Alex said. "There's not much of the human race left, is there? What makes you think we can survive if we don't do something?"

"Maybe we've developed an immunity," the thin man said.

"And maybe the tooth fairy is real," said Flash. "Come on, man, we've just been lucky so far. There's no reason to believe we're immune."

"Believe what you want. But remember, if you start trouble, you'll just draw attention to us."

Flash laughed bitterly. "Are you trying to tell me that you actually think they won't find us here sooner or later, if we just lie low and keep quiet?"

"I think we'll all live longer if we keep on the way we've been going."

"This man is telling you that it's everyone against everybody else," Alex said. "But we're all sitting here, without trying to rape, loot, or kill each other. All we're saying is that we ought to stick together. When we strike at the colloids, we'll do it so they can't trace where we came from."

"Safety in numbers, huh?" Jill said in a rasping voice. The pronouncement of this platitude seemed to animate her. "We just might be able to do something in a bunch, Elvin."

The thin man said nothing, seeming to have fallen back into a stupor. Riquelme was now paying strict attention to what the woman was saying.

"I mean, what have we got to lose? There's hardly any food even when the weather's good. And winter's coming

on, sooner than any of us would like to think. What are
we gonna do when its freezing, and we can't find a can of
beans to keep us going?"

"Look," Elvin said, without moving a muscle in his
face, "if one of us does find a can of beans, then he'll
have to share it with everybody else. If he keeps it for
himself, what happens then? I'll tell you what—somebody'll
shoot him for it. Only instead of one guy killing him, it'll
be the whole goddamn group. And they'll claim they've
got the moral authority to do it."

"Well, maybe a man ought to be shot for holding out
on his fellow human beings, if they're starving to death,"
Riquelme argued in hot Hispanic tones.

"We all have to look out for each other," the woman
said. "But the Lord helps those who help themselves."

The argument went on, the three newcomers almost
oblivious to their hosts. It seemed to Alex a positive
thing, even if they disagreed vehemently. At least they
were communicating. People were hungry for this kind of
thing. Three years without social discourse had been very
painful for everybody. Alex remembered how it was before the colloids—even in the hospital, conversation had
been a major part of everyday routine. After the world
had fallen, there was little communication besides bartering. People had simply become too fearful to associate
with each other except when absolutely necessary, and
most had kept their human contacts to a minimum. Alone,
a few had survived, but the masses had been swept away
like dust. Could the colloids have understood this from
the first? Could they have analyzed the group dynamic of
the human race and planned accordingly? It didn't seem
plausible, but then, neither did a telepathic virus.

"You talk about fighting back," Elvin said, addressing
Alex. "But some of us don't even have weapons. And
ammunition's in short supply even for those who have
guns."

"That's true," said Jo, arching an eyebrow at Alex.
"But we know where we might be able to come up with
what we need."

Elvin frowned, and the two others listened intently.

"I think I know what you're driving at," Alex whispered to her. "Maybe it's time we went back to look for Victor's stash."

"You read my mind."

"Not hard to do, in this case."

Jo smiled, but there was a hint of anxiety in her eyes.

"We should head out at dawn. Try to get some sleep first."

"Yeah."

"What's the matter, Jo? A couple of days ago, you were the one who was gung ho about taking another trip to West Philly."

"Don't remind me."

Riquelme and Jill ended up staying. But Elvin decided that he would continue on his own. When it became evident that he was not to be dissuaded, the others wished him well. Riquelme and Jill were already lying on a mattress together, dozing, when he cautiously opened the door and slipped out. It occurred to Alex that Elvin had been odd man out in a romantic triangle.

"Maybe it was a mistake to tell him so much," said Dr. Siegel.

"You think he's infected?" Flash asked. "No blue blotches or other signs."

"I don't know, but there's something odd about him . . . and he seemed determined to discourage us."

"I think I'll follow him for a while," Alex said, shouldering the Ingram. "Just to see where he goes."

Outside, Alex was dismayed to see that Elvin had not bothered to cover his route of egress. A wide path cut through the dead branches and logs like a trench. Alex quickly rearranged some branches and took the stone steps two at a time.

There was a new moon, and the shadows cast by trees made the darkness so deep that Alex was afraid to move very quickly. There was a chill in the air, and he felt himself shiver involuntarily.

At the top of the hill, he stopped for a moment to get his bearings. Through the foliage, he could see the river. Beyond it were the husks of destroyed buildings, protruding like gigantic tombstones in the night.

"Get away from me!"

The shout came from nearby. From his right. Alex

began to run in that direction, a tree limb slapping him painfully in the chest. He couldn't slow down, though. The urgency of that cry convinced him that Elvin was in serious trouble.

The ground sank quickly on the other side of the hill. At the bottom of the hill, Alex almost ran into their late guest. Something crawled through the darkness toward them. Something that gleamed and slid like oil in the darkness.

"Get out of my way," Elvin bellowed, running full tilt back toward Alex.

Alex stepped to one side, clicking the safety off the Ingram as he did so. He fired a quick burst at the undulating colloid, turned, and ran after Elvin.

He caught up with him at the top of the hill.

"It's all right," Alex said. "There was only one of 'em, and it can't move fast enough to get you now."

"I almost stepped in the fucking thing," Elvin said. In spite of his agitation, his voice remained calm.

"Why didn't it attack you, if it was that close?" Alex nudged him back toward the hideout, still suspicious.

"Beats the hell out of me," Elvin shrugged. "Maybe I'm not a choice cut of meat."

Alex chuckled, but as they made their way back down the stone steps in the dark, he considered Elvin's comment. Maybe it was true. Maybe the colloids left certain people alone, for some reason. But if so, why? He shook his head. The colloid had probably been lethargic, maybe because of the cold air.

Elvin never thanked Alex for saving his life. He merely allowed himself to be led through the trees to Flash's place. They went inside, Alex appreciating the warmth very much.

The others were surprised to see that Elvin was with him.

"Welcome back, Elvin," said Riquelme and Jill.

The hypnoidal man looked disapprovingly down at his two erstwhile companions, still enjoying each other's company on a mattress.

"Everything all right?" Flash asked.

"Our friend here almost tap-danced on a colloid," Alex replied. "Other than that, just ducky."

"Still want to make it on your own?" Dr. Siegel said to

Elvin. "Does the idea of being on the team strike you as more appealing now than it was a half hour ago, Mr. . . . ."

"Considerably," Elvin said in flat tones. He went to a mattress on the other side of the room from Riquelme and Jill and sat down cross-legged. "My name's Elvin, like I said before."

"Charmed, I'm sure," Siegel said, offering a sarcastic sidelong glance at Alex. "Doubtless, you're going to be an invaluable addition to our little group."

Ironically, Alex thought that she might be right. An unarmed man who had come that close to a colloid and survived might indeed be an invaluable ally.

CHAPTER NINE

The sun was climbing toward its zenith by the time Alex and Jo stood on the hill overlooking Ishan Street, but they could see their breath in the cool autumn air. Flash was with them, and so would Dr. Siegel have been, if they hadn't prevailed upon her to remain at HQ with the others. Alex thought there was a strong possibility that word had reached other survivors, word of a place where one could go for help and companionship. Such rumors would doubtless prove powerful incentives to the homeless few that still roamed the city's back streets and alleys.

Indeed, Alex wished that he and Jo and Flash were back in the park now, instead of here in the wasteland of West Philly, about to risk their lives.

"I don't see anything stirring down there," Jo said. "Maybe they've moved on."

"Yeah, and maybe they found Victor's stash *before* they moved on," Alex added.

"Pessimist." But Jo knew that he might be right.

"The question is," said Alex, "can the infected, while they are still more or less human in form, learn to use firearms?"

"There were rumors about that during the war," Flash said. "But I don't know anybody who ever saw them using weapons."

"Yeah, they don't have enough brain power left to use a gun. And even if they could manage it, why should the colloids destroy their own food supply? They can't feed on corpses."

"Logical enough, but what's to stop them from wasting us if they can't get to us any other way?" Alex said.

"Huh?" Jo said. "What does that mean?"

"I don't know. I've just been thinking about something sleepy old Elvin said last night."

"What did he say?"

"That he wasn't choice enough meat for the colloids, or something to that effect."

Flash chuckled. "He might be right."

Alex nodded. "Well, we can talk about Elvin's undesirability later. Right now, let's go down there and see if we can find something useful."

Clicking safeties off, the three of them held their weapons as if they were newborn babes, and advanced down the hill. Each time they passed the wreckage of a rowhouse, Alex peered down the debris-strewn alleyways. Nothing moved, not even a rat.

Methodically, they began to search the rubble for the planks covering the basement that Victor had described on his deathbed. There were several bombed-out basements, which could be discounted immediately. The house they searched for must have an intact ground floor, or there could be no hiding place. Thus they were able to eliminate half the buildings on the street immediately. Several of the remaining houses were little more than piles of bricks. These, too, could be eliminated. That left them with a few dozen houses to check out. Speed was essential, since infected people or colloids could show up at any moment.

The sun was overhead before they had gone through the first series of rowhouses. And though the light was blinding, the air remained crisp. Even so, Alex found himself sweating profusely. He remembered all too clearly the night he had been trapped in the tower in Center City. But if the colloids intended to ambush them here on Ishan Street, they were taking their sweet time about it. He tried to take comfort from this thought, telling himself that the enemy would have attacked by now, if aware that three likely victims were within striking distance.

"Alex!" Jo shouted.

Shielding his eyes from the sun, he scanned the rowhouses, but she was nowhere in sight. He ran to the house where he had last seen her. It was one of the least damaged structures in the neighborhood: most of the second floor was intact. He entered through a doorjamb—

the door itself missing—and found Jo standing in what had once been a back yard.

"Look!" she said. She had already removed the planks, revealing concrete steps that descended into shadow. "This has to be it!"

"It looks that way," Alex agreed. "But let's not be hasty."

He withdrew a stoppered bottle of kerosene from his knapsack, and a box of matches. If there were any colloids lurking down there, he was ready for them. Infected humans would be shot unceremoniously, but he would reserve the pleasure of burning any crawlers alive.

Cautiously, he went down the steps. Jo followed closely, her .32 in her right hand. At the bottom, they found themselves standing on a solid concrete floor, with enough light to show them that the basement was empty, devoid not only of enemies but of Victor's stash as well.

"I don't believe it," Jo said. "How could this *not* be the place? There's nothing else on this street like this, with the planks and everything. Alex, this has got to be the right house."

"Maybe it's hidden," said Alex, his voice rebounding from the cellar walls. "Or picked clean by the infected."

Flash was standing on the stairs, watching the streets for signs of movement. "Why would they cover up this cellar entrance, if they'd picked it clean?"

"Good question. Logically, they'd have no reason to do that . . . unless they were expecting somebody to come back here. In which case, they'd have them trapped."

"There's no sign of colloids so far."

Alex had to admit that Flash's point was well taken. Most likely, the basement had remained undisturbed. If so, the stash must be here somewhere. In the dim light, he studied the floor and walls.

"That section of wall over there," Jo said. "It looks as if it were built to accommodate a stairway, but the steps are over here."

Alex looked at the diagonal protrusion in the far wall, and saw what she meant. It seemed innocuous enough, but it might be what they were looking for.

"Okay, but how do we get to it?" said Flash.

"Maybe you have to go up to the ground floor and climb down," Alex reasoned.

"Then why cover the basement steps with planks?"

"Just so nobody would wander down here who wasn't supposed to, probably."

"I'll take a look." Flash disappeared, and a moment later Alex heard lumber being moved above them.

"Holy shit!" came Flash's muffled cry. "C'mere and have a look at this!"

Jo and Alex took the stairs two at a time. They joined Flash, who was on his knees before a section of floor that had come up like a trap door.

"I'll have a look," Alex said, climbing down into the secret room. "Not enough room down here to swing a cat."

It took his eyes a moment to adjust to the darkness, but he was delighted when he saw what was stacked on either side of the coffinlike space.

"Paydirt!" he yelled.

Boxes of ammunition lined one wall, and the other held medical supplies: first aid kits, Ace bandages, hypodermic needles, bottles of antibiotics, and even vitamins. There were several rifles and semi-automatic weapons leaning against the narrow wall at the end, four handguns, and—perhaps most useful of all—two drums marked "flammable."

"There's kerosene or gasoline down here," Alex said. "So don't light a match."

He began to hand up boxes of ammunition. "We'll take as much as we can carry today, and tomorrow we'll send out another group to get as much as they can bring back. We'll have to pour the kerosene into smaller containers to get it back to the park, but it shouldn't take more than a week with seven people working."

"What a find," Flash said, beginning to appreciate the enormity of their discovery as the material was handed up to him a bit at a time.

When they had as much as they could hope to carry, Alex clambered out with the help of Jo and Flash. The diagonal positioning of the wall made egress easy.

Jo smiled in wonderment. "How do you suppose Victor ever came up with that?"

"I'd say this house was built during the twenties," Alex said. "During prohibition. Bootleggers must have had this secret room built to hide booze."

"Thank God for devious minds," Flash said. "Bootleggers, dope runners, and all the other outlaws have their purpose in the scheme of things, just as I always suspected."

Burdened with bullets and medical supplies, each of them carrying one new semi-automatic and one new handgun, they started back toward the park.

"You know, if we go down this hill, we'll meet up with the tunnel just as quickly, and it'll be a lot easier on us," Alex said.

"I don't know," Jo cautioned. "Let's not push our luck."

"What do you mean?"

"I mean that we may run into infected people if we go that way."

"Why should there be any more of them that way than the way we came?"

"We know that the way we came is clear. So let's go back by the same route."

"Jo, you're still thinking of our first visit to Ishan Street. We have no reason to believe that there's any real danger around here today."

"I'd rather not, Alex."

"Look, if we're gonna fight back, we'd better start now. If we're afraid of our own shadows, we're not going to succeed."

"Aren't you infused with the spirit of revolution today," she said snidely.

"Come on," Alex said. "How about you, Flash?"

"I'll go down the hill, I guess," Flash replied. "Why not? Like you said, we got to start fighting back sometime."

"There you have it," Alex said. "You're outnumbered, Jo."

"Once again, macho adventurism wins out over reason."

The street curved down the side of the hill, obscuring what was ahead. Alex felt fortunate, as though things were at last going their way. Perhaps there was a chance after all. And then they came around the shell of a ruined rowhouse, seeing what was at the bottom of the hill.

Dozens of shambling figures milled in the street near a three storey, brick building with a peaked roof and red door. This rather large structure and the surrounding blocks had been left untouched by rocket fire during the war.

"Ironic," Alex said, drawing back behind the rubble.

"Ironic that we came this way?" Jo said sarcastically.

"That, too, I guess. But I was talking about that building down there. The big one without a scratch on it."

"What is it?" Jo demanded. "Some kind of government building."

"You bet your sweet patoot it's a gummint building," said Flash. "That's the armory."

"The armory!" Jo cried.

"Quiet, Jo," Alex said anxiously. "You want them to hear us?"

"They're too far away, aren't they?" she whispered.

"I don't know. You really want to chance it?"

"I see your point."

They withdrew, retracing their path and making their way back under the river the way they had come. Alex was silent much of the way, and when they emerged into the light on the other side, Jo said, "Stop sulking, Alex. You could have been right. It just turned out that you weren't."

"It's not that," he said. He frowned as Jo rolled her eyes. "No, really. It's a good thing we went that way."

"Oh?"

"Yeah, because now we know something about the enemy we didn't know before."

"And what is that?"

"The colloids are trying to keep us from getting in the armory, which must mean there are still weapons in there."

"Makes sense," said Flash.

"Does, doesn't it? And you know what else it means?"

Both Jo and Flash looked at him curiously.

Alex smiled. "It means that the infected don't know how to use them . . . at least not yet."

"How do you know that?"

"There were no armed guards down there. Why wouldn't the colloids just arm a few of those zombies and tell them to shoot anything that comes near the armory? I'll tell you why. Because their brains are not functional enough for hand-eye coordination that complex."

"Probably because the colloids eat away at the nervous system right from the beginning," said Jo. "Infected people can only walk for a few days, let alone chew gum or shoot rifles."

"And after a few weeks they start melting down into colloids," Flash said. "And the colloids look for food, which there is less and less of these days, now that the human population is way down."

"That means that if we can hang in there long enough, they might all die," Jo said.

"They might," Alex said. "But most likely some of them will survive, no matter what, just as some of us have survived."

"You're such an optimist," Flash said.

"Just a realist, I'd say," Alex replied. "Besides, Flash, we might only be seeing the tip of the iceberg."

"What do you mean?"

"Look how this epidemic has spread, and what it's evolved into in thirty-six months. Maybe it's some virus genetically designed to mutate rapidly, but got so out of control that the Russians, or our scientists, or whoever couldn't come up with a cure for it in time to stop it from spreading. Now that it's been out of control for three years, it's quickly reaching a crisis situation, since it's running out of host organisms."

"So what will it do next?" said Flash.

"The only thing it *can* do to survive," Jo replied. "Evolve into something new."

CHAPTER TEN

"Viruses don't necessarily die out," Dr. Siegel said as she leaned against the stone wall of Flash's hideout. "Some of them can lie dormant for extraordinarily long periods."

"So even if the entire human race disappears, this thing can still survive?" Elvin said.

"It might." Siegel assumed the air of a professor, stalking back and forth across the floor as she spoke. "We don't know enough about it to determine what will happen. We don't even know that it is a virus, not for certain."

"Well, where does that leave us?" Polly, the newest addition to the group, asked. "It's indestructible, and it's everywhere, and now it's immortal, too."

"Not immortal," Siegel corrected. "Just adaptable."

"We know that it can live on animals," Flash said. "I've seen it myself, eating away at pigeons and rats."

"But when was the last time you saw that?" Siegel asked. "No, that was only when the epidemic first started. They quickly learned to distinguish between humans and other mammals. Furthermore, so far as we know, they have never eaten anything cold-blooded."

"Right to the top of the food chain," Flash said. "You almost have to admire its *chutzpah*."

"We've known for quite some time that it's selective," said Jo. "But this recent development of massed attack is way beyond any virus I've ever heard of."

"Claire," said Alex. "The other day you expressed doubt that the colloids had been created in a lab. Do you think this epidemic can possibly be a natural mutation of some virus?"

"Virus or not, I don't think it originated on Earth," Siegel said simply.

Nobody said anything. It seemed to Alex that she had stated what they had all suspected for some time, but that no one had dared to say it aloud, perhaps out of some atavistic fear that saying it might make it come true.

"It's *Invasion of the Body Snatchers* time," Flash said, after a long moment.

"Something like that," Siegel nodded. "It's my guess that the virus drifts in space, until it falls to a planet with life on it. Then it infects some of the local lifeforms until it figures out which one is the most neurologically complex."

"Yes," Alex said, "it managed to do that rather quickly. But what's it been doing since the end of the war and the present? Why is it all of a sudden directing attacks, capturing armories, stuff like that? My guess is that the past few years have been a time of analysis for the colloids. Not only have they consumed their hosts, but they have studied them at the same time. Now they have mastered the nervous systems of their victims, perhaps even using areas of the brain that we have not developed ourselves."

"That might account for the telepathic communication," Jo said. "Maybe they're using the human mind as a kind of communication device."

"The human nervous system's electrical impulses might make a very good broadcasting system, if they could be appropriately channeled," Siegel said.

"But the broadcast time is limited, if the body is being used for food," Flash said.

"Which must mean that the brain is the last to be eaten." This came from the seemingly catatonic Elvin.

"Maybe not. Maybe there's some interaction between the colloid and neural tissue."

Flash shuddered involuntarily. "Inside the skull, man. We're talking about inside the fuckin' skull."

"Look," Jo said. "Can it be that we're making the whole thing too complicated? I mean, what about Occam's razor, or whatever you call that law? Why are we dreaming up this wild scenario, when there's a simple explanation?"

"Well . . ." Siegel stared at her.

"We've been attacked by groups of infected people, right? Does that prove they're telepathic? No, it just proves that some of them have banded together."

"What about the armory?" Alex asked.

"Maybe they have some dim idea that they could use the weapons kept inside. That doesn't prove that an alien virus is making them into its own personal army, does it?"

"Quite plausible," said Siegel. "Except for one thing. Why are the infected so intent on attacking and killing any uninfected human?"

"For God's sake, we've been attacking *each other* for three years. It's a kill or be killed world outside our little hideaway. These infected people are sick, dying, and yet they've banded together. They got it together sooner than we did, in fact."

"Good point, Jo," Flash said. "What do you say to that, Doc?"

Siegel said nothing, but went to a barred window and stared out at the shadowy branches.

Alex was puzzled by her desultory action. And he was a little surprised by Jo's plausible scenario. She had seemed to believe that the infected were working in concert this afternoon. And yet he had to admit that her theory was easier to believe in than an invasion from outer space.

"Doctor Siegel," he said, "do you have anything to add?"

The old woman seemed infinitely sad and lost, as she said, "No."

Alex glanced at Jo, but she avoided his eye. Flash jerked his head toward the window, as if to say that something was wrong with Siegel.

"Are you all right, Claire?" Alex asked.

"Probably not," she replied. "You see, Alex, I neglected to mention something that might be pertinent to this discussion."

"Something about the colloids?"

"No, something about me."

Alex moved closer, seeing a tear glistening on her cheek. "What is it?" he asked gently. "What's the matter?"

"I'll tell you what's the matter. I was once diagnosed as a paranoid schizophrenic."

Nobody spoke.

"How long ago?" Alex asked.

"Several years. Twenty years. Thirty. I don't know."

The tears were streaming down her face now. "I don't know what's real."

Alex put his arm around her. "You know as much as anybody else, Doctor."

But Siegel didn't seem to hear him. She just continued to weep, staring out the window into the gathering darkness. She gave no sign that she knew he was there.

Alex left her alone at last, retiring to the corner of the room where Jo was now sitting cross-legged on a mattress. "I think you opened a real can of worms there," he said. "What made you do that?"

"Well, it struck me that we're making too much of all this. What Siegel was saying really doesn't make a lot of sense, when you get down to it. Now we know why."

It seemed a harsh judgment, in a way, but it made sense. He pulled the curtain, a blanket hanging from a rope, that separated their section of the room, and lay down next to Jo.

"There's one thing that still bothers me, Jo," he said after a while.

"Oh?"

"If they're just sick people, why don't they go inside the armory and get those guns? Even if they couldn't use them, it doesn't make any sense. They'd try, wouldn't they? If they've been transformed into something else, though, something that isn't really human, they might not understand how firearms work."

"Alex, how could creatures that can cross billions of miles of space not understand something as simple as a gun?"

"Well, maybe they just don't think the way we do."

"They've had three years to learn."

"True, but they've done a lot of other things in that three years without guns. They've conquered the human race. Making their flunkies use M-16s might not have seemed that important to them."

"A disease has wiped out most of the population, Alex," Jo said with exaggerated patience. "That doesn't mean that there's some sinister purpose behind it."

"No, I suppose not." He rubbed her back.

"Alex, I think we're taking too many risks. If we lie low, this thing just might wear itself out."

Maybe she was right. Maybe the worst was over. Maybe they were among the lucky few who would survive this terrible plague. He wanted to believe that, but experience had taught him that things rarely worked out the way you wanted them to.

"I don't know, Jo. We've been lying low for years, and look what's happened."

"Yeah, we've lived while other people have died by the billions."

"That's one way of looking at it."

"That's the *only* way of looking at it, as far as I can see." She pulled away from him. "I want to live."

Alex tried to touch her again, and again she pulled away from him.

"Have you forgotten all the things we talked about yesterday?" he said sharply. "The future of the human race, and all that?"

"Listen to yourself," Jo said. "You sound like a megalomaniac. The savior of mankind."

"It does sound kind of stupid when you put it that way," he said. "But we've come this far. We have a group of people working together, and they're ready to fight."

"What kind of group? We've been listening to the ravings of a woman who, in one of her more lucid moments, admits to being a schizophrenic."

"She admits to having been diagnosed as a schizophrenic at one time. That doesn't mean that we should dismiss everything she says."

"Right." Jo emphatically rolled onto her side, facing away from Alex.

"Well, whether you're with us or not, I intend to take that armory away from the colloids," Alex said, anger rising in his voice. "I'm going to teach these people how to fight, just as though they were raw recruits arriving at Cam Ranh Bay in '68."

"I suggest you remember who won that war."

"Yeah, I haven't forgotten it for one minute in twenty years. This time, though, it's different."

"Oh, and why is that?"

"Because this time *we're* the North Vietnamese."

CHAPTER ELEVEN

They moved out in the morning. The light was still gray, as if they were living in a black and white movie. This effect was heightened by thick fog, which made the world seem grainy and insubstantial. But the wetness that lay heavily on the earth, and the rich odor of dying leaves braced Alex with the knowledge that this was indeed real.

For two weeks, he had been training refugees. The Fairmount Park guerrillas could not afford to wait any longer to attack. Sooner or later, the colloids would contrive to have their infected minions use firearms. Alex only hoped that it would be later. If the contents of the armory were in the hands of the infected, it was all over even before it started. Alex doubted that this was the case, however. After all, it had taken the colloids three years to get to this point. Manipulating brain-damaged, infected bodies just to walk and lunge must have been something of a colloid fine art. Getting them to do something as complex as locking and loading—not to mention hitting a moving target—might prove well nigh impossible.

Alex wasn't banking on impossibility, however.

Jo seemed resentful, unprepared for the military action that they were about to undertake this morning. She hadn't allowed him to make love to her since the argument following Dr. Siegel's admission of schizophrenia. He still didn't understand how their quarrel had come about; it seemed as if they were getting along just fine one moment, and the next it was all-out war. Well, he really hadn't known Jo for very long, when it came right down to it. On the other hand, they had been through so much together that it didn't seem right that she would suddenly turn on him. This struggle was just too important to back away from, and yet he couldn't seem to make her understand that anymore. She wouldn't budge an inch.

This was no time to be thinking about his relationship with Jo. They were already approaching the park's edge, along the cracked, weed-infested pavement of the East River Drive.

"Stay in the trees," he said.

They did as he told them, eleven women and eight men carrying the firearms they had found in Victor's stash, against perhaps seventy to one hundred of the infected. At least, that was the approximate number the one time he had seen the horde guarding the armory. God only knew how many there would be today.

During their training sessions, held about a mile from the hideout, Alex had welcomed anyone who had come to them. The shots had frightened the faint hearted, and only those who were ready to come in from the cold found enough courage to approach the clearing where Alex's guerrillas had been shooting at makeshift targets. Few colloids had been sighted since Elvin had returned that night. Perhaps they sensed that these people were not easy prey.

Most of the Spring Garden Street Bridge still stood by the ruined art museum. A car couldn't have driven across, but who had fuel to run a car? It was easy enough to walk, in spite of the twisted girders rising up like a steel flower on the north side of the bridge. The paved walk on the south side was intact. They were sitting ducks up here, but with all this firepower, Alex wasn't particularly worried about coming out into the open. The colloids weren't expecting a mass of people to emerge from the park on a military mission.

The wind slapped at them as they made their way single file across the bridge. They didn't see anything moving, but Alex was still relieved when they got to the other side.

Alex stood and watched his "platoon" file past. He wondered if some of these poor, benighted souls even knew where they were going. He had entrusted the most stable among them with their eleven guns, though even some of these he was none too sure of. Still, when the shooting started, people had a way of surprising you.

The most unlikely souls often performed heroically in combat. And his soldiers had been living under combat conditions for over three years, in a very real sense.

Fifteen or twenty minutes passed before they drew up in sight of the armory.

"Some of my buddies used to spend some time in there," Flash said. "Weekend warriors who didn't want to go to Nam. The armory was loaded for bear three years ago, which is probably why this is the only few blocks standing in West Philly anymore. Dumb fucks blew the city to bits, trying to stop a virus from spreading."

Alex remembered. His faith in the American military mind had not been restored by the Army's actions during the colloid war. The regular Army had taken the armory out of the National Guard's hands, creating a haven for themselves and killing an ungodly number of civilians with their seemingly random rocket fire.

"Let's do it," Flash said, looking at Alex for the command.

"Keep down," Alex said, just loud enough for all his people to hear. They did as they were instructed, all of them realizing that their lives were at stake. They were depending on Alex to see them through this thing, and he didn't intend to let them down.

"Flash, see if you can get a little closer. See how many are down there."

Flash scrambled off the broken sidewalk, and started moving toward the smashed rowhouses along the way to the armory.

"If you think there's a chance you'll be seen, just come back," Alex said.

Flash nodded, and disappeared behind a crumbling brick wall. They waited in silence for his return. Once, Alex stole a glance at Jo. He sensed that she knew he was looking at her, but she didn't even glance back. He hoped that neither of them died today. He didn't want to leave her like this.

Ten minutes later, Flash was back. He was out of breath, but he managed to say between puffs: "Must be a couple hundred infected down there."

"So their numbers have increased." Were they expecting an attack? Alex thought better of voicing that dark thought.

"What do you think, Alex?" Flash asked.

He wished that he could talk to Jo, ask her advice about this, but she sat like a statue, staring down at the armory.

"Any sign that they've gone inside the building?" he asked Flash.

"Uh, uh." Flash shook his head. "Those big red doors are locked up tight as an iron drum."

Flash referred to the twenty-foot-tall front entrance, twin doors painted a faded blood red, its size designed to accommodate tanks and armored cars. There were other doors, of course, and it was preposterous to assume that the infected had not been able to get inside.

"Well, if we go straight for it," Alex said, "maybe we can kill enough of them to scare off the others."

Flash's expression was doubtful, but he nodded. They had to do something. Things weren't going to get any better if they waited.

"Give the word, boss." Flash smiled at him, and Alex thought that here was a brave man. Maybe Flash wasn't afraid simply because he had lived with death for so long.

"All right," Alex said to the others. "We've got a limited supply of ammunition, so don't just shoot at anything. Make sure you've got a target. It's best to go for the head, because a wound that would shock an uninfected human being might not stop these people. There's another reason, too. They're better off dead, and a gut shot, even if it knocks one off his feet, might not finish him. You're doing him a favor by killing him quick. Remember that."

Elvin stared at him with his usual vacant, hypnoidal expression. "We'll remember," he said slowly and deliberately.

Alex took a long look at the grim faces of his guerrillas. Misfits, society's rejects, drug addicts though they might be, they wanted to strike back for the years of fear and misery the colloids had brought to the earth. They might never get another chance; the rebellion could end right here where it started. They were afraid, but they were still ready to fight. That was the best attitude a soldier could have.

Alex raised his hand, but Flash pointed toward the armory before he could give the signal.

"Look," Flash said.

Alex turned and saw what had caught Flash's attention. One of the big, red doors was opening. The infected milling about 33rd Street turned and stared dumbly as the armory was opened to attack.

"Let's go!" Alex shouted.

They were on their feet and running down the hill, outnumbered at least five to one. The element of surprise, as Alex had anticipated, was on their side. The red door was open all the way now, revealing a dark, cavernous room inside. The infected, staring at the armory like the faithful at a shrine, still did not see the guerrillas coming.

A gunshot exploded behind Alex.

Without slowing down, he glanced over his shoulder. Jo was holding her .32, smoke streaming from its barrel. She had stopped running, and fell behind the others.

The guerrillas were only halfway down the hill, but the infected were turning, awareness rippling through their numbers. The gunshot had taken their attention away from the armory door. Still, the infected were not organized. They stood dumbly as the attack force reached them.

Alex was almost on top of the nearest one before he fired. The infected man's head burst open, his body tumbling away upon the shock of impact. Gunfire popped all around Alex, but his people kept their heads and stayed together. Three more infected bodies fell before he could find another target.

The guerrillas broke through into the armory. Alex tried to push the door closed, but found it to be very heavy. Somebody screamed. He saw Elvin being dragged back outside by four or five of the infected, his fingers clawing at them ineffectually.

"Flash!" Alex shouted. "Find a way to shut that door!" And he was on Elvin's attackers, clubbing them with the butt of the Ingram. It was too risky to shoot at such close quarters, but he caught a woman squarely in the temple. She clung tenaciously to Elvin in spite of the blow. Three more well placed jabs had loosened her hold, however, and now several other guerrillas had come to Elvin's assistance. His attackers were beaten to the ground, and then their bloody bodies were shot, gunfire echoing through the huge open room.

The sound of creaking wood caused Alex to look back and see Flash closing the thick, red door. More of the infected were staggering inside before he could shut it, though.

"Faster, Flash!" Alex shouted. "Faster!"

But the weight of the door made it slow going. Alex fired at three advancing infected, and shouted, "Form a line here! Don't let any of them through!"

The guerrillas stood abreast, shooting into the advancing enemy bodies. The faded red paint was spattered with a darker crimson as the door moved slowly, ponderously. Closing it could not have taken more than twenty seconds, but it seemed like hours. The concrete floor was awash with blood, and twitching fingers were crushed between the two doors as it finally shut.

The screams of the dying echoed through the armory, and Alex ordered his people to finish them off. The last gunshots were deafening in the enclosed space. The place reeked of burnt gunpowder and blood.

Doctor Siegel dropped her gun. It clunked onto the floor and she followed, kneeling before them all, staring at the corpses with emotionless eyes.

"This is no time to quit," Alex said. "There might be more of them in here. Somebody opened that door while we were coming down the hill, and it wasn't one of us."

He started back into the shadows, where tanks rested like slumbering dinosaurs. Flash went with him, and Riquelme. It was only then that he realized that Jo was no longer among them.

"Where's Jo?" he cried, suddenly very frightened. "She didn't get left outside, did she?"

"No, man," Flash said. "She made it inside. But she said she was gonna take a look to see if there were any colloids back here."

"You mean she came back here *alone*?"

"Yeah, I was gonna go with her, but you told me to shut the door. It seemed like a good idea at the time."

Alex nodded. Why would she do something so stupid? Fifteen minutes ago, she didn't even want to fight, and now she was going on point. It didn't make any sense.

They had worked their way deep into the armory now, and were creeping through the armored cars, when Alex heard something move.

CHAPTER TWELVE

Alex crouched next to the armored car. He heard Flash and Riquelme breathing raggedly behind him. Whoever or whatever he had just heard, it was moving closer. A soft sliding sound, just around the front end of the armored car. In another second it would be in sight.

It stopped.

Alex held a palm up, signaling Riquelme and Flash to stay where they were. They would wait until the thing came out where he could see it.

But it didn't show. Sweat made Alex's forehead itch, as he waited for something to happen. Several seconds passed, and no sound came from the front end of the armored car. Carefully, Alex lowered his head to see past its wheels. There were two boots there in the shadows. Should he shoot this person in the foot? It might be the smartest thing to do, under the circumstances.

"Alex," Jo's voice called out. "Where are you?"

"Jesus," he breathed. Standing up, he said. "Over here, baby."

Jo stepped into sight. "What are you doing over there?"

"Oh, just playing hide and seek."

Jo laughed. "Really?"

"Yeah . . . and what have you been doing?"

"Checking the place out with my little friend here." She waved the .32 nonchalantly.

"Find anything?"

"Just a second storey door in the north wing that goes out to a fire escape onto Cuthbert Street. It was wide open, as if somebody had just left in a hurry. I locked up after them."

"You didn't see anything else?"

"No. We're the only ones in here now."

"How can you be sure?"

Jo shrugged. "Check it out for yourself."

"I will."

Jo started to walk back toward the others, but Alex grabbed her arm.

"You almost blew the whole raid," he said.

She jerked her arm away from him. "What do you mean by that?"

"You know what I mean. Firing that shot."

"I thought I could hit one of those guys."

"With a handgun? That far away? On the run? Are you kidding?"

"No, I'm not kidding."

"I don't know if everybody made it inside. If they didn't, you've got a lot to answer for, Jo."

"Fuck you," she said, and walked away.

He watched her for a moment, and then turned to Flash and Riquelme. "See those catwalks up there?" he said. "Let's go up and take a look through those windows, see if we can find out what's going on outside."

A shaft of light from one of those very windows revealed a stairway. Alex bounded up, with Flash and Riquelme right behind him. Directing each of them to a separate window, on the north and south sides of the armory, Alex made his way down the catwalk to the west side. The glass in the windows there was smoky, but few of the panes were shattered. Alex rubbed a clear circle onto the glass at eye level and peered out.

There were infected people milling about on the sidewalk, as before. Other than a few corpses sprawled onto the pavement and in the gutter, there was no sign that there had been a battle here a few short minutes ago. Perhaps the infected understood that their enemies were now trapped inside the armory, and that waiting was the best strategy. They didn't appear to be any kind of coherent force. But why were they here at all? There was no food for them here; nothing, in fact, but weapons.

Starting back down to the ground floor, Alex thought about what those weapons could mean to his guerrillas—if they could ever get out of this building.

Halfway down the stairs, he heard a commotion coming from inside the armory. His people were struggling with somebody near the door. He heard them shouting and saw a robed, bearded man striking at his attackers with a pipe. It was Samuel!

Alex rushed down and stopped them from hurting the old man. He had to forcibly push two people away. In the din of screams and imprecations, they couldn't hear him say that he knew Samuel, but the violence soon quieted. Jo stood off at a distance, leaning against a tank's treads, watching silently.

Alex faced Samuel's attackers. "This man is not the enemy," he said. "I know him. I don't understand how he got in here, but let's give him a chance to explain."

"I am the hand of the Lord," Samuel thundered, raising his pipe on high. "I smite the enemies of Israel."

"Israel?" someone said. "What's he talking about?"

"The mouth of Baal has opened, and the Children of Israel have been delivered."

"You opened the door, didn't you?" Alex asked, grinning. "You saw us from one of those windows up there, and you opened the door to let us in."

"If he did that, why was he hiding?" a woman named Mavis asked.

"He would have been killed if he hadn't," Alex pointed out. "He doesn't have a gun."

"It was the Lord's wish that you find shelter here," Samuel allowed. "I was the hand of God."

"Maybe you were, at that." Alex turned to the others. "You almost killed this man, and he was the one who made our victory possible."

"How do we know that?" Jo stepped forward. "We found him hiding in here. How do we know that he didn't just take credit for opening the door?"

"Well, if he didn't open it, who did?" Flash said.

"Even if he did open it, how do we know he did it to help us?" Jo persisted. "What if he was trying to let the infected in here, to arm them?"

"Good point," said Jill.

"What do we really know about this man?" Jo turned a cold gaze on Samuel.

"For Christ's sake, Jo," Alex said, "Samuel helped us before. Have you forgotten that he put his life on the line for us?"

"A lot could have happened since then."

She was right. It was possible that Samuel had been infected since then. He didn't seem any different, though. No blue blotches on his skin, and he spoke articulately, despite his obsessive religiosity. "He's not the enemy," Alex said.

"Would you stake your life on it?" Jo asked.

Alex looked deep into Samuel's eyes. There was madness there, but it was a human madness. "Yes," he said. "Yes, I would stake my life on it."

The guerrillas, who had been listening intently, seemed to relax a little. They trusted Alex enough to know that he would not make such a claim lightly. They withdrew to the building's corners, leaving Alex alone with Samuel.

"Don't blame them," Alex said. "They have reason to be suspicious of strangers."

"As do we all," said Samuel.

"Stay with us. There's safety in numbers."

"The Satanic forces have been smitten by the hosts of the Lord this day," Samuel said. "If the Lord's people have mistaken me for a demon, perhaps it is because I have for too long lived away from other men in the wilderness."

"Then you'll join us?"

"Yes."

Alex put his arm on Samuel's shoulder. He turned to see Jo's disapproving glare. She looked away as he called to the others.

"Listen up, people," Alex shouted. "We're well protected by these walls, but we need food. Obviously we can't all go, so I suggest that a couple of us slip out, go back to the park and get some supplies. Any volunteers?"

"I'll go," said Flash.

"Good idea. You know where everything is stashed. Anybody else?"

"I'll go with him," Jo said.

Alex didn't know if he liked this. But he had argued with Jo enough for one day. He wouldn't try to stop her from accompanying Flash. There was too much to do, without worrying about what she was going to do next. At least she wouldn't be screwing things up around here.

But, as he helped the others pile up the bodies, he began to wonder if it was such a good idea.

"Three dead," said Elvin.

Alex looked up from the mound of human flesh. Clearly, Elvin wasn't talking about these infected corpses. "Three of our people didn't make it?"

"That's right. Annie, Leslie, and Leonard are all out there." Elvin showed no expression, as usual, but there was a catch in his voice.

"Too bad, but at least there were only three. We gained our objective with only fifteen percent losses."

Elvin stared at him, perhaps finding Alex's reaction questionable. Alex didn't like it, either, but he knew from experience that if they didn't celebrate their victory, there would be nothing left for them to do but mourn the dead. Chaos would follow, that way. It was best to go on and plan new strategies.

There were two large store rooms on the ground floor of the armory, in the south wing, each containing several padlocked metal bins. Breaking them open, Alex and Riquelme found M-16s, portable rocket launchers, a great deal of ammunition, napalm B canisters, and flamethrowers.

"These flamethrowers are battery-ignited," Riquelme said.

"Is that good or bad?" Alex said.

"Probably bad, because the batteries haven't been charged in a couple of years. But they tend to last a pretty long time, so maybe we'll luck out and find one that still works."

"See what you can do." Alex went out to announce their find to the guerrillas. After the cheering died down, he said. "Our two volunteers should be leaving right after dark. They can go out by the door that Jo locked this morning. In the meantime, we should drag those bodies up and drop them out of a window."

"Aren't you afraid of infection?" a man named Irv Finney asked.

"We're more likely to get sick if we keep the bodies in here with us, wouldn't you think?"

"Yeah, I guess you're right."

Just after sunset, the bodies were dragged up and pushed unceremoniously through a briefly opened window. The infected on the street below looked up, after the first corpse thudded down onto the sidewalk, some of them shuffling awkwardly out of the way of the falling corpses. While this ugly job was underway, Jo and Flash left by the Cuthbert Street fire door. The distraction seemed to work: no gunshots were heard.

A few minutes after they had gone, Alex unlocked the same door and went out into the darkness. He had instructed Riquelme to lock up behind him, and to say nothing to the others about where he had gone.

Standing on the fire escape, Alex could see his breath in the moonlight. A few infected people were half a block away, but they didn't see him. The sickening thump of another body hitting the pavement drew their attention toward 33rd Street. Alex hung from the fire escape's bottom rung by one hand and dropped, sprinting for the nearest rowhouse. Once he was in the shadows, he slowed long enough to take a look back, trying to determine if he had been seen. Satisfied that he had not, he started toward Fairmount Park.

CHAPTER THIRTEEN

He was too far behind Jo and Flash to catch up. But that was all right. He knew where they were going, and he had a pretty good idea of how long it would take them to get there. He tried to convince himself that he was only following them to make sure they didn't get into any trouble. The real reason was much more disturbing.

Taking the long way around, through the trolley tunnel, would be wise tonight. But Alex was going to take the bridge. The risk was worth it, if he could get to the park ahead of Jo and Flash. Once he was satisfied that everything was all right, he would sneak back the same way, and they would never know that they had been followed.

There was little moonlight, but Alex was used to getting around in the dark. He stayed alert, watching for any signs of life. Once, as he passed an abandoned railyard, he thought he saw the glistening hump of a colloid, but he couldn't be sure.

In ten minutes he was on the bridge. If he was attacked here, his best bet would be to jump into the river. But he was not attacked. He crossed over into Fairmount without incident. In another fifteen minutes, he was heading down the hill toward the hideout.

It was then that he heard Flash screaming. Alex didn't hesitate for an instant. He sprinted toward the sound of his friend's voice as if his own life depended on it.

It wasn't hard to find Flash. He was lying on the ground, in the path of the hideout. Glistening, shapeless things clung to his arms and legs and torso.

"Flash!" Alex cried in an anguished voice.

But Flash could not answer. His body trembled and his limbs flailed ineffectually. Colloids had eaten into his skin, and were swiftly corroding his flesh, muscles, seeking the nerves. He shrieked until a pseudopod slid into his mouth. Flash gagged, but the vomit did not stop the colloid from vanishing down his throat.

Alex opened fire, using many more rounds than was necessary. He did not intend to let his friend suffer for one second longer than he had to. His finger grew numb on the trigger, and his hands and forearms ached by the time he stopped shooting.

The colloids, feeding on Flash's nervous system, trembled with the shock of his death. In a moment, they would reject the dead body and crawl away. Alex had better not be anywhere near them when that happened. There must have been six or seven of them on Flash's body. God only knew how many more were lurking in the overgrown woods surrounding the hideout.

But he had to find Jo, no matter how many of them were here.

"Jo!" he cried, crashing through the underbrush. He reached the hideout and kicked open the door.

There was nobody inside. Apparently, Jo must have escaped. Alex tried to feel relieved, but he knew that there were other possibilities. He preferred not to think of them right now, but he couldn't help it. He could only hope that Jo would find her way back to the armory. He lit a kerosene lantern and searched for signs that she had been inside the hideout tonight. As far as he could tell, the stores of canned goods were untouched. He found a sack and filled it with as much food as he could carry.

Just before he turned out the lantern, he took one last look around. The corner of the room that he and Jo had used for their private quarters was covered by the curtain. He could not resist going over in the darkness and lifting the curtain for a moment.

There was Jo, lying on the mattress. Was she dead? His heart grew huge in his chest.

Before he could move or make a sound, he saw that something was on the pillow beside her head—something that quivered gelatinously. A thin stream rushed from the colloid's main mass, across the pillow and into Jo's right ear.

Even in the darkness, he could see the rise and fall of

her breast. Her eyes were wide open, staring straight up at the ceiling.

Alex gripped the Ingram. He hadn't thought twice about killing Flash, but this . . . this was Jo. He backed away, letting the curtain drop. He could not penetrate Jo's soft flesh with bullets. Turning, he ran from the hideout, retching.

He did not stop running until he had climbed up the fire escape and was pounding on the iron door for someone to let him into the armory. There were infected people standing on the pavement, but none of them came near. If they had, he would have killed them. He didn't want to—he only wanted to be among humans, away from that hellish sight at the hideout. He had never panicked like this, not even in the worst days in Nam. "Let me in!" he shouted. "For Christ's sake, let me in!"

He almost fell as the door opened inward. The worried faces of Elvin and Dr. Siegel peered at him.

"It's Jo!" he cried. "She's—"

"What is it, my dear boy?" Dr. Siegel said, embracing him. "What has happened to Jo?"

"Oh, God!" He buried his face in her breast and wept.

The others began to gather around them, astonished that Alex could break down like this. Elvin shushed them to silence, as Siegel talked to Alex. "Alex, tell us what happened."

"A colloid," Alex said. "She's infected."

Siegel looked at him skeptically. "There was no sign of infection."

"No, it's something new. An infection that hides in the brain, controlling her. I saw . . ." He covered his face with his hands.

"What, Alex? What did you see?"

"A colloid, its pseudopod entering her ear. Communicating with the one inside her."

"How do you know?"

"I know. She's been different these past few weeks. The thing has been inside her."

"But the colloids eat away at a person. There is a noticeable physical change."

He grabbed her by the shoulders, looking deep into her

eyes. "Don't you get it, Claire? They've learned how to do it without showing themselves."

"It's impossible." But Siegel looked frightened.

"But that's what they've done. They've adapted, developed this new capability to get at the last few survivors, to get at us."

Elvin stared at him with his sleepy eyes. "You mean Jo is one of *them* now?"

"I don't know." Alex slumped against the wall. "She might not even know what she's doing. But she led Flash right into a swarm of colloids."

"Jesus, Mary, and Joseph," Polly muttered.

"Then Flash is dead," said Siegel. "Is that what you're saying, Alex?"

"Yes, he's dead. I shot him myself."

Everyone was silent now. There was no need for an explanation. They understood what Alex meant, when he said that he had killed Flash. They had all seen people devoured by mature colloids.

"Jo led Flash into a trap?" a woman said. "Didn't I hear you say that?"

In utter misery, Alex nodded. "Yeah."

"She *was* pretty anxious to leave here tonight," said Irv. "It seemed kind of funny that she would volunteer, the way she's been acting."

"I thought I was the only one who noticed that," Alex said.

"Well, once you left, we couldn't help talking about why you went out after them. We knew it couldn't be Flash you were suspicious of."

"How do we know what he's saying is true?" Elvin asked. "Maybe something else happened, and Alex doesn't want us to know about it. Maybe he killed both of them."

"Right," Riquelme said. "And rather than just let things be, he comes back here and announces that Flash is dead and Jo is infected. Sure."

"Why was he so suspicious of them in the first place?"

"Don't you remember what happened this morning? Jo fired a shot, warning the infected that we were attacking," said Riquelme, his dark face showing anger. "That seems like a pretty good reason for him to be suspicious."

Nobody argued with that. Seeing that Alex had brought

something back with him, a man opened the sack. "Canned goods," he said. "And lots of 'em."

"Never mind that," Alex said. "We've got to do something."

"What can we do?" Siegel asked. "She is lost."

They didn't understand. No, how could they? He loved Jo, far more than he had ever realized. He could have killed her back at the hideout, but he hadn't been able to bring himself to do it. Now she would be one of the infected. But maybe Siegel was right. Maybe she was already dead.

"Come, Alex," Siegel said. "Maybe Jo is better off now. At least she won't suffer."

"No." This was all wrong. "She's not dead yet. I shouldn't have left her."

"You couldn't help her," said Riquelme, not unkindly. "I've seen it a thousand times."

"I've got to do something!" Alex screamed at them. "I never ran away like this before. I've got to do something!" He sprinted to the room where the napalm was stored. He unlocked the bin and lifted out one of the smaller napalm B canisters. It was heavy, but he would manage to carry it up and drop it out on the vile things that lurked outside. He wanted to see them burn. To hear their screams.

But he didn't. Instead, he fell to his knees and wept uncontrollably. "Jo," he said, over and over again. "Jo, I love you. Don't leave me."

He cried for a long time, until he felt a hand on his shoulder. It was Claire.

"Alex," she said. "I'm sorry."

"I thought I was ready for this. My wife and son . . . I didn't think anything could hurt me like this again."

"You're still human. That's not a bad thing."

Alex wiped his eyes with the back of his hand. "In this world, maybe it is a bad thing. It was different before the colloids came. We could afford human emotions then, but not now."

"Alex, don't."

He stood and faced her. "I won't waste this napalm. Better to save it for a time when I can do some real damage." He was under control now. Hearing Claire speak rationally helped, especially knowing that she had been in a schizoid state earlier today. They had to go on, no matter what happened. This was war, and you couldn't lose your head.

Stooping, he picked up the canister and set it back inside the bin.

A commotion was starting up on the second floor. Alex and Siegel went to see what it was. A crowd had gathered by the Cuthbert Street door.

Alex pushed through the gathered guerrillas. Elvin stood by the door, a frightened look on his face.

"Somebody's out there," he said. "Somebody who wants to get in."

CHAPTER FOURTEEN

Alex pointed the Ingram at the door. "Open it."

Riquelme opened the door. A lone figure stood silhouetted on the fire escape, the moonlight at her back. She stepped inside.

Nobody spoke.

The door slammed behind Jo. She looked around her and said, "Flash is dead."

Alex wasn't sure how long he stared at her. Gradually, the realization came that he was gaping. This couldn't be. He had seen her violated by a colloid. She couldn't be standing here talking to him like this. This just wasn't right.

"I couldn't help him," Jo said. "I managed to get to the hideout. I stayed there until I was sure nobody was around, and then I came back. The long way around."

"Is that all that happened, Jo?" Siegel asked.

She turned to the older woman. "What do you mean?"

Siegel said nothing. She seemed to go off on one of her schizoid fits again, perhaps set off by this inexplicable incident. She wandered off into the armory's shadows without speaking.

"Jo," Riquelme said, stepping toward her and extending his palms. "What Siegel meant . . ."

"Take her gun!" Alex ordered, cutting him short. He pointed the Ingram directly at Jo. "Elvin, take it!"

Elvin looked frightened and confused, but he did as he was told.

"What do you think you're doing, Alex?" Jo directed a withering glance at Alex.

"I'm making sure you're not armed," Alex said. "You see, I followed you tonight."

Jo showed nothing. Her cold stare transfixed Alex,

made him feel weak. "Why did you follow us? Did you think we weren't up to the job? You could have gone yourself, you know."

"I just had a hunch," Alex said.

"A hunch?" Jo snarled.

"I saw you." In spite of the chill, he was sweating. "In the hideout. In our bed."

She didn't even blink. "After they got Flash, I ran into the hideout, sure. I thought they might not find me in the dark, so I hid on our mattress behind the curtain. If you saw me, why didn't you say something, Alex? What's wrong with you?"

He felt the others' doubts as if they were palpable, as she twisted things around. But he had to think about what he was doing. What had he really seen behind that curtain an hour ago? Only the kerosene lamp had lit the scene, and even that light had been obstructed by the curtain. Was it possible that he had only *imagined* the colloid there?

"No, it won't work, Jo. I know what you are." But there must have been some doubt, some hesitation in his voice. She gave no ground.

"Alex, are you going to let our personal problems stand in the way of your leadership? You've been acting so distant lately. I thought it was because you were planning the raid, but this . . . ."

The words came out of him, slowly, deliberately: "I saw a colloid crawl inside you."

"What?" But her defiant tone didn't work. The guerrillas could take no chances. "Who ever heard of an infected person getting up and coming home, talking to people like I'm doing?"

"It must be a new stage. They've been studying the human body, analyzing their victims." It was Siegel, trying to come to grips with this new problem, and with her madness at the same time. "They've learned how to manipulate the entire organism."

"Prove it," Jo snapped.

"We don't have to, Jo. We know Alex well enough to believe he saw something."

"Take her into that room," Alex pointed at an office

across the hall. "I want an armed guard with her at all times."

"Have you lost your goddamned mind?" Jo shouted. But she followed her captors without a struggle. As soon as she was under lock and key, Alex said. "I know what I saw."

Siegel nodded. "They've got her, all right. I can sense it, too." She gestured for him to follow her. "Come, Alex."

He was grateful for this, even if Claire Siegel's perceptions could not always be trusted. There was an alien organism in control of Jo's body, manipulating her nervous system, her mind. But what could he do about it? He rubbed his temples, trying to fend off the headache that had been building, as they walked to the C.O.'s office in the south wing of the armory.

"When the colloid was inside her," Siegel said, "it must have absorbed information about our fortifications."

"Yeah, we can expect some sort of attack soon." Alex slumped into a swivel chair. "They know we're organizing people into an active resistance."

"They can't ignore us."

"Christ, why did it have to be Jo?" Alex buried his face in his hands. "I love her."

"It might not be final, Alex."

"What?" He looked up at her sharply.

"If this is a different sort of infection, as we suspect, there might be a way to fight it."

"How?"

"Well, we have some drugs back at the hideout."

"First aid stuff. What good is that?"

Dr. Siegel smiled. "There's more than iodine and Ace bandages in those first aid kits."

"Huh?"

"Your friend Victor had some recreational drugs in his possession, too."

"I don't understand how that's going to help us."

"I have a theory, Alex."

"Doctor, there's an old expression—a theory is like an asshole, because everybody's got one."

"Hear me out."

Alex shrugged. What did he have to lose? Some cockamamie theory wasn't going to change things. Jo was still infected, controlled by some virus created in a lab, or a mutation that had run wild, or. . . ?

"Have you noticed a common trait among all the survivors in our little group?" Siegel asked.

"No. We're of varying ages, men and women from different social and economic backgrounds. I don't see any common ground at all."

"There is one thing. Jo was the only exception."

"I still don't see what you're talking about."

"Every one of us has had some severe pyschological illness. I have been treated for schizophrenia. Many of the others are street people, who suffer from the same disorder. You have been diagnosed as a manic-depressive, to use an out of date term. Flash was an addict. Do you see what this might mean?"

Alex thought he did. He remembered what Elvin had said the night he almost stepped in a colloid, about not being meat choice enough for infection. But he said nothing, permitting Siegel to go on.

"I believe that the virus enters a human body and seeks out the nervous system, an electro-biological network where it can thrive. If it finds an imperfect network, it cannot grow. Perhaps it leaves its inhospitable human host then, or perhaps it simply languishes and dies. Whatever happens to it, we have reason to believe that it can't dominate the neurologically damaged host."

"You're saying that even if we're infected, the virus can't hurt us."

"Right." Siegel smiled at him.

Alex leaned forward. "But even if your theory is correct, it won't help Jo. She's already infected."

"True, but the infection has not corroded her nervous system as yet."

"How can we be sure of that?"

"If that were the case, she would not be able to act as she has. The virus has infiltrated the gyri of her brain that control behavior, but thus far it is *only* manipulating her. She may not even be aware of it."

"Is that possible?"

"Sure. As you said earlier, this is a new phase. The colloids have refined their puppetry skills. Those poor, decaying souls stumbling around out on the street are to Jo what heavy metal rock is to a Mozart symphony. I don't even mean that as a value judgment, just an analogy comparing the levels of complexity and sophistication."

"But why did they target Jo?"

"We can't be sure that they did, Alex. But, on the other hand, we cannot dismiss the possibility, either."

"Another thing I can't get out of my mind. If Jo's not neurologically damaged, how did she go for so long without becoming infected?"

"There are bound to be a few survivors who haven't suffered from mental illness. Perhaps a severe neurosis is a partial deterrent . . . or perhaps the virus is building up an immunity to irregular nervous systems."

Alex cringed. If that was the case, there was no hope for any of them. Something had to be done—right away.

"What do you think the drugs can do to help Jo?"

"Induce an artificial schizophrenia. It might drive the virus out, or even kill it."

"And if it doesn't work?"

"We will have to . . . to think of something else."

"We'll have to kill her," Alex said, his voice barely above a whisper. "That's what you mean, isn't it?"

"Yes, that is probably the only alternative."

Alex felt as though he were paralyzed. There was only the slimmest chance that Jo could be saved. He had to do something, though. He couldn't just let her be eaten slowly by a colloid. But there was one other thing that troubled him.

"If we drive it out of her body," he said, "how do we know that she'll be the same? I mean, this thing has got its hooks into her brain. How do we know it won't destroy her mind?"

"We don't."

Bowing his head, Alex prayed that he would find the strength to kill Jo, if Siegel's plan failed. The odds seemed overwhelming that he would have to do it. He had been unable to shoot her earlier tonight when he had stumbled upon the truth, but he couldn't afford to be so squeamish a second time.

"What do you say, Alex?" she asked. "Are you willing to give it a try?"

"I don't see what choice I have," he said. "Bring the drugs here, and I'll get Jo."

"I'll only be a minute."

Taking the lantern, Claire left him alone in the darkened office. He sat there for a little while, dreading what he must do. At last he gathered his strength, stood, and went after the woman he loved.

CHAPTER FIFTEEN

"What do you want?" Jo said. Her expression seemed to come from across the galaxy, though she stood not five feet away from him.

Siegel glanced at Alex, and it occurred to him, not for the first time, that all of this might be madness. They both could be utterly wrong. He could even be mistaken about what had happened tonight at the hideout. No, he had seen Flash eaten alive, and he was certain Jo had led his friend to his death. But it wasn't Jo who had done it, not really. It was something growing inside her—a virus, an evil humor, an avatar, a demon. It wasn't Jo, the woman he loved. He had to destroy it.

"Jo, Doctor Siegel's got a pill I want you to take," he said.

"A pill?" she narrowed her eyes in suspicion. "Why? I'm not sick."

"Maybe not, but we think you might be. The pill won't hurt you. Think of it as preventive medicine."

"I don't want any pills. Goddamn it, Alex, what is all this bullshit?"

"As Alex told you," Siegel said, "this is just a precautionary measure."

"Then why don't you take it, Claire?"

"I think I'm immune to the illness that concerns us."

"Oh, yeah? What kind of illness is that?"

"A virus."

"Had it before?"

"No."

"Then what makes you think you're immune?"

"Logic."

"Something you're not strong on, if I remember correctly."

"You're referring to my schizophrenia," Siegel replied.

"But you forget that I managed to get a doctorate. That required a certain amount of discipline."

"Oh, it's discipline we're talking about, is it?" She glared at Alex. "Like holding me prisoner and forcing me to take drugs against my will. Pretty kinky."

"We're at war," Alex reminded her. "Unusual times call for unusual measures."

"Bullshit."

"You're stalling, Jo."

"Now why would I do a thing like that?" She sneered at him.

"It doesn't matter. We'll use force, if necessary."

"Wait just a minute." Jo's tone abruptly became conciliatory. "There's no need to get nasty about this. If it'll make you feel better, I'll eat the drugs."

"It's just one drug, one pill."

"Well, lay it on me."

Did she know? Did she understand what they were about to do to her? Did the thing inside her understand? Was it laughing at them, envisioning their bitter disappointment when this long shot failed? There was only one way to find out.

Siegel held a tiny, black film can in her right hand. With her left, she unscrewed the top and shook a single blue tablet into her palm.

Jo looked from one to the other. The door was locked, and there was an armed guard right outside. She had to take the pill, though she didn't know what it was, or why they wanted her to take it. The look in Alex's eyes must have convinced her—or convinced the thing living inside her—that she would die if she did not take it. She extended her hand and accepted the pill.

"Would you like some water with it?" Siegel asked.

"No, thank you." Jo popped the tablet into her mouth unceremoniously. "Now what?"

"Now we wait."

Jo sighed and sat on the floor, cross-legged. It would take at least thirty minutes before the psychoactive drug would take effect. At least, under normal circumstances it would take that long. There was no way of knowing how long it would be with an infected person.

For Alex, the minutes passed with excruciating slowness, marked only by the swift beating of his heart.

"Can you turn that lantern down?" Jo asked, after several minutes. "It's bothering my eyes."

Siegel nodded, and Alex turned down the light. This, he suspected, was the first sign that the drug was working. The faint rays of the lantern should not have been troublesome. Perhaps he and Claire wouldn't have to wait much longer. As much as he feared what was to come, he wished for it to happen soon. He could barely stand this. Cool as it was in the unheated room, he felt a drop of sweat form on his temple and trickle down into his beard.

"What is this drug?" Jo suddenly asked. "What are you doing to me?"

"You'll be all right, Jo," Doctor Siegel said soothingly. "Don't be afraid."

"Don't be afraid?" Her face remained oddly expressionless in the dim glow of the lantern. "How can I not be afraid? Everything is changing."

"Changing? What do you mean?"

"The colors coming out of that flame," she said. "They weren't there before."

"Certainly they were," Siegel replied. "Only your perception of them has changed."

Jo's chin fell onto her chest. "I won't let this happen," she murmured.

"Why not, Jo?" Alex said, as if she were one of the guys in his outfit back in Nam. "Just go with it, and see what happens."

"No, I can't. The pattern is rearranging itself. I don't know how to manipulate it when its changing."

Alex and Siegel looked at each other. Was this the colloid talking now, or merely Jo, babbling in a psychedelic stupor? The muscles of her face grew taut, teeth bared in a fearful grimace, as she sank ever deeper into the trip.

The sound of shattering glass broke the spell. Jo cowered as if her mind had fragmented into shards. Alex was unable to look away from her. This distraction from outside might ruin everything, but it had to be dealt with.

"Stay with her." He pulled Jo's .32 from underneath his coat and handed it to Siegel. Leaving them, he rushed out of the room, the Ingram in his hands. Riquelme, just outside the door, was shouting, "Alex, they're trying to break in."

"Come with me," he said. They hurried down the corridor, toward the sound of popping gunfire and breaking glass. Screams of rage and pain followed, and as they entered the north wing's second floor, Alex saw why.

Elvin was struggling with one infected man, while another crawled through the broken window. Two more lay dead on the floor, while Samuel calmly fired at the window with a handgun. A bullet hit an infected man in the jaw, and his twitching body fell across the window sill.

Running across the room, Alex pushed the corpse outside, seeing three more just outside the window. Riquelme fired a burst at them, hitting two of them in the chest. One of the infected pitched to the sidewalk below, while the other managed to hang onto the fire escape, legs dangling in the air.

Alex saw what had happened. The infected had formed a human pyramid, and one of them had climbed up onto the fire escape to pull it down. Now dozens of them ascended toward the open window, thick as maggots on the black, metal ladder.

"The flamethrower!" Alex shouted. "Get a flamethrower!"

Samuel started toward the door. Almost as an afterthought, he turned and shot the infected man struggling with Elvin. Then he ran off in search of the flamethrower, his cassock trailing behind him. Alex, Elvin, and Riquelme stood shoulder to shoulder, firing at those who tried to come in through the window. Fortunately, only one could enter at a time, and the bodies that didn't fall to the ground were piling up on the fire escape landing, making it difficult for the others to get past them. By this time, several guerrillas were standing behind Alex, firing while he reloaded.

It seemed like hours before Samuel returned with the flamethrower, though it was probably more like ninety seconds. Riquelme took it, as Alex prayed that there was still some life in its battery. Hands clutched at them through the open window as they helped Riquelme into the straps holding the tanks on his back. Just as the infected were

coming over the sill, Riquelme turned to face them. In
another few seconds there would be too many of them
inside to deal with. Alex held his breath as Riqueleme
squeezed the trigger. A brilliant orange jet flared and
enveloped the squirming infected. Their screams were
ghastly. Smoke billowed back into the cramped room,
choking Alex with a foul stench—burning human flesh.

Tears came to his eyes, and he gagged on the nauseat-
ing odor, as Riquelme moved closer to the window and
blasted another fiery spurt at the infected. Several of
them leaped off the fire escape and ran away, their tattered clothing on fire.

He kept burning them until the fire escape was cleared.
By this time, the corridor outside the room was crowded
with guerrillas, all anxious to join the fight.

"Get axes, chisels, anything you can find," Alex ordered, stamping at small fires inside the room. "Dislodge
the bolts holding that fire escape and pull it inside the
building."

But before they could get started, a thunderous pounding echoed through the armory.

"What the fuck is that?" Alex said. He picked up the
Ingram and headed down toward the main room, several
of the guerrillas following him. The pounding sounded at
intervals of every few seconds, and Alex soon saw where
its source lay.

The big door on 33rd Street was under attack. Moving
fast, Riquelme and Samuel right behind him, Alex
climbed up to the catwalk and looked out the dirty windows to the street. Dozens of the infected were carrying
a fallen telephone pole, ramming it into the red doors
again and again. One door was beginning to buckle, the
sound of cracking wood echoing through the enclosed
space.

"The flamethrower won't work very well from up here,"
Alex said.

"Napalm," said Riquelme.

"Right," Alex agreed. "Get me a canister. That ought
to do the trick."

Alex watched tensely through the window as Samuel
ran down to get the canister. It wouldn't be much

longer before the enemy were surging through that door.

He prayed that he could stop them. If the infected burst into the armory in their hundreds, his guerrillas would not last long.

CHAPTER SIXTEEN

Alex heard Jo screaming as he dropped the napalm from the center window of the armory. He lost sight
of the canister in the dark swirl of bodies below, but then
the fire spilled out of it, flowing brilliantly over the cracked
pavement like a time-lapse film of the brightest flower in
creation. Flaming chunks of the canister's magnesium
casing flew through the air and burned through diseased
flesh like blazing bullets.

The infected who carried the telephone pole were
shrouded in flames. In mid-charge, they continued to
rush toward the door for a couple of seconds before
dropping the pole with a resounding thud. They scattered
in all directions, some of them falling onto the asphalt,
others running in circles, the fire clinging to them. Their
screams seemed inhuman, as if animals were dying down
on the street, not men and women.

Samuel hoisted a second canister, preparing to toss it
out the window as soon as Alex gave the word. But Alex
saw that the telephone pole was on fire. The assault had
ended. The infected who were not burned milled aim-
lessly about the smoldering corpses. Smoke plumed up
into the night sky past the window, but the fire was not
close to the wooden door, and it seemed unlikely that it
would damage the brick front of the armory.

A scream issued up from the depths of the building,
jolting him back to what he had been doing before the
attack. It was Jo.

He ran back to the little room. Jo's screams grew
louder, more hysterical. As he drew nearer, he heard
Siegel's voice, too, insistent and firm. He opened the
door, almost out of breath.

Jo was against the wall, flattening her body as if she
were trying to be absorbed into the concrete. Her face

103

was a grotesque mask of fear. She shrieked as if she—and not those outside—were being burned alive.

"She's incoherent," Siegel said. "In her suggestible state, she has been badly affected by all the violence."

"Jo, it's over," Alex said, gulping air. "The fighting is over."

"They wanted to kill me!" she screamed. "They were trying to kill me!"

Siegel shrugged in exasperation. "That's all she says."

"You don't understand," Jo said breathlessly. "They really want me dead."

"Who wants you dead, Jo?" Alex asked.

She rolled wild eyes toward him. "The colloids. They know you've got me."

"Didn't they send you here tonight?"

"Yes, but everything's changed now."

Siegel was silent, realizing that perhaps Jo was not raving. This wasn't what they had expected, but it might be a breakthrough, nevertheless. Alex tried to keep Jo talking.

"Why has everything changed?" he asked.

"Because you know about me."

"What do we know?"

She whispered, "I'm infected."

Alex said nothing. So blatant an admission disarmed him. Only an hour ago, Jo had fended off all implications that anything could be wrong, and now she admitted knowing she was infected. But why did she think the colloids wanted to kill her?

"Why are you afraid, Jo?"

"There's a colloid inside me," she said in a heart-breaking voice. "It's been running things. I didn't even know it at first."

"It's that subtle?"

"Yes, it's that subtle. Only when it was too late for me to fight did I realize. But by then it had complete control of me. Now it's confused, sick."

"Sick?"

"It's a parasite," she said. "It lives in the nervous system, redirecting the fields of the brain. But the wiring has suddenly changed. It can't manipulate me, and it's having trouble feeding."

"What does it feed on?"

Jo looked like a small child, her eyes huge with terror and wonder. "It feeds on thought."

"On thought . . ." Siegel grasped Alex's bicep. "No wonder we couldn't understand the nature of this thing. It isn't attracted by living tissue, but by neural energy."

"Once it has absorbed all the host's thought energy," Jo said, "it can start to consume the body whenever it chooses."

"Why did it let you know this?"

Jo began to sob. "It wants me to know that it's the master. While it was controlling my body, my tongue, my mind, I was buried somewhere deep inside, watching this thing fool you."

Alex went to her and put his arms around her. "My God, Jo," he said, his voice breaking with emotion. "This is a nightmare."

"I wish it were," she said. "When your personality, your ego, is pushed into some secret place in your mind, it is like a nightmare. But it's real, Alex."

"We're gonna beat this thing, baby," he said, caressing her soft hair. "We'll beat it together."

"I think I understand what you're going through," Claire said softly. "I know what it's like for your consciousness to be pushed into a dark prison."

"I'm afraid," Jo cried. "It's going to gain control over me again, once the drug wears off."

"Fight it," Alex said.

"Tell us all you know about the colloid," Siegel said. "The more we learn, the better our chances of defeating it."

Jo trembled against Alex's chest. "It's hard to . . . clarify what I know. I didn't learn about this the way I'm used to learning."

"It's all right. Just say it any way that comes into your head. We have to work fast."

"I know that there's a limited communication with other colloids."

"What are the limitations."

"Distance is one, even though they are in communication all over the world. But the farther away one is, the fainter its transmission. Once it's distant enough, one colloid only knows another's thoughts at a remove, through an intermediary colloid. Events happening in Europe or Asia or New Zealand are rather vague, but they receive enough information to know how the war is going all over the Earth."

"Then they do think of it as a war?" Alex said.

"Yes, a war of survival."

"But why? What did we ever do to them?"

"It's what we *have* that matters to them, not what we've done."

"The Earth, you mean."

"Yes. Their own world is long gone, but before they left it they found a way to transform themselves."

"Into a virus?"

"Yes, dormant while traveling through space, attracted by the light of suns. As they drift through a solar system, billions of viral cells are pulled down by the gravity of the planets. The sun's actinic rays revive them, and then they actively seek out living creatures to infect."

Alex saw that it was a strain for Jo to talk at all, much less maintain the rational tone required for explaining the life cycle of a colloid. Her face was gleaming with perspiration, in spite of the room's chill. Still, she seemed less distraught than before. Perhaps the virus had been defeated; perhaps it was dying now, or even dead. Or perhaps it was merely lying in wait in Jo's synapses, regaining strength.

"I think you should try to get some rest, Jo," he said.

"Alex," she said, laughing for the first time since she had returned, "how can I rest while I'm tripping my brains out?"

Alex laughed, too, and so did Siegel. It didn't seem possible that Jo could say something like that. A colloid couldn't have a sense of humor, could it? She must be all right. But then Alex remembered that they had been fooled by her parasite for days, maybe even weeks, before he had stumbled onto irrefutable evidence of her infection. Even then he had not wanted to believe what he had seen.

Nevertheless, Siegel went out in search of something

for Jo to lie on, and returned in a few minutes with a roll-away cot. Alex helped her to unfold it, and Jo, overcome with exhaustion, stretched out and closed her eyes. Alex kissed her and sat cross-legged on the floor.

"You'd better get some sleep, Claire," he said. "I'll stay with her tonight."

Siegel nodded. "The worst seems to have passed. I won't be far away, though. Just call for me if there's any trouble."

"Yeah, I will."

Siegel went out and closed the door behind herself.

Dousing the flame on the kerosene lamp, Alex sat in the dark and listened to Jo's breathing. She seemed to be sleeping soundly, peacefully. He wanted to believe that the ordeal was over, that she was going to be all right. But that was the sort of wishful thinking that he had indulged in when Sharon and Billy had fallen ill. If anything, it had made the heartbreak even more intolerable. That was one of the reasons he had gone over the edge. You had to look at things realistically, no matter how painful it might be to do so.

But it didn't seem realistic to believe that the colloids were the result of a virus from another planet. It seemed like a wild science fiction story . . . a story in which he was one of the characters. . . .

He remembered a quote by a guy named J.B.S. Haldane that summed it up nicely, something about the universe not only being stranger than we imagine, but stranger than we *can* imagine.

He dozed, his consciousness spiraling down into an abyss that opened onto the stars. All infinity stretched before him, but he could only dimly perceive the grandeur of the galactic vastnesses. He drifted through a limitless void, asleep but imbued eons ago with a consciousness.

His world was erupted, opening like a bloody wound in the darkness of space and hurling its detritus outward. The fragments had cooled and fallen into an eccentric orbit, forming an asteroid belt out past the fifth world in the solar system. The cells that had been propelled sunward had drifted immense distances, a few billion falling toward the first sun they approached, a few billion more falling towards the second. And so on, until the journey had gone on for so long that it began to seem like eternity.

Millions upon millions of years had gone by, but at last a myriad of viral cells had reached a world where they could survive . . . and that world was the Earth.

CHAPTER SEVENTEEN

Alex's dark dream was disturbed by a cry. He jumped up, his right shin colliding painfully with the desk. By the faint moonlight, he saw Jo writhing on the cot. Was it the drug? Or the colloid?

"Jo," he said. "I'm here."

She grasped his hand, squeezing with such ferocity that it hurt him. She screamed, a loud, high-pitched sound that hardly seemed human. The metal legs of the cot scored the linoleum as she squirmed in agony.

"Jesus," Alex breathed. Was she losing the battle? The colloid was attacking, trying to regain control. The drug's effect was wearing off, or the alien was learning how to work around it. Either way, Jo was in danger of losing. He knew it to the core of his being.

"Jo," he said, leaning as close as her lashing body would allow, "fight it. *Fight it.*"

Jo opened her mouth wide and emitted a long, miserable wail. She might have been a beast in an abattoir, as she tossed her head back and forth, tears streaming from her eyes. They were trying to take away her humanity, and he would not permit it.

"Fight, Jo. For God's sake, *fight.*" He grabbed her shoulder, trying to keep her from falling off the cot. He was amazed by the rigidity of her muscles, the power that was in her—unharnessed now, as she struggled for possession of her own soul. He would help her ride this thing out, help her win. Because if she lost . . . if she lost, he didn't want to think about it, but he had to.

If she lost, he would have to kill her. It wouldn't really be her, but it would be her body, her face, her voice, her hair, her sweet smell that he would kill. But it wouldn't be Jo. He had to keep telling himself that. It wouldn't be Jo anymore. It would be a thing from another world.

He had to remember that. Even as his muscles ached with the effort of keeping her on the cot, he kept it in the forefront of his consciousness. Even as he urged her to fight the colloid, he did not forget what he must do if the battle went against the woman he loved. He would owe it to her, to kill the thing that had robbed her of her soul.

She stopped struggling abruptly, her sweat-soaked face relaxing. She was silent but for her harsh breathing, her breasts rising and falling from her recent exertions.

Was she all right? Or did this mean that the colloid had succeeded? Alex would have to wait and see. He went back to sit on the floor, slumping against the wall, exhausted. He had to get some sleep now, because the battle might start up again at any moment. For all he knew, the alien was playing possum, gathering its strength for another onslaught.

He was awakened by Jo's screams an hour later, and again he rushed to her. Frustrated, he watched her agonized flailings as she resisted the colloid. How much ground had it gained? Even if she survived, would it destroy her mind? She had been one of the last sane people on the face of the earth, and now she might lose her mind even in victory.

But this was no time to be thinking the worst. He had to believe that it was possible for her to win, to survive the virus intact. When she was at last becalmed, he collapsed onto the floor once again.

He was awakened by her screams twice more during the night, and twice more he held her until the seizure subsided. Her body seemed weaker each time. Alex began to fear that she could not prevail. He would have to kill her.

He fell onto the floor for the fourth time, losing consciousness almost instantly. The next time he woke up, he would have to do it, would have to kill her. He prayed that he would never wake up, then. If only his aching body gave out before Jo was conquered by the alien. . . .

"Alex."

Someone touched him, and the Ingram was in his hands. He was on his feet before he realized that it was Claire.

"Alex," she said, "don't shoot."

Morning light illuminated the room, revealing every

wrinkle in Siegel's aging face. Behind her, Jo slept peacefully. She was pale and drawn, but she breathed regu-
larly. He went to her.

"She's going to be all right," Siegel said.

Alex wept silently.

"Let her rest now," said Siegel. "Why don't you join
us in the briefing room, if you're feeling up to it?"

"I'm okay. What's the meeting about?"

"You'll see." She ushered him out, closing the door
behind them. Alex was reasonably alert by the time he
took a seat among the other fourteen guerrillas. The briefing room in the south wing was quite large, holding about
eighty or ninety seats. All the guerrillas sat in the first
two rows, near the pull-down maps and the blackboard.
A sense of military order pervaded the scene, in spite of
the appearance of Alex's tatterdemalion troops.

"We've learned a great deal about the enemy in the
past few hours," Siegel said, gaining everyone's attention. "First of all, we now know that the virus is not man
made, intentionally or otherwise."

Alex waited for murmurs of incredulity, but there were
none.

"It's from another planet," Siegel continued. "It is
here to conquer the Earth for its own purposes. The
invasion requires at least four phases to be successful.

"The first is a tiny, living mote, set free into space from
its home world to search for likely planets to conquer. It's
dormant in that stage, but in the second phase it becomes
parasitical—a colloid—as the mote enters the body through
a pore and searches for healthy tissue in which to grow,
activated by actinic rays and fueled by neural energy.
The third and most recent development is a remote-
controlled probe with the ability to invade and manipulate healthy neurological tissue without damaging it, and
thus to infiltrate our ranks."

Siegel paused to let them chew on this. Except for a
cough, the room was silent until Polly said, "You said
there are four phases, but you only named three. What's
the other one?"

"We don't know yet, but I suspect that it will be the
culmination of the colloid's life-cycle. Its purpose is to
dominate the earth. It needs hosts, but the stock of

healthy human tissue has just about been used up. They have to find some other way to survive now."

"Maybe they'll just die out," said Irv Finney.

"Doubtful."

"Maybe they'll go somewhere else, then," said a man named Dick Philips.

"I don't think they can. It looks as if they're stuck on Earth for good."

"So why are they sending the infected after us, when they've got the whole world?" Riquelme asked.

"Good question. The colloids are in communication all over the planet, and they know we're not really much of a threat to them. It only goes to show how merciless these creatures are, to attempt to destroy even this small, imperfect enclave of human beings."

"Maybe it shows something else," Alex spoke up.

Siegel looked at him respectfully, as did the others. He stood and said, "Maybe it shows that they're desperate."

"What do you mean, Alex?"

"I mean that time is running out for them. The next phase, whatever it is, has got to be achieved soon, or they're finished."

"What can we do to stop it?" Samuel asked in his booming voice, "if indeed the good Lord wants it stopped."

"You must believe that He does, Samuel," Alex replied, "or you wouldn't be with us, would you?"

"You haven't answered my question."

"Okay, I'll answer you as truthfully as I can." Alex shook his head. "I don't know what we can do to stop it, but I suspect that *it* thinks we can do something. I don't agree with Dr. Siegel that we are harmless to the colloids. They fear us for some reason, or else they would ignore us."

"Why do they fear us?"

"Look at how they've reacted. They kept this armory under guard. They knew that we were going to try and capture it, and they had already targeted one of us in case we were successful. The colloid inside Jo almost caused us to botch the assault, and later led Flash to his death. When we discovered that Jo was infected, they attacked the armory so that we couldn't question her. Well, we drove the colloid out of Jo's body. There's a way to do it, and that means we don't have to fear the colloids anymore."

The guerrillas all started talking at once in excitement, but Siegel shushed them.

"No, Alex," she said, "I'm afraid you're wrong. There are few psychoactive drugs left. Once those are gone, we are at their mercy."

"Unless your immunity theory is correct."

Alex was amused to see annoyance on several faces. Even at civilization's end, society's rejects were still shunned—by organisms from outer space.

"If Siegel is right, we are only in danger from external attack," said Alex. "That means that we, and other people like us, are the last chance the human race has got."

"But even if she is right," Elvin said in typically flat tones, "that doesn't mean that they can never find a way to infect us."

"If they could have done it, they would have by now," argued Mavis. "They're fresh out of healthy people, so they should have started in on us a long time ago."

"That seems to be a reasonable assumption, given what we know now, but we can't be sure they won't find a way to start in on us once their food supply is completely gone."

"That means that this abomination has to be driven from the face of the Earth," Samuel intoned.

At any other time, Alex might have smiled at Samuel's declaration, but not now. Samuel was right; the only way to win was to drive them from the earth. That, however, didn't seem to be possible.

Nevertheless, the guerrillas were stirred up. They had won a few skirmishes in recent days. Even if these were not major victories, the little group had taken heart from them, and the setbacks they had suffered had not discouraged them. Alex considered this a healthy trend.

"What about that woman of yours," Polly asked Alex. "Are you sure she isn't infected anymore?"

"I don't think she is," Siegel answered for him. "We'll know for sure when she wakes us, though."

"You mean you left her alone? She could be opening the front door of the armory right now."

"Unlikely. She's physically exhausted. She won't be up

for at least twelve hours. We'll talk to her then, and we'll find out if the colloid has left her body."

That assertion seemed to quiet them, but a dark, repressed fear mushroomed again in Alex's consciousness. What if Jo's mind had been destroyed by the colloid?

CHAPTER EIGHTEEN

"Do you think you can hold down some food?" Siegel asked.

"I'd sure like to try," Jo said, smiling wanly.

Alex smiled, too. She seemed to have shaken the colloid. Unless it was even cleverer than they believed it to be, it was gone. But did that mean that it was dead, or merely that it had left Jo's body in search of another host? Well, it would have to travel quite a distance to find a healthy brain, and it was no longer in its drifting, dormant stage. Most likely, it couldn't live outside the host for even a brief period.

"There are some jars of baby food in our stores," Siegel said. "Those would probably be the best thing for you right now."

"Pabulum?" Jo said. "Sounds great."

"I'll get it in a minute." Siegel shook a thermometer. "In the meantime, stick this in your mouth."

As soon as they were left alone, Alex bent and kissed Jo on the cheek. She put her arms around him and held him to her with what little strength she still had.

"Thank you for staying with me through it all, Alex," she said. "I don't know if I could have made it without you."

"You would have made it, Jo," he said. "You've got a will of iron."

"Alex," Riquelme's voice came from outside the door, "there's something you should see."

"I'll be back," he said to Jo. Taking the Ingram, he went out to see what it was. They went to a window, where Riquelme pointed down at the street. Nobody was out there.

"They're gone," Riquelme said. "For the first time since we came here, they're gone."

Alex opened the window and stuck his head outside. There was nothing moving. This should have been a welcome sight, but he found it disturbing instead. Why would the colloids want to surrender the armory to the guerrillas, without leaving even a token force to continue the siege?

Siegel approached. "Alex, what is it?"

"The infected are gone. The streets are empty."

"Then the fourth stage must have begun," Siegel said. "That's the only logical explanation."

"But why would all of them leave?"

"Perhaps they are all needed somewhere else now."

"Needed? For what?"

"I don't know, Alex, but I suppose we'll find out in due time."

Siegel and Elvin went off, leaving Alex to ponder this unexpected turn of events. It occurred to him that the smartest thing for him to do was to go outside and try to find out where the infected had gone. It seemed a sensible plan, but he hated to leave Jo alone so soon after her ordeal. He supposed that she would be safe enough here, though, with Siegel to look after her.

He gathered enough provisions to last a few days, cleaned the Ingram, and slipped out through the fire exit on Cuthbert Street. Except for a scurrying rat, he saw no signs of life at all in the mid-morning streets. It was a cloudy day, though it didn't look to Alex as if it were going to rain. The weather was unseasonably warm, in fact, somewhere in the mid-fifties as he set out.

It seemed logical to ford the river and find out what things were like in Center City these days. Since there was nobody around, he saw little risk in crossing by bridge instead of passing through the tunnel.

Half an hour later, he stood in the shadow of One Liberty Place, a sixty-one storey skyscraper built just a few years earlier. The huge, neo-deco tower had been left miraculously untouched during the war, except for a few broken windows. Its silver-blue spire was luminous against the glowering clouds, a gigantic tombstone overlooking a cemetery that had once been a thriving city.

"Shit," Alex said softly. "Where is everybody?" At this point, he almost would have been relieved to see a colloid. The city seemed picked clean of life, as if nothing could exist here ever again. A barren garden, sown with salt.

He wandered through the side streets and alleys, hoping to find someone, anyone. He could almost believe that the entire population of the Earth had vanished, except for his little band of guerrillas. But that seemed highly unlikely. There were many others like them, neurologically damaged people everywhere. They all had a chance; they might die by the hands of the infected, but they could not contract the disease themselves. There were thousands of mentally ill people in Philadelphia alone, millions in North America. Perhaps tens or even hundreds of millions worldwide. If they could come together as a fighting force, then the colloids would have something to worry about.

"You alone?" The voice came from behind him.

Alex turned quickly, crouching and looking for cover. But there were only stone walls on either side of the narrow alley. He pointed the Ingram at the person who had spoken.

"Don't shoot," the bedraggled oriental kid said. "I'm not one of them, please believe me."

Alex lowered the barrel of the Ingram. "I'm sorry," he said. "But you shouldn't have come up behind me that way."

"I was afraid you'd get away before I could talk to you. You don't know how long it's been since I've had somebody to talk to."

"Well, you'll have plenty of people to talk to, if you come with me. What's your name?"

"Tony. Tony Chang. What's yours?"

"Alex Ward." Alex stepped forward and extended his right hand. Tony's grip was firm, but he was so thin that Alex suspected he hadn't eaten for days. "If you know a good place to sit down, Tony, I've got some rations. Why don't we eat and compare notes?"

"Sounds good to me," Tony said. "I know just the place."

Tony led Alex to a Burger King. The front wall had been blasted inward, but in the back were a couple of intact booths. They sat down at one and Alex opened the rations, offering some to Tony before he took any for himself. Tony ate slowly, in spite of his intense hunger, savoring every bite.

"Do you know where they all went?" Alex asked.

"No, but I saw them moving toward the river."

"How many?"

"There must have been thousands of them. Others were joining them all the time, like they were migrating or something."

"Heading south, like snowbirds?"

"No, it looked like they were going north."

"Going north for the winter. Not very smart."

Tony looked at him as if he didn't understand, and then he burst into laughter. "No, not very smart."

"What could they be up to?" Alex said.

Tony shook his head. "I don't know, but I'm glad to see them going away from here."

"Yeah, but where do you suppose they're headed?"

"To hell, I hope."

"Look, Tony, I'm going to follow them, try to find out what's going on. Do you want to come with me?"

"Come with you? Look, we just got rid of them. Why push our luck?"

"Because they're probably planning something worse than what's already happened."

"Shit, what could be worse?"

"Whatever it is, it will be the final blow to what's left of the human race."

"You think so?"

"They haven't got far to go."

Tony smiled. "You really think we can fight back, don't you, Alex?"

"I know we can. We've won several battles already. And we've found a way to fight infection."

"How?"

"We've got a drug that can drive a colloid out of a human body. It's been tried successfully once."

"Really? That's fantastic."

"We also think that some people are immune to infection. You might be one of those."

"You mean all this time I didn't have to worry?"

"I don't know about that. A lot of people who weren't infected have been killed."

"Tell me about it." Tony loked as if he were not ready to buy this theory. "Why are some people immune?" he asked.

"The colloids tend to stay away from people who have suffered neurological damage."

Tony stared straight at him, and then burst into laughter. "You mean, after growing up my whole life with people not accepting me, now some virus doesn't accept me, either?"

"Something like that." That had crossed Alex's mind more than once; he and Tony were on the same wavelength.

Throwing back his head, Tony laughed until tears came to his eyes. "Wow! I always knew I had been put on this Earth for some special purpose. But when I told people that, they said I was nuts and put me away."

"Well, you're alive and those who said you're nuts probably aren't. Maybe you *were* put on earth for some special purpose. I'm not very religious, but if I were, I'd probably believe that God, in his infinite wisdom, had created us poor unfortunates to save the world."

"I know you're not serious, but it's the sort of thing a smart preacher or politician could make work for him," Tony said. "Rhetoric to get the blood boiling among the masses."

"Who can argue with a little well placed fire and brimstone?" said Alex.

"We could probably use some of that fire and brimstone, if we're going to follow the infected on their Conga Line to New Jersey, or wherever they're going."

Alex smiled, realizing that Tony intended to go with him. "You don't have a gun, do you?"

"No, and I don't want one."

"Let me guess . . . you're a secret master of Tae Kwan Do?"

"Something like that." Tony grinned knowingly, and Alex didn't know whether to take him seriously or not. That was the trouble with crazy people—you never knew if what they said had any basis in reality.

"So," Alex asked, "you coming with me, Tony?"

"Why not?"

They finished eating and walked through the blasted wall of the Burger King, out onto Chestnut Street. They headed north to Race Street and made their way east, toward the Delaware River. The remains of the Benjamin Franklin Bridge was a cat's cradle of twisted, blue girders on the Pennsylvania side; over on the New Jersey side, the riverfront was a gaping hole where the bridge's pilings had stood.

"Camden has never looked lovelier," Tony said.

"If I saw before-and-after photos, I could hardly tell the difference," Alex agreed, enjoying the old Philadelphia game of making fun of New Jersey, "except for that crater where the bridge abutments used to stand. Those bombed-out buildings behind it don't look much different than they used to."

"The Walt Whitman Bridge is still standing in South Philly," Tony said.

Alex nodded. "I'm relieved to know that I won't have to swim to Jersey, if I ever get the urge to go over there again."

"An old Chinese proverb: 'Every cloud has a silver lining.' "

"Is that Chinese?"

Tony shrugged. "Who knows?"

They walked a little further before Tony said, "We'll be coming up on the interstate in a few minutes. We should get out of sight as soon as . . ."

Alex shushed him, pushing him into an alleyway. Someone was walking in the street ahead. Not one, but several people. They were shambling up the ramp toward the interstate highway.

And on the highway, like an insectile army, thousands of the infected moved toward the north, slowly but with unmistakable purpose.

CHAPTER NINETEEN

"It looks like these are the stragglers," Alex said. "Once they've gone, the city will be deserted, except for the uninfected."

"What about full-grown colloids?" Tony said.

Alex thought about that, and realized that he hadn't seen a single colloid all day. "They seem to be gone already. I don't know how they did it, though."

"Maybe they're hibernating in the city someplace."

"Wouldn't that be great? If we could just find their hiding places, we could burn them all alive."

"That would warm our hearts, wouldn't it?"

"We better get closer, instead of daydreaming."

"Closer?" Tony said.

"How else can we find out anything about them?"

"Yeah." Tony seemed resigned to go through with this. Perhaps human companionship was more important to him than safety. In any case, Alex was glad to have his company, not to mention his help.

Keeping themselves out of sight as much as possible, they advanced by fits and starts. Now hiding in the shadow of an abandoned car or building, now dashing quickly to a shattered wall, they attempted to minimize the time spent in the open as much as possible, while they methodically approached the highway.

Zigzagging in a northeast direction, they soon found themselves at a complex of old, brick storage buildings, rusting rails leading away from them like blood trails. They walked on packed gravel blackened by a century of soot and oil, climbing a hill that led to a concrete wall. The wall bordered the west side of the interstate for a couple of miles where the six-lane highway stretched toward the northeast. It was brightly painted with colorful murals depicting city life, a relic of the sixties.

"There's a break in this wall somewhere along here," Tony said. "It happened during the war. A stray rocket or something. . . . The usual military ineptitude."

They soon found it, a jagged gap in the concrete from which they could look down on the throngs of infected who moved slowly away from Philadelphia.

"There goes my hibernation theory," Tony said.

Alex peered through the gap, and saw what Tony meant. Each of the infected had become hunchbacks, growths swelling underneath the ragged clothing of those who wore anything at all. Those who were naked revealed not curved spines, but gelatinous parasites clinging to their flesh.

Passengers. Every one of the infected carried a colloid on his or her back.

"It's a clean sweep, all right," Alex said, leaning back out of sight of the infected. "The meek have inherited Philadelphia, if not the Earth."

Tony nodded. "This is wild," he said. "Where the hell do you suppose they're all going?"

"Broadway?"

Tony laughed as they clomped down the hill away from the interstate, and it occurred to Alex—not for the first time—that as long as they could laugh, they would never be completely beaten. They sought refuge behind a windowless brick building.

"I wonder," Alex said, as soon as he had caught his breath, "if we could just sort of fall in at the end of the line and march along behind them."

Tony tried to laugh, but he seemed unsure of whether Alex was serious or not. "You know what they'd do to us if they found out?"

"If we were at the end, we could just shoot the nearest of them and make a run for it. I don't think they could catch us."

"You're crazy as a shit house rat, man," Tony said.

"So they tell me."

"Look, for all we know they're going to jump off a cliff like a bunch of lemmings. Why not let them go?"

"I already explained all that to you, Tony."

"Yeah, but you seem to be looking for ways to get us in trouble."

"You don't have to come with me."

Tony fell silent. Alex knew that he was putting the kid between a rock and a hard place. If he didn't tell him where the guerrillas were holed up, Tony would remain a solitary wanderer in a deserted city. Of course, Alex could tell him about the armory and let Tony go join the others, but then Tony's incentive for helping him would vanish. Maybe he was being a little ruthless, but it seemed necessary. This was, after all, war.

"You'll take me to your friends if I go with you?" Tony asked. "Provided we live through this?"

"You have my word on it."

Tony looked dubiously at him, but he nodded his assent. "You sound like that lawyer who used to advertise on TV."

Alex laughed. "You know what happened to the lawyers, don't you? Sane and logical as they were, they were among the first to go."

Tony permitted himself a smile. "Maybe the colloids aren't *all* bad."

"Well, pretty soon we'll find out just how bad they are, won't we?"

Tony didn't look at him, as he said, "Yeah, I guess so."

"Let's do it then."

"What about your gun?"

Alex looked down at the Ingram nestled in his arms. "What do you mean?"

"As soon as they see it, they'll know you're not one of them. Then what's going to happen?"

"Maybe I can strap it on my back and cover it with my clothes. It'll look like I'm carrying a colloid."

"It might work."

"Sure it will. You should look for something to put on your back, too."

"But you said that they communicate telepathically, Alex. How are we gonna fool them?"

"There are thousands upon thousands of them. They won't bother about a couple of stragglers."

"I hope you're right."

Alex removed his shirt and arranged the Ingram's strap around his left shoulder, with the barrel pointing toward the ground. Then he put the shirt back on and pulled it up over the gunbutt.

"How does it look?" he asked.

"Lovely," Tony said, tearing strips from his own bedraggled jacket and stuffing them under his collar. "You should have been featured in *GQ*."

"You'll pass muster, too. Let's go."

They hustled back up the hill, taking care not to be seen. Coming to the gap in the wall, they waited until the last of the infected staggered past, and then stealthily walked out onto the crumbling asphalt. They took their places at the end of the line and pretended to be part of the exodus.

Alex felt a sense of awe as he looked ahead, seeing the infected walking four or five abreast as far as the eye could see. Perhaps Tony had been right; this might not have been a very good idea. After fifteen or twenty minutes, they came to an exit ramp. More of the infected were joining them, coming up from Girard Avenue. Alex tried not to stare at the blotchy blue faces as the newcomers fell in behind him and Tony.

Tony glanced at him resentfully, as if to say that he had told Alex so. It was too late to get out now, though. Now they were stuck here, and would have to see it through till the end.

It was eerie, marching silently in this army of the dead. The infected made gurgling sounds, similiar to the noises some inmates had made when Alex was in the hospital. The scuffing of rotted shoes on the asphalt was the only other sound. A strong breeze swept the sickly odor of the infected away most of the time, but every now and then it assailed Alex and Tony. It was so repellent that Alex wanted to gag every time he caught a whiff, but he tried to show no reaction. Nevertheless, he became preoccupied with the smell. It was a death stench, but not like after a jungle firefight, or even like the dying in a hospital. It was a unique and—for lack of a better word—alien smell.

As time passed, and they marched into Philadelphia's northeast, the wind died. Surprisingly, Alex became more accustomed to the odor. He was reminded of a summer job he'd held when he was a teenager—garbageman. His first day on the job, he had made the mistake of standing under the enormous trash crusher blade after the truck had deposited its disgusting contents at the dump. Suddenly a stinking rain had fallen from the blade, drenching his hair and running down onto his face and shoulders. He had shouted out in anger at the driver, but the more experienced garbagemen had only been quietly amused by his discomfiture. After a few more days, he had gotten used to the smell . . . though his mother had not enjoyed washing his work clothes.

He found comfort in this memory now, assuring himself that he would get used to the terrible stench of the infected. The trick was simply to take your mind off it, to think of more pleasant things. He tried to occupy himself by looking around him, taking note of the odd detail, or trying to determine what the wrecked buildings had once been used for.

Tony walked slightly ahead of him, to his right. He seemed as preoccupied as Alex was trying to be, and his face was so dirty it was impossible to tell that he had none of the telltale blue blotches on his skin.

Terror seized Alex's heart then. There was a trail of cloth strips falling from the tail of Tony's jacket. His fake colloid was coming undone.

Alex dared a glance at the infected behind them. Their dead eyes were on the trail of rags behind Tony. The nearest of them advanced clumsily but swiftly toward him.

CHAPTER TWENTY

Three of them were on Tony before Alex could even think of reaching for his gun. More were behind them, grasping and grunting, trying to get in on the kill. Tony screamed as they wrestled him to the ground, overpowered by the sheer weight of their numbers.

Alex's hand was reaching for the Ingram's shoulder strap, but he made a conscious effort to stop it. They didn't know that he wasn't one of them. Only Tony was in danger.

But could he stand by and watch the kid die? If it wasn't for Alex, Tony wouldn't even be here. But there were hundreds of the infected behind them now, and those ahead were turning to join in the fray. The Ingram could only kill a few of them, and then he would be trapped. He had to let them kill Tony. With a resigned motion, Alex turned toward the north and continued walking.

"No!" Tony cried. "You can't do this!"

Tony was screaming at his attackers, but it seemed as if he were talking to Alex. He kept on screaming as Alex shuffled slowly forward, trying to show no sign of the horror and heartsickness he felt. He should never have forced Tony to come with him. The kid had trusted him.

As the infected horde moved slowly onward, Tony's shrieks faded and then stopped altogether. Had he been killed outright, beaten to death by the infected? Or had the colloids instructed their hosts to place some of them on the poor kid, so that they could devour him alive? Alex might never know, and he didn't want to. It was enough to know that Tony was dead . . . and it was all Alex's fault. Tony had survived on his own for three years, and now he had been done in by his need for companionship. Alex had played to that need like a master manipulator.

But why? He hadn't needed Tony's help. It wasn't like him to enlist other people in his causes. He should have just sent Tony to the armory and left it at that. Now he had to live with this.

The day wore on into dusk. As the stars came out, Alex noticed that the odor of the infected didn't really bother him so much anymore. Tony's death and the physical effort of the long walk had numbed his senses, he supposed. Would he ever have a chance to get away? Maybe he should work his way over to the edge of the highway. Then he might be able to slip onto the embankment of an overpass and make a run for it. He tried, but the infected were so close around him that he couldn't do it without arousing them.

No, his only chance was to act just like them. He had to keep shambling along as if he were under the power of a colloid, no matter how long it took. Alex despaired to see that, even as darkness descended, they were not yet out of the city. Perhaps the night would be his salvation, though.

Again, he was disappointed. The infected often jostled him now, drawing closer to one another—and consequently to him—for warmth as the temperature dropped. Alex felt the cold seep through his rags, and through the holes in his boots. He exhaled vapor. Against his back, the Ingram was like ice.

As the night deepened, he remembered Tony's comparison of the infected to lemmings marching to the sea. Well, they were going the wrong way to reach the Altantic, but the walk probably would turn out just as ill-fated . . . for Alex, at least. And, when he got right down to it, what did it matter? In his most secret heart, he had often thought that the Earth was better off without humankind. Under the colloids' rule there was no pollution, no threat of nuclear war, no regional conflict. There had once been billions of people on the planet, it was true, but if he became truly objective about it, he had to admit to himself that, by and large, his fellow creatures had done a good job of little besides fouling their own nest.

And it was entirely possible that the colloids, once they

had secured their position as masters of the Earth, would accomplish great things. The holocaust might prove to be the salvation of the planet.

Alex stared up at the clear night sky, wondering if the star the colloids had come from was even visible from earth. Might their arrival have been foreseen in the world's religions for all these millennia? Gods and angels, celestial visitors, UFOs. . . . Perhaps this was the destiny of the human race, the origin of all religions, somehow glimpsed by the prescient from the dim beginnings of civilization.

But this was fatalistic bullshit. Why had he fought the colloids if he believed that they were the rightful heirs to his own world?

He was very tired, but there was no chance of stopping to rest. The infected just seemed to go on and on without ever sleeping. No wonder they died so soon after the organisms invaded their nervous systems. Alex might be able to walk all night, but he would have to stop sometime tomorrow. He'd had so little sleep in the past few days. First the raid on the armory, then the death of his friend Flash, his discovery of Jo's true nature. . . . He had been so horrified to learn that she was host to a colloid. It didn't seem so bad to him now. After all, the colloid hadn't harmed her, had it? She was alive and well back at the armory, recovering from the intense struggle induced by the LSD. But had she been so much different under the influence of the colloid?

Her motivations had given her away, of course. Suddenly she was not working for the guerrillas anymore, and he had become suspicious of her. Not right away, though. He had to admire the cleverness of the enemy, to devise this new and subtle method of infection. They had come up with a refinement that even the host might not be aware of.

The realization came at that moment, shriveling his guts with terror. He was infected.

But no, it couldn't be. He was the proud possessor of a bipolar disorder. He was a nut case. The colloids had never wanted people like him.

At least they hadn't up to now.

In spite of the cold, sweat began to form on Alex's

brow, under his arms, in his crotch. He wanted to cry out, deny what he feared; scream to the stars that it wasn't true.

But with each passing moment, he knew with more and more certainty that it was. He had led Tony Chang to his death, at the behest of the colloid growing inside him. He had to remember that it was the colloid who had forced him to do it. He had believed himself to be no less at risk than Tony, hadn't he? If Tony had not carried a gun, was that his fault? And even if he had not joined Alex, Tony could as easily have died in the streets, couldn't he? Alex could have sent the kid to the armory, sure, but the guerrillas had little enough food as it was. Tony Chang was no great loss.

But this couldn't have been Alex thinking these things. This was contrary to everything he believed in.

It was the colloid, attempting to control his thoughts.

Alex looked around for the first time since Tony had been attacked, seeing that the infected paid no attention to him. They had doubtless been instructed by their masters not to harm him. He was one of them now.

How long had he been infected? Since the moment the colloid had been driven from Jo's body and mind? He estimated that at eighteen to twenty hours ago, but he could not be sure. He was losing track of time, borne along by thousands of the infected, moving endlessly into the shadows of night. The saurian necks of mercury vapor lamps rose up on either side of the broken asphalt, seeming to gesture towards the stars.

How could he defy a life form so old, an organism that had crossed such a vast distance in space and time? He had no choice but to obey it now, or he would be destroyed. He resigned himself to the alien's domination.

It was then that the colloid revealed itself.

Alex understood its reasoning. He had not been so unsuspecting as Jo, and so it had been forced to act artfully to lure him away from the armory and from the guerrillas. He must have no opportunity to take psycho-active drugs, and he must be permitted no contact with any of his friends, ever again. Or at least while the drugs lasted.

The colloid inside him revealed this to him with impunity. There was nothing Alex could do, was there? *It* was in control now, and had been for some time. He had foolishly walked away from his one hope of salvation and placed himself in the clutches of the colloids, utterly oblivious to the alien's influence over him.

And, oh, how the creature was enjoying itself. The delicious irony of being driven out of Jo and immediately entering the nervous system of the guerrilla leader, why *that* had made the entire ordeal worthwhile.

"I'm glad you think so, you son of a bitch!" Alex bellowed. With a furious effort, tearing the clothes on his back, he wrenched the Ingram around under his arm and pointed it at the nearest of the infected. "Maybe it's not so fucking easy as you think!"

But what good would it do to shoot the infected? There were so many of them. He could only kill a few, and then he would be alone with an empty gun against thousands.

The infected masses to his right parted, and he staggered through the crowd, not really certain if this was his idea or the colloid's. Sitting down by the side of the road, he held the Ingram gently, as the gap closed, and the infected continued to move toward the north.

He almost laughed, to think that a wish of his had come true. Many times, while he hid in the sewer like vermin, he had wished that the infected would not be able to harm him. He was one of them now; a higher order of the infected perhaps, but one of them nonetheless. But he was still fighting the colloids. In that he was different from the rest of them. Their minds were gone, useful for nothing more than beasts of burden. Thus far, he was unharmed, just as Jo had been unharmed. He would resist this invasion of his innermost being.

Hardly realizing what he was doing, he clicked off the Ingram's safety and raised the barrel in his mouth. As if he were performing fellatio, he closed his lips on the icy steel and shut his eyes.

His index finger gently touched the trigger.

CHAPTER TWENTY-ONE

Sweat poured from his face, and he trembled so badly that he wondered if he would be able to pull the trigger. He was uncertain whether this was his idea or the colloid's. He only knew that he wanted to do it. Did he deserve any better, after what he had done to Tony Chang?

He strained to pull the trigger, but his finger would not cooperate.

"I want to die, you bastard," he said.

But the colloid wasn't through with him . . . not yet. He lowered the gun from his face, commanded by an intelligence that was not his. He sat cross-legged by the side of the highway, waiting.

The colloid pushed his consciousness into some unused part of his brain, a dark cave from which he could see only the shadows of the world outside.

Don't leave me in here! he screamed. *Please! I can't survive in here!*

The colloid was not moved by his entreaties. It had gained complete control over him, and it would do with him as it pleased from now on. It would not dispose of his consciousness entirely, for then he would be of no more use to it than the infected hordes that moved endlessly before him. His new master would dip into his mind as if it were a well, taking what it required while keeping him alive.

Now he was sure that *he* had wanted to kill himself, but the colloid had prevented him from pulling the trigger. His last chance for freedom had been taken from him. Confused by contradictory emotions, he had hesitated for an instant, and the colloid had surged into complete dominance. He was imprisoned far away from his friends and the drugs that might save him.

What was worse, he could *feel* the alien crawling through

133

his brain like some loathsome spider. It lingered where it found what it considered pertinent information, sucking it up through some sort of bio-electrical field and relaying it to the other colloids.

It had apparently separated his motor functions from his other brain functions. Alex's body sat motionless, watching nothing.

A figure emerged from the infected army that marched endlessly before his staring eyes.

It, too, stared. The eyes were blank, dead. On its back it carried a glistening hump. It shuffled toward Alex and stood over him, unseeing, a marionette whose strings were pulled by the alien thing inside him.

It was Tony Chang.

One of the worn-out infected had been replaced by Tony, and the colloids had brought him out of the crowd to show him off to Alex. Perhaps they wanted Alex to see how lucky he was, one of the chosen few who would be allowed to retain some vestiges of their former selves.

Tony, he cried from deep inside his prison, *forgive me.*

The colloid found this amusing. It showed him why. Linking with the colloid in Tony's brain, it revealed a vision of desolation so total that even a glimpse of it was painful. There was nothing left of the bright kid Alex had first met—when?—the day before. Nothing at all. Tony would never forgive him, because Tony no longer existed. And it was all Alex's fault.

No, the alien had already been inside Alex's mind, insidiously manipulating him to feed it another victim. Tony had become a beast of burden, not because of Alex, but because of the colloids. Alex had to remember that, or he would lose what little reason that remained to him.

What are you going to do with me?

The colloid did not show him its intention, of course. It was the master, and he was the slave. It need reveal nothing to him, unless it desired to do so. This much was made clear to him.

It was trying to break his spirit.

Maybe you're surprised that you haven't broken me yet, maybe even a little disconcerted.

The colloid did not respond. It was probably unwise to

be so demonstrably defiant, Alex considered. The colloid controlled most of him, but not the essential core of his being. It had tricked him at first, until he had become aware of it . . . largely because of what had already happened to Jo. It occurred to him now that it might not have figured out a strategy.

Perhaps it was consulting with other colloids about him at this very moment. That would explain why it had left him sitting here with the possessed body of Tony standing over him. Physical paralysis and guilt were doubtless intended to immobilize him, inside and out.

Trying to put out my electrolytes, huh?

The colloid showed no reaction to his little joke. It wasn't likely that it had a sense of humor, he supposed . . . although it did seem to understand irony, in a sadistic way. Perhaps it did not comprehend the meaning of his mock question at all, but it surely understood the spirit in which the question was asked.

Well, I'll just wait in here until you see fit to do something. After all, what good am I to you if I just rot away?

The colloid indicated that it had plans for him, which seemed something of a minor victory to Alex. It was confused by his behavior, and as a result was showing its hand—or pseudopod. Alex was cheered by this ludicrous image.

The colloid was not.

Too bad. If you don't like my attitude, all you have to do is finish me off. Oh, but I guess you can't do that until you find another host, right? You can still take away the last vestige of my personality, though, can't you? Why don't you do that?

The reply was not forthcoming.

It couldn't be that you need me, could it? Saving me for a little espionage, just as you did with Jo?

But the colloid no longer responded to his goading. He would get nothing out of it now. It left him alone, perhaps to contemplate his guilt as Tony's body stood watch over him.

Alex had never minded solitude that much. After he got back from Viet Nam in '69, he had taken an apartment by himself. And he had done the same thing after he got out of the hospital three years ago. He had needed

time by himself to sort things out. There were worse
things than being alone . . . up to a point.

When you reached that point, you started to go stir
crazy. The colloid was probably counting on that fact of
human nature. Or maybe it didn't care. Maybe its power
over him would grow and grow until he had no recourse
but to do precisely what it wanted, right down to the
tiniest detail. Not just physically, but mentally, and even
emotionally.

But if it went that far, he wouldn't be Alex Ward
anymore, and he would be useless as an infiltrator. No, it
seemed likely that some element of his personality must
remain, if the job was to be carried out properly. He had
to go on hoping that this was the case. It was his only
chance.

Alex thought about his guerrillas, and especially about
Jo. Were they all right? Had Jo recuperated from the
infection? She had appeared to be recovering, but he
hadn't spent so much time with her before he left the
armory that he could be *absolutely* sure.

He sensed the colloid, lurking outside his mental prison.

*That was your idea, wasn't it? I would have made more
plans than that ordinarily, but you planted the idea in my
mind that I should move quickly, find out where all the
infected are going. Well, where the hell are they going?*

The colloid was not about to tell him, of course. At the
moment, it wanted to show him something else entirely.
It was linking with another colloid, and there was something disturbingly familiar about this creature. Its presence seemed to inundate Alex's mind, as if he too were
linked to it.

I know you.

Yes, and it knew him. Though it had been transformed
since he had last communicated with this entity.

It was Flash.

You're still alive!

But Flash didn't answer. He seemed unfocussed, swirling about inside Alex's prison like liquid. And yet, this
was unmistakably Flash. A memory of Alex himself fleetingly manifested itself among the vertiginous remnants of
Flash's consciousness. Did that mean that Flash recognized him?

How can you still be living? I must have been too late to save you from the colloids.

Flash couldn't answer him, but the colloid showed him that the host became a part of the colloid as it consumed him. Flash was not only alive, but his essence was alive in all the colloids who had come into contact with what was left of him.

In a very real sense, he had become immortal.

Alex tried to absorb this new knowledge. If he gave up, he could go on and on in the same way. All those he had assumed dead were still living, their memories somehow stored in colloidal suspension. The parasite in his brain had sought out Flash to demonstrate this fact.

But he can't think. He's not really Flash. It's some kind of trick. You've stored his memories, and now you're showing them to me like an old videotape.

But he sensed that there was more to it than that. This thing that spun about him like a living whirlpool was not just a recording, or even a memory. It existed here and now, and it was aware of Alex. But why couldn't it communicate with him. What had happened to Flash?

The colloid told him that this was what had happened to the infected, until the recent past. The intelligence of the host need no longer be impaired. But he would have to work with the colloid, in the creation of a new species.

A new species?

For the moment, the colloid would reveal no more of its secrets. Just enough had been shown to intrigue Alex and make him fearful. A new species? Part colloid and part human? Was this the fourth stage that Claire Siegel had guessed at?

Show me more . . . please.

Unexpectedly, the colloid did as it was asked. It began by breaking the link with the creature that had once been Flash, and bringing forth another ghost.

And this one was infinitely more painful for him.

It was his son, Billy.

CHAPTER TWENTY-TWO

Alex stood in the eye of a hurricane that had once been his own flesh and blood. Billy was raging, unlike Flash; he was full of youthful energy that had been stolen from his human body and stored in colloidal suspension. Now he sensed that his father was here with him, but he could do nothing but flail ineffectually with the abandon of a child. Alex felt his boy's agony as if it were his own. Billy cried out, the wail of a lost soul.

Billy, no.

Alex was uncertain of whether he was speaking to the colloid or to his son. This was so monstrous that he didn't think he could stand it. He would shrivel up and die, this little piece of him that was left somewhere in a corner of his mind.

You took him from me, you bastards, and now you torment me with his ghost! I'll kill you for this! I'll kill you all!

Now the colloid was truly amused. It had awakened passion in Alex at last: passion, anger, hatred. It had need of such strong emotions if it were to use him successfully. The colloids had proven themselves to be even more ruthless, more monstrous than Alex had believed possible. He was astonished by the depths of their ugliness, and he let them know how much he loathed them.

The colloid remained unaffected. He realized that it would goad him further if its purpose were served, and yet he could not control his rage.

His son's soul—there was no other word for it but soul—was a Catherine Wheel of blazing emotion. Billy blamed Alex for what had happened to him: the irrational belief of a child in his parent's omnipotence. And it seemed that Billy was stuck, that he would never know better because he could never learn anything again. He was in limbo.

Alex's anger turned inward, and he accepted the pain for what it was. It would do him no good to castigate the colloids. They didn't care. He had to face his own feelings about his son, which had been transformed now that he knew Billy was still partly alive.

Billy, do you hear me?

The childish rage did not so much answer him as it washed over him. Billy might understand what he was trying to do, if Alex could make him understand that his death was unavoidable. But how could you make a nine-year-old boy comprehend something like that? Death was not part of a child's life; even a grandparent's death was not altogether meaningful when you were that young. How could Billy ever have come to grips with the idea that he was going to die?

And he had been right. In point of fact, he had not died. His father had allowed him to be eaten away, to be changed into some half-human, half-alien monstrosity. But Alex hadn't understood what was happening. He had only wanted his son to live.

It wasn't fair. It just wasn't fair.

Son, what you don't understand is that I'm no different from you. Alex was pleading with him now. The colloid might take Billy away at any moment. He had to achieve some sort of rapprochement before that happened, because he might never get another chance to communicate with Billy. *I'm only a human being, just like you. I know I'm your father, but you have to understand that I wanted to stop what was happening, but I couldn't. I couldn't and it almost killed me. I love you, Billy. I always loved you and I always will. I love you now, son.*

Billy's rage flickered and died. Perhaps, even in this mutated form, he remembered the times Alex had nurtured him and taken him places and taught him things that a boy had to know to get along. This was his father, who had come at last to take him home.

I won't let you down, Bill. Hang in there, kiddo.

But already Bill was fading, pinwheeling out of Alex's brain and into oblivion.

He was immediately replaced with another suspended

soul. And this one was every bit as painful to Alex as the last. It was Sharon, the woman who had helped Alex recover from the mental wounds of war. The woman who loved him. The woman he had married. Billy's mother.

But this time he was ready. He projected love to his wife, and would permit himself no other emotion, no other thought. She was like the morning sun in her response, warm and hopeful. Her surprise at finding him in this most unexpected place only suffused her spirit with a luminescence that made him love her even more.

Sharon, I've found you again. I've dreamed of you so many times since you died, but I never thought I'd be with you again. I love you so much.

And she loved him, too. There was no misunderstanding on her part. She, after all, had suffered their son's infection and death with him, and she had understood his anguish when she too became infected. She nearly drowned Alex in her love.

And she was taken away immediately.

Alex remained in his minute prison, bereft. Somewhere outside this place, his vacant eyes shed tears. He felt them stinging his eyes and rolling down his cheeks. His face was hot despite the early morning chill. He had broken free of his prison!

But only for a moment . . . and then he was back inside.

He was exhausted. And yet he was certain that he could shore up his resources again. He was not beaten. He had not let them break him. Instead of being horrified by what they had revealed to him, he had expressed love to Sharon and Billy. The colloids had hoped to turn his love to hatred, and better yet, to fear. Without even thinking about their intentions, he had expressed his honest emotions toward his wife and son, not as mutations, not as colloids, but as the human beings they had once been, and in some essential way, still were.

I told you before, you'll have to kill me to win. I won't let you beat me.

The colloid did not respond. Perhaps it was beginning to believe him. It was probably linking with other colloids, trying to devise a strategy to deal with his obstinacy. That would give him a little time to shore himself up.

They had tried their big guns on him, and they had failed. What could they do now? Torture him? What torture could have been as effective as bringing his loved ones back from the dead? No, he had won. He was almost certain of it.

Almost.

He must clear his mind, prepare for the last desperate siege. This was war, and the colloids had almost made him forget that single, overriding fact.

He still loved Sharon and Billy, something the colloids had never suspected. Nevertheless, his wife and son were part of the past, and Alex had obligations in the present. There were people who depended on him, uninfected people who needed him. It was his duty to get back to them, one way or the other, or die trying. He could not help Sharon and Billy anymore. He had reminded them of the past, when they were entirely human, and Sharon at least had seemed grateful for that. Billy, too, had felt something at the end of his forced visit. Alex was certain of it.

He yearned for more contact with his loved ones, but he knew it was no good. The colloids would only come up with some devious new way to use them against him. Perhaps Sharon and Billy were not dead in a physical sense, but they were dead to him. If not, then he would have to become like them. That was one thing he would never allow.

Do your damnedest.

The colloid rose to the challenge. It revealed to him that he would never again communicate with Sharon and Billy, and that was merely the beginning. Jo, and all the other guerrillas would be consumed, and their souls—the colloids enjoyed the concept of the soul—would linger in an alien purgatory for what would seem an eternity.

The colloids had conquered their fear of neurological damage, and would soon infect every brain left on earth, no matter what its condition.

You're trying to frighten me, but you're only giving me strength. You wouldn't want to wipe us out unless you were afraid of us.

What would it matter, when the last humans were gone from the Earth?

Never. We will never be driven from the earth. Even if you consume us all, there will still be a part of us living inside you. The seeds of your defeat have been sown in your own biology. You cannot win.

Alex felt himself growing, battering at his prison cell door. He sensed the colloid's alarm at this unexpected turn, and he exulted in it.

I'm crazy, and you're gonna see how it feels to be crazy, too!

He gloried in the manic rush that seized him, the wild and reckless expansion that filled the tiny space in his brain and more. He was seeping through the prison, into the labyrinthine contours of the cortex, through the hypothalamus, spreading outward through the reticular activating system. Every neuron charged by a firing synapse, one after another coming under his control once again.

He felt his own heart beating.

He felt his own lungs breathing.

He felt the electric charge fire along the optic nerve, and he saw once again.

The asphalt was hard against his buttocks. His back ached from sitting in the same position all night.

He was drooling. He closed his slack jaw and wiped away the spittle. Above him stood the mindless body of Tony Chang. Somewhere, hidden inside it, was a remnant of Tony as he had been, but would never be again.

Alex lifted his weary, sore body off the pavement and stumbled past the colloid master under whose weight Tony's body was bent.

One last sensation of the dying colloid that had tormented Alex passed fleetingly through his consciousness, guttered, and then was snuffed out. Its dark light was no longer within his body or mind.

Alex walked out onto the empty highway and watched the sun rise.

CHAPTER TWENTY-THREE

The wind whistled along the highway.

It took several minutes for Alex to remember where he was. And even then he didn't know how far he had walked. He appeared to be in the suburbs somewhere north of the city, and he had a long way to go back home. He felt very weak, though his spirits were high indeed.

He turned around, seeing Tony standing by the side of the road. The kid's spine was cruelly curved by the weight of the colloid, and he looked more dead than alive.

Still, Alex didn't shoot him. The colloid would have nowhere to go if its host died, and consequently would have no recourse but to attack Alex. If he just left it alone, perhaps he could walk away from it and return to the armory. It was also possible that the colloid would force Tony to attack him, of course. Alex thought it best to move away warily.

But Tony turned slowly toward the north and began to walk stiffly. Apparently there was more important business afoot than dealing with Alex.

Had the colloids written Alex off as a freak? Surely there were others besides him who had resisted them. He might never know the reason, but he suspected that the colloids considered him beyond the pale. If he were truly untouchable, then he would be able to strike at them in ways that they might never suspect. It was something to think about.

Just now, however, he could only think of food and shelter. His joints ached from exposure, and his hunger seemed to course through his entire body. He had never felt so frail and weak in his life.

He started the long walk home, the activity gradually warming him a little against the morning air. But after an hour or two walking on the deserted interstate, it occurred to him that he might be better off going cross country. He might even find something to eat in the ruins of northeast Philadelphia, though it was not likely. The scavengers had picked the city clean a long time ago.

Alex stepped over a guard rail and stumbled down the embankment, into the abandoned streets with their rows of tract houses. Most of the two storey buildings were still standing, miles from Center City, where the action had really gotten hot during the war.

Alex entered a house, finding it almost empty. The wooden floors had been eaten away by the weather, since the windows were all broken. The kitchen shelves were empty.

He left the house and continued in a general southwesterly direction. Every now and then he stopped to look in another house, or neighborhood store, and each time he was disappointed to find nothing to sustain him.

As the morning wore on, the sun warmed the streets somewhat, though an occasional breeze chilled Alex. Most of the time, he was uncomfortable but all right. If he hadn't been so weak and hungry, he could have made good time. He estimated that it would take days for him to get back to the armory at this rate. He was very thirsty; if he didn't get a drink soon, he would keel over. But it hadn't rained in several days, and there was no sign of water anywhere. Alex didn't know how much longer he could keep going.

The wind picked up, snapping at Alex's face, but he thought he heard something between the gusts. A buzzing, droning sound . . . quite distant but coming closer all the time. It seemed familiar, but it had been so long since he had heard such a sound that it took him a moment or two to realize what it was.

A motorcycle!

Alex started toward it as quickly as he could. He crossed the street and walked behind some deserted rowhouses, and there it was, a chopped-down Harley-Davidson with a girl riding it.

Without hesitation, she barreled toward him and stopped not five feet in front of him. She lifted her goggles and let her raven hair stream behind her. She could not have been more than fifteen years old.

"Got any water?" Alex asked, the words coming more easily than he expected after his ordeal.

"Sure." She pulled out a bottle fastened to one of the chopper's struts and tossed it to him.

Alex managed to catch it. Lifting it in a toast, he drank long and deeply.

"You can drink the whole thing, if you want," the girl said. "I got plenty more back at my place."

"Thanks." Alex took another long draft.

"They're all gone, huh?" the girl said, glancing toward the east.

"Yeah," replied Alex, wiping his chin. "I watched the last one go."

"Shoulda shot the motherfucker."

"Like shooting the ocean."

"My name's Ronnie Carilli," she said. "What's yours?"

"Alex." He eyed the bike. "Where'd you get the gasoline to run that thing, Ronnie?"

"Down in South Philly. Scavengers raided the refineries, but they were too dumb to get the tanks the executives used to fill up their own cars. There's still a lot of gas down there."

Alex smiled.

"I don't know why I told you that."

"Don't worry. It'll be our secret."

Ronnie frowned. "Where'd you come from anyway?"

"I was . . . following them."

"Where'd they all go?"

"North. That's all I know."

"Maybe they'll go to Alaska."

"Maybe."

"Think they'll come back?"

"Not for a while." Alex finished the water, and said, "Do you know where I can get some food, Ronnie? I'm starving."

"Jump on, and I'll take you back to my place."

Alex nodded, and got on the back of the motorcycle. He held onto the strap as Ronnie revved up the engine with obvious relish and roared off to the south. She drove like a maniac, but that was all right. There wasn't any traffic to worry about.

Alex had assumed that Ronnie lived somewhere nearby.

By the time they had crossed Market Street and were headed down 9th toward the old Italian Market, however, he realized that she was a South Philly kid, through and through. This girl had grown up in the neighborhood where her parents and grandparents had grown up, probably from the time that her ancestors had found their way here from Ellis Island. She had only been twelve when the colloids came, and had watched all of her loved ones die. Perhaps she had been a problem child, the victim of a disorder which had been her salvation while all those around her succumbed to the terrible disease from the stars.

Ronnie took him to a narrow street, little more than an alley off Passyunk. Alex was relieved when she cut the Harley's engine. He blew on his numb fingers and tried to hear what she was saying, deafened as he was by the wind and the cycle's powerful motor.

"This way." She led him up a flight of marble steps to an apartment house. The door was unlocked, and they walked into a spacious lobby. "Posh, huh Alex?"

She took him upstairs to an enormous apartment with boarded up windows. There was one chair, and there were cushions on the floor for sleeping. Next to the fireplace was a pile of cardboard and wood. Ronnie put some boards in the fireplace and lit a match to a bit of the cardboard, which she stuffed into the hearth until she got a blaze going.

"Cook you some beans?" she said.

"That would be great."

Ronnie used a pair of tongs to hold the can of beans over the fire, after opening the can with an old fashioned can-opener, running it around the top of the can with surprising speed.

"Had to get used to this thing," she said. "My mama always used an electric can-opener."

Alex nodded. And as soon as the beans were heated, he accepted them gratefully. Ronnie handed him a Swiss Army knife with the fork extended, and he began to eat.

She watched him in silence. She was a pretty girl, in an appealing Mediterranean way. There was a toughness about her that was belied by her youth and soft features.

She made Alex wish that he were twenty-odd years younger.

"It's great now that the colloids are gone, you know," she said. "I mean, I just ride my bike wherever I want. Hardly ever see anybody. When I do, I stop and talk to them, but they usually don't make any sense. You talked just like a normal person."

Alex grinned. "Don't let that fool you, Ronnie. I'm just as crazy as anybody else."

She looked at him warily.

He spoke quickly to reassure her. "Harmless, though."

"Yeah." Ronnie used the tongs to heat up a can of beans for herself. As she leaned forward over the fire, a scapular fell out of her fatigue jacket and dangled over the hearthstones. "I guess it doesn't make much difference anymore if you're crazy or not," she said. "It's enough to just be human."

"Ronnie, how did you survive all this time?"

"My Papa hid us first one place and then another, until he got infected. Then my Mama and I ran away from him so he wouldn't kill us. Mama got infected last summer. I been on my own ever since she died."

"I'm sorry." Alex hoped that she would never learn that her parents weren't dead, not completely. It was better to believe that they were in heaven, or even in hell.

"That's okay." Ronnie removed the can of beans. "I guess you must of lost somebody too."

"Yeah." He handed her the knife. "I lost everybody."

Ronnie sat cross-legged on the floor, eating. She stared at the fire, remembering.

"Look," said Alex, after a while, "I know where there are people who are putting together something. A family, kind of. Would you like to go and live there?"

She looked at him strangely. "It's not some kind of cult, or anything like that?"

"No, just a bunch of people who got tired of being alone, that's all."

"Are they hiding out in the underground? I almost got raped down there once, and never went back."

"No, there's nobody in the underground anymore. My people are in West Philly."

"Is that where you were headed when I found you? To join up with them?"

"Yeah. I left there yesterday . . . at least I think it was yesterday. Or it might have been the day before. I'm not really sure."

"What happened? Get hit on the head?"

Alex laughed. "Something like that."

"These people you're talking about," Ronnie asked. "Want me to drive you to them on my bike?"

"I'd appreciate it, Ronnie. But right now I think I ought to get some sleep."

"Just curl up over there." She gestured toward the cushions.

Alex set the Ingram on the floor, laid down on the cushions next to it, and closed his eyes. His entire body was so aching and tired that he could not get comfortable. He should have been able to fall asleep, but it wasn't working. He closed his eyes and tried to drift off, to no avail.

After a half hour of this or more, he rolled onto his side, and felt a gentle touch on his shoulder.

"Alex," Ronnie whispered. "Wake up."

CHAPTER TWENTY-FOUR

Had she heard intruders? Had the infected returned? He detected no urgency in the girl's tone, and heard nothing himself. What, then, was the trouble?

"Anything wrong?" he asked, reaching for the Ingram.

"I need to know something," Ronnie said. "That's all."

Alex's heart resumed beating at a nearly normal rate. There didn't seem to be any imminent danger. But what did the girl want?

"Will you hold me?" Ronnie asked in a child's voice. "It's been a long time since anybody's done that."

"Sure." Alex put his arms around her and her warm face pressed against his shoulder.

"My mom would of said this is a mortal sin, but I gotta tell you . . . "

Alex waited.

"See, I never knew what it was like to . . . I mean, I had a boyfriend, but we were only twelve, see. And he got sick. And then it was like just trying to survive. People were dying, and you couldn't get food and water, and colloids were everywhere. So I never learned about . . . you know."

Alex thought he knew what she was driving at. "And you want me to teach you? Is that it, Ronnie?"

She raised her little face so that she could look directly into his eyes. "Yeah, that's it."

He hugged her tightly. "You don't want an old fart like me."

"You said you lost everybody." There was distress in her voice. "Don't you like me?"

"Of course I like you. It's just that I'm old enough to be your father. My son would be almost your age now, if he had lived. It wouldn't be right, Ronnie."

He felt her hot tears soaking through his clothes. "I'll probably die before anybody makes love to me," she bawled.

"No, no. There are lots of young people around. I met one the other day who was only five or six years older than you, Ronnie. A lot more will come out of hiding now that the colloids are gone."

That seemed to calm Ronnie a little. "What happened to him? The guy you ran into, I mean?"

Alex shook his head. "He didn't make it."

"Young people never make it. I must be the only one left in the whole world." She started crying all over again.

"Oh, come on." It seemed to Alex that she was right, though. There did seem to be a preponderance of middle-aged and even elderly people still surviving. Perhaps it was simply because they had learned to be more cautious during their longer lives, or perhaps it was because the brains of the young tended to be healthier.

"Come back with me to my friends, and soon there'll be other young people joining us, I'm sure of it."

"Really?"

"Cross my heart."

Ronnie seemed to brighten a little. "Think maybe if I come back with you, I'll get a boyfriend, huh?"

"I know you will, Ronnie. Look, right now I've gotta get some sleep, though. I know it's early in the day, but I haven't had any rest for quite a while."

"I know. Sorry." Ronnie, her virginity still intact, extricated herself and left Alex to his dreams.

His dreams were not pleasant. He spiralled down to a dark place where armies of the infected marched endlessly through the night. In each of them was a thing that had come from a distant world, a thing that had no intention of letting him go until he was consumed.

Alex remembered a dream he had had while Jo was recovering from infection. He had been a viral cell, dormant, drifting through space. He had come to earth with billions of other cells, seeking the most advanced nervous systems on the planet.

He knew now that this had not been a mere dream. He had already been infected, the colloid driven from Jo's body into his. Even then, in the earliest stage of infection, its memories and his had become entwined. It had not shown itself while he was conscious, but while he was asleep . . .

But was he dreaming all this now? He was asleep, wasn't he? Strange images flickered across the insides of his eyelids, making him wonder what the vanquished colloid had left behind.

Was it possible that he still retained some vestige of the parasite's memory? Was he, in some indefinable way, *still* infected?

He fell through space, a long drifting descent through the cloudy atmosphere. This world's gases were almost ideal, and the sun's rays provided an adequate actinic exposure for the active seeking of sophisticated neurology. He felt himself awakening, already hunting, tumbling toward an unwary, bipedal creature who had never dreamed that such things could be. . . .

The biped's resistance was futile, and a new home was found amid the heat of its firing synapses. Its thought processes were complex enough to provide food, though much of it was ill suited to the purpose of its nervous system's invader. Social impulses were short-circuited, except for a rough herd instinct. The infected were easily programmed to attack the healthy.

Alex dreamed these things not as incidents, but as ideas, colored by the memories he had shared with the colloid. His own memories surfaced from time to time.

He entered a door and found a man being eaten by a colloid. The man resisted, half his face gone. He resisted until Alex shot him dead. Victor, and then Flash had resisted, and Alex had killed them. Jo was a Janus-faced entity who aided him on the one hand and worked against him on the other.

In the darkness, he ran from her. But as he moved through the terrain of his nightmares, he always found her just ahead. She was his beloved . . . and he feared her.

She embraced him, and he struggled, screaming in terror. But as her warmth enveloped him, he succumbed. And he knew that Jo was no longer the creature he had feared.

She released him and he lurched forward, falling . . .

And sat bolt upright. Late afternoon light streamed through the apartment's windows. The room was cold, but he was coated with his own sweat.

Ronnie was bending over him, stroking his forehead.

"You had a bad dream," she said.

It occurred to Alex that he might always have bad dreams from now on. He clung to the memory of Jo—the Jo he had known before her infection. The Jo who could never have led Flash to his death.

Alex bitterly remembered the remnant of Flash imprisoned inside a colloid, robbed once and for all of the defiant spirit that made him a unique human being.

Those swirling ghosts were not his loved ones, not anymore. He would go mad if he believed otherwise.

"Are you okay?" Ronnie asked.

"Yeah."

"Can I get you something?"

"No, I just want to go home."

Ronnie nodded. While he had slept, she doubtless had been thinking of what he had told her about the people at the armory. He wanted her to go with him, to be with other people.

"I'll get my stuff," she said.

An hour later they roared up to the big red doors of the armory, finding them wide open. Riquelme sat on a folding chair just inside with an M-16 propped against the jamb, warming himself at a fire in an iron drum, its smoke escaping from the entrance. He stared in disbelief as Alex got off the back of the chopper and walked toward him.

"Man," he said, getting up and bear-hugging Alex, "we thought you were dead."

"Not yet."

A woman Alex didn't know came out of the armory, and Riquelme said, "Liz, this is Alex." He turned back toward Alex, saying, "Liz joined us the morning after you disappeared."

"Glad to meet you, Liz."

Others were emerging from the depths of the armory, no longer afraid to come out in the open now that the colloids and the infected were gone. They gathered around Alex.

"It is the Prodigal," Samuel intoned, "returned from the land of the wicked."

Claire stood next to the cassocked prophet. She stepped forward and hugged Alex. "Welcome back," she said.

Alex said nothing until Jo appeared. She stayed back at the group's fringe for a moment, as if unsure that it was really him. Then she ran to him tearfully, embracing him with all of her renewed strength.

"You're alive," she said over and over again. "You're alive, you're alive, you're alive."

"Shaky, but still alive," Alex said. "I want you to meet a friend of mine." He turned to Ronnie and introduced her to the guerrillas. "I think she saved my life this morning."

"Let's go inside and talk," said the usually less than garrulous Elvin.

Everyone laughed at that, and though Elvin seemed puzzled by their mirthful reaction, he smiled a little, too. Alex, his arms around Jo and Ronnie, went inside the armory for the first time in days. Just how many days remained to be seen; he was almost afraid to ask how long he had been gone.

"We missed you, Alex," Polly said. "Where have you been all this time?"

"In hell." Overcome by emotion at this reunion with his friends—no, his family—he felt physically weak and exhausted, in spite of the food and sleep he had enjoyed earlier today. It would take more than a few hours to recover from the living death he had endured.

CHAPTER TWENTY-FIVE

Alex had another bad dream, and as a result he awakened sometime during the night. The room, an office outfitted with a cot, was still. He lay without moving for some time, staring at the ceiling. A sweaty film dampened his face and neck, moistening the pillow. The blanket was on the floor.

The nightmares would probably stay with him for some time. He was reminded of the years immediately following his military service, when he'd dreamed repeatedly that he was back in the Marine Corps, on his way to some unnamed tropical combat zone, where he would surely die.

But what if he were wrong about that? What if there were still some vestige of the colloid inside him? What if his victory had been nothing of the kind, but a ruse to make him infiltrate his own people once again?

He might never know . . . until it was too late.

Well, there was one person who might be able to help him learn the truth. He stretched his limbs and got out of bed gingerly, bumping around in the dark while he looked for his clothes.

Soon he was dressed and out in the corridor searching for Jo. The last time he remembered seeing her, she had been covering him with the blanket, just after she had washed his body with a damp cloth and dried him with a towel. He must have dropped off almost immediately after that.

Alex walked down to the big motor pool on the ground floor. He was amazed to see that nobody tended the front doors. They were closed, but appeared to be unlocked. A few days of peace had made the guerrillas very lax, it seemed.

He couldn't blame them. There was no sign that the

infected would return. They had lived in fear for such a long time that the chance to breathe freely once again must have been irresistible. The colloids and their slaves were gone; if there was an enemy among them, it was Alex.

Or possibly Jo. Where could she be?

Alex went over to the south wing and tried a few doors. On the third try, he found a most surprising sight. Claire and Samuel slept together on a mattress, their entwined limbs loosely covered by army blankets.

Gently, Alex closed the door, hoping that he had not disturbed them. He had missed a few things while he had been gone, apparently. But he found this unexpected union strangely appealing. It was a wedding of science and religion, after a fashion. He chuckled a little as he continued his search for Jo, opening one door after another until he came to the briefing room where they had once discussed the nature of the colloids hypothetically.

In the glow of a Coleman lantern, Jo and Ronnie sat talking in the large, empty room.

"Mind if I join you?" he asked.

They turned toward him.

"Alex," said Jo, "what are you doing out of bed?"

"I couldn't sleep. Nightmares."

Jo looked at him tentatively, as if she had heard something that recalled a memory she had believed lost to her. "Nightmares," she repeated.

Alex nodded. "Have you had them, too?"

"Yes. Ever since . . ."

Ronnie looked from one to the other questioningly.

"Ever since. . . ?" Alex had to hear her say it without prompting.

"Ever since I got sick."

"Me, too." He moved closer to her. "What are the nightmares like?"

"Like . . . like that thing left part of itself behind."

"Its memories? Maybe not all, but at least some of its memories?"

"Yes." She looked very frightened, and Alex put his arms around her.

"What are you two talking about?" Ronnie demanded to know.

Without looking at her, Alex said, "We were both infected, Ronnie."

"What?"

"It's true," Jo said. "It happened to me first, and we managed to get it out of my system, and then . . ."

"And then I got it," Alex said.

"The same one?"

"Yeah."

"Wow."

"Don't worry, Ronnie," Jo said. "We're not going to turn on you."

"I don't get it," Ronnie said. "I thought that once you were infected, that was it."

"It's a new strain," Alex replied.

"Gnarly," Ronnie said.

"That's a good word for it."

"You both got infected, and you got better. I still can't believe it."

"That's the trouble, Ronnie," Alex explained. "We don't know if we really are better."

"Well, you're not trying to kill anybody, are you?"

"Not yet."

"Look," Ronnie's pretty face frowned, "would you be telling me all this if you were planning to wipe this place out?"

Alex felt Jo's body quaking. He looked down at her face and saw that she was laughing. "She's right, you know. Why *would* we be standing here talking about it in front of her?"

"It would have to be an extremely subtle form of mind control, wouldn't it?" Alex agreed. "So subtle that the host not only reveals the nature of the parasite to every person he comes in contact with, but even reveals his doubts about being cured."

"Reverse psychology," Jo said, evoking a popular term Alex had not heard in many years.

"Besides," Ronnie said, "if you've got the colloid's memory, Alex, that means you've got its memories of Jo, too."

"You may be right," he said, hugging Jo. "We'll see if I can dredge it up a little later. Right now, I think we have some catching up to do."

"Well, I'll see you guys later," Ronnie said. Smiling, she stood up and left the briefing room.

" 'Bye," Jo said.

As soon as the door closed behind Ronnie, they kissed long and deeply. Both of them knew that it would not end there, but neither of them wanted to take the time to find a more comfortable room for their love making.

The floor would have to do. Their clothes formed a cushion underneath Jo. Alex rubbed her all over, kissing her. He licked her ears, her face, her breasts, slowly working his way down. At last he found her sex and worked it with his mouth, revelling in her hot, sweet taste. He teased her with the tip of his tongue, until she began to quiver ecstatically. Her shuddering grew ever more intense, and he worked harder and faster, until Jo exploded into orgasm, bucking and writhing with the greatest pleasure a woman can know.

Grinning, Alex lifted his head. Jo took his face in her hands and drew him toward her, kissing him lovingly. He mounted her then, lying still between her smooth thighs for a few sweet moments. And then he moved, kissing her neck. He thrusted, at first very slowly. At last he drew back, his movements almost imperceptible, like those of a minute hand on a clock, and then he pushed his loins into hers, and she moaned appreciatively. Building and building toward his own climax, the tempo faster and faster, reaching new heights of ecstacy with each thrust. They were locked in a sensuous dance that seemed as if it would never end.

And then it happened. All of Alex seemed to well up and escape through this tiny part of him, like a hot flood through the eye of a needle. It was eternal, exquisite.

He closed his eyes. And yet he could see, looking down at him, *his own face.*

"Alex!" Jo cried, from somewhere inside *him.* "Alex, I'm . . . I'm you!"

She was right. He was inside her, too. Seeing with her eyes, tasting with her tongue, feeling with her tactile sense. He knew how she felt at that moment, encircled in warmth with this big man between her legs, secure in the knowledge that she was giving all of herself to the one she loved.

It was fleeting, but they both knew that it had really happened. There had been some sort of psychic exchange, a visitation one to the other. A brief, unfocussed moment had followed, and then they were back inside themselves.

They collapsed, gasping and touching one another as if they were both part of the same person. In fact, they both realized at that moment that they *were the same entity*.

"Jo," Alex said, breathlessly, "the colloid did leave part of itself in us."

"Yes," she replied, "but we've turned it into something beautiful." She smiled at him in a way that he could only have described as beatific.

"It was wonderful." He kissed her.

"Let's see if we can do it again," Jo said, kissing him back. "For the purpose of scientific study only, of course."

Alex laughed. "Seems as if it's our duty, doesn't it?"

"Mm, hmm."

She drew his face toward her again and kissed him passionately. Alex responded, his heart full of a love that he had never known before, not even toward his mother, or toward Sharon, or not even Billy. This was love to the nth power.

As they made love for the second time, they went even deeper inside one another than before.

The third time, they knew that they would never be separated again.

CHAPTER TWENTY-SIX

"This is too good to be true, Alex," said Claire Siegel. "Once you two figure out how to schematize the knowledge inside you, and combine what you've inherited from the colloid . . . well, there's no telling what we'll learn."

The guerrillas were gathered in the briefing room, listening intently to the exchange between Alex, Jo, and Siegel. Samuel stood next to Claire, and Ronnie sat in the front row next to Riquelme, Liz, and Polly. Clearly, none of them knew quite what to make of this new development; not even Siegel, though she tried to make some sort of sense out of it, good biologist that she was.

"Well, we seem to be limited to certain moments for the mind link," Alex said.

"Oh," Siegel looked a little disappointed.

"But we don't mind stimulating each other to get results," Jo added.

Siegel looked puzzled. "Stimulating each other?"

"You see, Claire, we are linked only at the moment of orgasm."

Dr. Siegel's face registered consternation. "Only at the moment of . . ."

"Orgasm," Jo repeated happily.

"I see." Siegel seemed a little disappointed. "Well, perhaps we can still compile some data."

"Be glad to help," said Alex.

Many of the guerrillas were laughing now, in spite of Claire's sense of desuetude.

"There's more to it than that," Jo said. "We both have dreams, too."

"Dreams?" Siegel brightened a little.

"Yes, dreams which seem to be some sort of residue left by the infection."

"What are these dreams like?"

"They seem to be about the experiences of the colloids. Mostly about the one that infected us, but there are others involved, as a result of their telepathic network."

"I see."

"It's my guess," said Alex, "that they opened up parts of the brain that aren't usually used. They broadcast with these—for lack of a better term—psi centers, never imagining that any of their hosts would escape their domination."

"And now you and Jo are able to use those centers," Claire said cautiously. "Surely this can be useful."

Alex shrugged. "Hard to say."

"Well, at least we can be sure that the colloids didn't intend for you to have this power," Claire said.

"If it is a power. We still don't know for sure what good it is."

"Surely the Lord has provided us an opportunity to strike back at the heathen," Samuel said.

Claire looked a bit embarrassed, but said nothing. Alex was confident that she would remain resolutely rational, even if she were having an affair with Samuel. Perhaps she would be even more rigorously logical, in compensation for his religiosity. In any event, she might not have wanted the others to know that she and the street prophet had become an item.

"We'll try to find something," Alex said. "But this psychic linkage might not lend itself to a military application."

"If they don't come back," said Elvin, "it won't matter."

"They'll be back," Jo said with certainty. "And when they do, they'll be more dangerous than ever."

The room became very quiet. Alex knew that Jo was right, but he didn't know *why* he knew it. It was more than just a deduction. There was something left in her mind that told her the colloids were not yet through with the remnants of the human race.

"What do you mean, Jo?" Claire asked.

"It's the fourth stage you predicted," Jo replied, looking both frightened and distant at the same time. "They're almost at that point now."

And Alex knew that it was true. He had been witness to the colloid migration; more than a witness. He had been a part of it, and their purpose had been entrusted to the colloid who had ridden his nervous system. He knew what Jo knew, though it was hard to dredge up the memory.

"I can't tell you any more now," Jo said. "Alex and I will have to concentrate."

Smirks and sexual innuendo were not forthcoming now. All of the guerrillas sensed that something was happening, something that might be of the greatest significance. They disbanded, leaving Alex and Jo alone.

Jo and Alex looked at one another, with a far deeper understanding than they could have ever known before.

"They're counting on us," said Jo.

"I know, but it's all so . . . so inchoate," Alex said. "I can't make much sense out of it."

"Not yet, anyhow." Jo smiled at him, and he thought at that moment that things might work out. But the next moment, his doubts returned.

"Claire is excited because I managed to throw off the colloid," Alex said. "But for all we know, it was weakened when it was forced out of your body. She seems to think that we can shake them through sheer will. I have my doubts about that."

"Oh ye of little faith," Jo said, laughing. "You've got to admit that we're better off than we were just a few days ago, Alex."

"Immeasurably."

"Well, let's just do what we can to help the war effort." He put his arm around her. "Okay."

They walked to a room which they'd been staying in, with mattresses covering much of the floor. It seemed a good place for them to work on their new "powers."

Alex shut the door and they lay down. They were still for a little while.

"There's something I haven't told you," Alex said. "When I was infected, the colloids brought my loved ones back from the dead."

Jo's eyes widened. "Yes, they did it to me, too. My father and mother, and my husband. It was horrible."

"How can we fight them, knowing that our loved ones are alive in them?"

"We saw them die, Alex. They're not alive."

"But they are. Their memories, their emotions."

"That's all it is, just memory."

"No, there's more. They reached to me, to what I thought."

"Impossible."

"No, it happened. I told myself that they were dead, too, but they're not. They're in Limbo."

Jo looked deeply into his eyes. "It's our responsibility to put them to rest."

She was right, of course, but Alex was hurt to think that these last remnants of his wife and child must be destroyed. "Why do you think the colloids preserved them?" he asked.

"Isn't it obvious? They had analyzed human emotional states thoroughly enough to realize the value of keeping these pitiful bits of our loved ones alive. It's nothing but a dirty trick."

Softly, Alex wept. Jo held him tight. "I'm sorry, Alex," she whispered.

"When you were infected," he said, "I thought that you didn't love me anymore. I know that you were being manipulated. Still, the memory of it is very painful."

"Oh, Alex, I'll always love you."

They made love, slowly, tenderly. And at last, as they came, Alex saw through Jo's eyes once again. This time he held onto the dark, round image of his own shoulder as she pressed her face against his chest. Determined to see more, he squeezed her so tightly that she cried out.

The image became clearer.

"Jo," gasped Jo.

She was not only seeing through his eyes, now she *was* Alex, making love to herself. And there was nothing for Alex to do but to become Jo. He filled that place in her that had been vacated, while she simultaneously entered him.

And he was her.

Even after they lay panting next to each other, each still retained part of the other's persona.

"They must have used emotions to broadcast to one another," Alex said. "Channeled human passions."

"I don't think they can communicate very well without the nervous systems of their hosts," Jo said. "That's why they don't want animals. Only a pretty sophisticated nervous system enables them to branch out."

"Yes, I got an image of a world where there were no higher animals. The colloids remained isolated and died out. They broadcast as much as they could, and the others were in a kind of one-way communication with them until the last of them disappeared."

"They're in contact with other planets that they've invaded," Jo said. "That much is clear."

"Do you realize what this could mean?" Alex said, excitement growing inside him.

"Yes, that we could learn more about the galaxy by just lying here than all the space probes could bring back in centuries, maybe even millennia."

"It seems as though we really can do that, doesn't it?"

They lay together, listening to each other's heart beat, thinking about this. At last Alex spoke.

"Maybe we should be worried about things a little closer to home right now, though."

"What do you mean?"

"I think you know."

"Alex, you know where the colloids went, don't you?" This was not a question.

"Yes," Alex said, "and we have no choice but to go there, too."

CHAPTER TWENTY-SEVEN

"There's no time to talk about this," Alex insisted, grabbing the attention of everybody in the briefing room. "Their mobilization means that they've already started."

"Started what?" Elvin demanded. Like most of the others, he was content to live here at the armory in peace rather than tangle with the colloids once again.

"Creating a . . . superbeing, for want of a better term."

"A *superbeing?*"

"Yes, a kind of colloid-human hybrid. This has been their plan all along."

"Yes, it makes sense," Claire agreed. "They have been analyzing their victims, and preserving the tissues for their own purposes."

"They're going to make a creature of their own," said Jo, "using the human race as their modeling clay."

"An abomination," Samuel intoned.

"Well," Alex said, "it's probably safe to say that it won't conform to our idea of a bouncing baby."

"We've got motor vehicles," said Jo, "and Ronnie can show us where there's gasoline. We've got to start moving today."

"But where are we going?" Polly asked.

"New York City. It has the largest amount of material for them to work with in North America, and there's plenty of sea water available, which they need for the birth."

"One question," Elvin said.

"Shoot."

"Alex, how do we know you and Jo are completely clean? You were both infected, and you might still be. This could all be a load of bull designed to get us killed."

"Do you want to take the chance?" Alex said, his

169

anger flaring. "Do you want to stay here while the colloids create a race of adaptable new creatures to carry on their work? No one's going to force you to come with us."

"Who's going to join us?" Jo cried.

"I will," said Riquelme, silent up to now.

"Me, too," said Polly.

"I will," Claire said.

Within a few seconds, all of them had agreed to risk it—even Elvin. He shook his head as he said, "Why not?"

Alex quickly began to explain his strategy. Nobody among them knew how to drive a tank, and there wasn't time to learn, so only jeeps and trucks would be taken from the armory. And Ronnie's motorcycle would come in handy for reconnaissance, since it was fast and maneuverable.

They would stock all the weapons they could carry, including some of the remaining canisters of napalm, a mortar, and a flamethrower. M-16s would be passed out, with all the ammunition in the armory's stores. This was a last ditch effort, and they all knew it. They must throw everything they had at the enemy this time, and hope that they would emerge triumphant. Alex and Jo knew that this birth would not be the only one, but they also knew that there were bands of guerrillas in other parts of the world, willing to fight until they were all dead or until the earth was reclaimed. There was no middle ground, no compromising anymore.

This was either the end or the beginning.

First, they had to gas up all the vehicles that would carry the thirty or forty guerrillas to New York. Alex sent Riquelme with Ronnie, carrying a five gallon drum strapped onto his back. The gasoline they brought back would be more than enough to get the rest of the vehicles down to the refinery where the cache of fuel was located.

While Riquelme and Ronnie were gone, the ordnance was cleaned and oiled, and ammunition was doled out. There was little talking today. Indeed, now that their offensive was about to begin, the guerrillas seemed to be glad that they would again see some action. They had welcomed the peace, but they all had sensed that it was deceptive. The colloids were not about to share the Earth with them, and they knew it.

There was no way of telling how long it would take to reach New York. It was a mere one hundred miles away, but nobody knew what the condition of the roads was. That was one reason why jeeps might come in handy.

Alex really didn't have any idea of what they would do, even if they got to New York in time. They would strike as effectively as they could, and do as much damage as possible. But their chances of victory were slim.

The guerrillas would most likely all be killed.

He tried not to think of it as he shouted orders. Jo was beside him, radiating strength while she came up with many viable suggestions. Alex wished that they could stop fighting, live decently and raise a family. If they succeeded with this raid, maybe others would have that opportunity. That was really the best they could hope for, he supposed.

But it was best not to think about it. Ronnie and Riquelme returned after an hour or so, and the gasoline they brought with them was doled out to the seven vehicles that they had decided to take with them. After sitting for three years, the motors were not eager to start, but a few drops of gasoline in carburetor valves and a push start downhill got the requisite number of jeeps and trucks running. They were driven to South Philadelphia posthaste.

While the vehicles were gone, plastic containers were filled with water, and food was rationed. The guerrillas sat eating in grim silence, looking forward to the work they had to do. When they had awakened this morning, they had expected another quiet day of uncertainty, just like the preceding days. And now they were about to embark on a mission that might very well cost them all they had left. Alex hoped that they enjoyed their beans.

"Maybe next spring, we can plant a garden in that lot up the street," Riquelme said. "Maybe grow us some fresh vegetables and fruits."

"Yeah, right," Elvin grunted.

"You don't sound very optimistic, Elvin," said Polly.

"I'm not."

"Then don't come with us."

"I said I'm coming, and I meant it," Elvin said slowly and emotionlessly.

"Try to make the best of it, then, will you?"

Elvin seemed a little surprised to be upbraided in this fashion, but he said nothing. Alex knew that Elvin would perform when the time came, but he did like to complain. There was no need for the others to listen to it. Not this time.

They sat in the great hollow space of the motor pool, making coffee on a Coleman stove and speaking only when necessary. Alex was relieved when he heard the roar of motor vehicles in the distance.

Five jeeps and two trucks pulled up to the armory, followed by a dejected looking Ronnie.

"The kid was wrong," a new guy named Judd said. He had driven one of the armored cars. "There wasn't even enough gasoline left to fill all seven tanks."

"How much did you get?" Jo asked anxiously.

"Less than half a tank in that last one."

"We'll siphon a little out of the other tanks. It'll probably be enough to get us there."

"I'm sorry, Jo," Ronnie said. "It seemed like a lot of gas to me. But I guess I was wrong."

"It *was* a lot of gas when you were alone," Jo said.

"Sure as hell wasn't what we expected," Judd said bitterly.

"Where do you get off with an attitude like that?" Jo demanded. "Ronnie could have kept all the gas for herself, you know."

Judd backed off, and Ronnie looked appreciatively at Jo.

"Listen, everybody," Alex said, after witnessing the exchange, "we're all working together. If somebody fucks up, they fuck up. Don't rag them about it. This isn't a picnic we're organizing here, we're going to fight the son of a bitches who've taken our world away from us. Maybe we didn't used to think it was much of a world, but it was the only one we've ever had. We were the losers, the street people, the schizophrenics, the addicts, and the heavy-duty neurotics. Now we're the last, best hope of the human race. We all know what that means. We've got to give it everything we've got. We've got to be willing to die for the future of our planet. I know better than any of you, except for Jo, what the colloids are *really* like. I had one inside me, and I still feel what it did to me. The only thing we can do to save ourselves is to destroy them, because they'll never leave us in peace. They believe that we'll just repopulate and crowd them out if they allow us to survive. They don't want to share the Earth, they want to own it. I say we won't let them."

Alex's voice had been rising in pitch, and the others now let out a chorus of approving shouts.

"Let's hit them *hard!*"

This time their shouts were deafening, as they piled into the armored cars and jeeps, started the engines, and turned onto Market Street. At the ruins of City Hall the little convoy turned left and made its way to Race Street. A few minutes later they were driving up the interstate highway, where Alex had marched with the army of the infected.

Alex drove Ronnie's motorcycle at the head of the column, Jo riding behind him. Ronnie hadn't protested; she rode with Riquelme and Polly under the canvas top of the first jeep. The air was cold and the clouds were low.

They drove at fifty miles per hour, Alex watching out for potholes and damage to the asphalt, tears coming to his eyes because of the powerful wind. They left the city behind in a few minutes, the autumn brown Pennsylvania hills undulating on either side of them. They passed a shrine on the east side of the highway, a marble statue of the Virgin Mary. The Virgin's head was missing.

As they drove steadily toward the north, the first snowflakes of winter began to fall.

CHAPTER TWENTY-EIGHT

Forty miles into New Jersey, they had to slow down. The pavement had been blasted during the war, and they had to drive overland for a few miles. Fortunately, the terrain was not treacherous, and they soon found a road that parallelled the Jersey Turnpike. They followed it, steering around the many potholes and wide cracks in the asphalt.

The snow hadn't amounted to much, though it, too, had slowed them down for a few miles. As they cruised through deserted hamlets and untended farmland, it occurred to Alex that this much noise had not been heard in these parts for at least two years. Their convoy boomed over the hills and announced their movements in advance. The Harley alone made a terrific racket. Except for the occasional staccato din of gunfire, they had lived in a quiet world for many months. The change was exhilarating.

Alex brought the Harley around a big, looping curve. He came very near to a collision with the hulks of four cars that had been pulled out into the road. Behind the junkers were several men and women armed with rifles and shotguns. Alex pulled up within a few yards of the makeshift barricade and raised his hands. The convoy came to a halt behind him.

"Hold it right there!" a man shouted from behind a dented 1978 Oldsmobile. His breath steamed out of his bearded face as he spoke. "We'll shoot if you come any closer!"

"Don't shoot," Alex said in as calm a voice as he could manage under the circumstances.

"You go back the way you came," the bearded, slender man said.

"We've got to get through," Alex said.

"Why?" their interrogator asked suspiciously.

Why beat around the bush? "We've got a war to fight."

The bearded man squinted. "The war's been over for a long time. Haven't you heard?"

"We're starting a new one."

"With who?"

"Not with you. With the colloids."

"They're gone." But in spite of his words, the barrel of the bearded man's shotgun moved slightly to one side, much to Alex's relief. Perhaps he was getting through to this guy. "We're all that's left around here."

"The colloids are only a few miles away," Alex said. "And they're not finished with us yet."

The bearded man glanced at his companions, and then back at Alex. "How do you know that?"

"I know."

For some reason, that non-answer seemed to satisfy him. Now the shotgun was pointed at the ground, instead of at the convoy. "Just you and these few people are gonna fight 'em alone?" he asked.

"Yeah. We're going to be seriously outnumbered," Alex said. "But we've got a lot of firepower."

"Looks like you've got half the goddamn army back there," the bearded man said, gesturing at the convoy. "Where the hell did you get the gas?"

"There was a little left in a refinery in South Philadelphia," Alex said. "We used the last of it to get this far."

The bearded man came out from behind the Olds. Holding the shotgun in one crooked arm, he walked toward Alex and extended his hand. "I'm Pat Crowley," he said. "That's my son Jack there, and these folks are the only survivors we know of in central Jersey."

"Alex Ward." The man's handshake was firm. "Do you know if there are any roads open all the way to New York?"

"The city? Yeah, you can still get there. But there ain't much left in New York. A few street people, some raving loonies, and maybe a couple of flea-bitten cats."

Alex almost laughed. The first two categories pretty well covered him and the convoy. He wondered if Pat weren't a little off center himself, in spite of his flinty attitude. There was a wild look in his eye, but he seemed a straightforward guy, and he was clearly the leader of this group of survivors. It seemed that he had done a pretty good job of organizing them.

"If we get to New York in time," Alex said, "we might be able to stop the colloids."

"Stop 'em from doing what?" a woman asked from behind a leafless tree, off to Alex's left. "Seems as if they've already done their damnedest."

"Yeah," Pat said. "Lil's got a point. The colloids ain't bothering us anymore, so why run up to New York and look for a fight with them?"

"Because they're definitely going to bother us again," Alex said. "They're planning something that just might wipe out the few people who are left on earth."

"What are you talking about?" Pat demanded.

"They're making a baby," said Alex.

"A baby?"

"*Their* kind of baby. They can't live on Earth much longer the way they are now, so they're creating something that can. If we can stop them, then maybe they'll die out."

"Just like that?" Pat asked sarcastically.

"No, they'll try this more than once. But I have a way of knowing when and where they'll do it. And I'm confident that there are pockets of survivors all over the world who will help us fight them."

"Can you hold on a minute?" Pat retreated behind the barricade and talked in low tones with his people. After a minute or two, he re-emerged, and said, "Want us to go with you?"

Alex felt himself grinning like a fool. "I thought you'd never ask."

"Well, we got eleven people here. If you can help us start these cars, we'll go along. We've got some jumper cables."

Alex instructed Riquelme to bring one of the jeeps around. While the batteries were being charged, Alex looked Pat straight in the eye. "It's going to be rough," he said.

"Usually is." Pat pronounced it "youzhully."

The Jersey guerrillas got their gear together, and climbed into their cars. The convoy was soon back on the road,

and spirits were higher than ever before, though the odds
had only been infinitesimally improved.

Crowley's comment about the dejected survivors in
New York made Alex a little more optimistic, too. He
suspected that people would fight for their world, no
matter how unlikely it seemed that they would triumph.
If he could find and arm enough of them, maybe the
Earth still had a chance.

He found that the more time passed, the less knowledge he retained about the colloids. Still, he remembered
more than a few things, and his link with Jo had strength-
ened whenever they made love. Each time he felt a surge
of emotion he sensed the stirrings of her mind, though
the communication ran only one way in such instances. Jo
had confided in him that she experienced the same thing
when her passions ran high. But only when they achieved
orgasm together were they totally, truly linked—mind to
mind and soul to soul.

As the convoy roared along the country roads, Alex
wondered what would become of them. He had come to
love the guerrillas like a family, and now he was leading
them to death. Was it his right to do this?

The best rationale he could come up with was that he
had not forced anyone to go on this junket.

A dip in the road, leading down to a swampy mudhole,
brought his ruminations to an abrupt end. They had been
approaching the so-called meadowlands, hundreds of square
miles of marshes through central and northern New Jersey. Pat had voiced some concern about the inevitability
of such obstacles, so they weren't completely unprepared.
The mud, however, ranged from the woods on the left
side of the road to the rocks on the right. It appeared to
be impassable.

Alex cut his engine and held up his right hand, signal-
ling the rest of the convoy to stop. In a moment, all the
motors were still, pinging with internal heat. Alex's ears
rang in the abrupt silence. Stretching, the guerrillas got
out of the jeeps and trucks, some of them walking up to
the mudhole.

"This is worse than I thought," Pat said, peering down
at the obstruction. "Not even your motorcycle could get
through this."

"Maybe we can put enough logs over it to get across," Alex said. "There's a hatchet in one of the jeeps."

Pat nodded. "Worth a try."

Working fast, Alex chopped down a slender birch tree while the others gathered branches. As soon as he got tired, Riquelme took over with the hatchet. In an hour, they had cut down four trees and laid them across the mudhole.

Chopping down a fifth tree, Alex stopped for a breather and handed the hatchet back to Riquelme. In spite of the cold air, he was sweating profusely and was nearly out of breath. Jo joined him and they walked a few yards into the woods. Occasionally they heard the shouts of the guerrillas and the hatchet ringing steadily against the wood.

"Do you think this is going to work?" Jo asked.

"I think there's a chance."

"Those logs look awful flimsy."

"Yeah, they might snap."

"And I used to think traveling to New York was bad in the old days," Jo said ruefully.

Alex laughed in spite of everything. "Even Amtrak was better than this."

Forty minutes later, they were through working. They had laid down three more tree trunks, and the first jeep was brought forward. Riquelme was driving.

"Take it easy going across," Pat advised him. "But if it starts to go, gun the engine and try to get over before it's too late. You don't want to sink into that mud."

Riquelme nodded and revved up the engine for a minute or two, and then began to inch onto the makeshift bridge. His wheels spun against the slick wood, and Alex felt himself sucking in breath as white bark was stripped and flew through the air.

"Easy!" Pat shouted.

Riquelme eased up on the gas and suddenly his wheels caught. He drove across the log bridge and stopped on the rise on the far side.

Everyone cheered and shouted for a moment, and then the rest of the vehicles were driven across the logs.

CHAPTER TWENTY-NINE

The road went to higher ground for a few miles, but they continued to drive cautiously. They had stacked the logs in one of the trucks in case of another mudhole. Alex sensed a positive attitude about their journey that left him a little incredulous. It was as if their success at fording that little mudhole was perceived as some sort of good omen.

Well, why not? It might have been a minor victory, but it *was* a victory. Anything that helped them now was good, as far as he was concerned.

They came to the crest of a hill, and spread out before them were the seemingly endless marshes of New Jersey. The tall grass was yellow and brown, and the road wound past white snow patches like a serpent. Crowley and his son joined Alex and Jo, as the convoy cooled their engines.

"Yeah, old Route Thirty-One didn't youzhully have much traffic," Pat said. "Farmers and local people used it, though. It runs between the Garden State Parkway and the Jersey Turnpike, and used to come in handy for tractors and such."

"We're lucky you didn't just watch us go on by instead of stopping us with your barricade," Jo said.

"Well, we thought about letting you go. We could hear you coming for twenty minutes before you got into Larkin. That's the town we were in, Larkin. Anyway, we decided to face you. Even though we haven't seen many marauders lately, we weren't about to welcome an armed convoy into town."

"Seems like you've got pretty good reconnaissance, Pat," Alex said.

"My boy Jack scouted ahead. We knew how many of you were coming, and that you were loaded for bear." Young Jack Crowley grinned and shook his blond hair from his eyes as his father slapped him on one brawny shoulder. Alex estimated his age at sixteen or seventeen. He seemed a bright and earnest sort of kid, and his skills might come in handy when they got to New York. "In fact," Pat added. "I'm going to send Jack out now, to try and find out what's in store for us."

"I don't know," Alex said. "It might be pretty dangerous."

"Not on the Harley," Ronnie said, clearly hoping to get her bike back. She was sitting on the warm hood of a jeep. "We can outrun anything on my hog."

Jack looked eagerly at his father, and then at Ronnie. The idea of riding off with a pretty young girl obviously appealed to him.

"Seems like a good idea," Pat said. "If they see anything, they can head back. If something happens, they can fire a couple of shots in the air and we'll go after them."

"Sounds like a plan, Dad," Jack said.

"Well, I guess it'll be okay," Alex agreed reluctantly.

Ronnie eagerly hopped off the hood and joined them.

"I want you to take Jack up ahead," Pat said, "past the marshes, and see what you can find."

She looked at Alex for confirmation, and, when he nodded, she said, "Okay."

"Grab some chow first," Alex said. "The rest of us will take a rest here and let you get a good head start."

"Jack," said Pat Crowley, "you know what to do if you get into trouble."

"The usual, Dad? Fire two shots and run like hell."

"Yeah." Pat nodded grimly. "Don't be a hero. Just get back here in one piece."

"How far you want us to go?" Ronnie asked.

"When you're getting close to the river, or when you see the city, then you've gone too far. If you haven't run into anything before that, then we can take the initiative and head right into the Big Apple."

"And if we have run into something, we'll make a U-turn and come back here real fast," Ronnie said.

"Right, the Harley will be the best vehicle for that. It can turn on a dime and goes a lot faster than any of these other vehicles. Another consideration is that it will be a lot easier to pull out of the mud than one of these jeeps."

"Let's eat, so we can get going, okay?" said Jack, looking admiringly at Ronnie. "We want to get started pretty soon, don't we?"

"Yeah." Ronnie smiled shyly at Jack.

The two kids bolted down their food and roared off on their mission. Alex, Pat, and Jo watched them go, and then joined the others just as Claire propounded a new theory.

"Alex and Jo were not infected in the same way as previous victims," she began, "but they still—"

"Infected!" One of the Jersey people shouted, a man named Dan Galouye. "They were infected?"

"Yes, but they threw off the infection," Claire explained.

"That's impossible," said Pat.

"Concerning the infection that you are familiar with," Claire said, "that may very well be true. But they were infected in a different way. Neurotropic, yes. But not tissue-devouring. We assumed that the colloids developed this refinement to infiltrate our ranks, but I think there was another reason for it."

"What?"

Siegel paused for a moment. "The colloids had analyzed billions of human bodies, studying them even as they consumed them. But they had a need to study a functioning nervous system that was untainted, or as nearly so as they could manage. The creature which they are about to unleash on our long-suffering world, which I will refer to as the *neonate*, will require a highly developed mental ability. Since it will be composed of mostly human tissues, they must use the human brain as their model."

"I see what you're driving at, Claire," Jo said. "The colloids themselves are nothing without their hosts. They might not be able to survive on Earth if there were more to them. Consequently, they can't use themselves as the model for the, uh, neonate's nervous system. It has to resemble a human brain."

"It's speculation," said Alex, "but it makes more sense than our previous theory about why they infiltrated us."

"True as far as it goes, but there's more to it than that." Claire smiled knowingly.

"Well?"

"Try not to get a swelled head, Alex, but I think the

new infection was designed to invade only the more . . . shall we say *sophisticated* minds."

"Then yours should have been one of the first, and yet you weren't infected, Claire."

"Perhaps my mind is a little too unbalanced, even for this new refinement. Or perhaps they have somehow found a way to identify those with leadership capabilities. Who can say?"

They all mulled this over, Pat and his little group sitting off to the side of the road together. It occurred to Alex that the Jersey people were disturbed by what they had just heard. Claire had not considered their reaction when she had begun her little speech, which might turn out to be a costly mistake.

"Pat, Dan, and the rest of you, I want you to know that I'm all right," Alex said. "It's true, what Dr. Siegel was just saying."

"You look pretty healthy, all right. But I never heard of somebody getting *un*infected."

"Well, remember how I told you that I *knew* certain things about the colloids and their plans?"

"Yeah."

"I know these things because of my infection. They didn't know they should keep things from me, because they didn't realize I could get rid of the infection, either."

Pat shook his head. "Jesus Christ."

"You and your friends can turn back," Alex said.

"My boy's gone ahead with that girl," Pat said angrily. "How the hell can I turn back?"

Alex looked down at the dirt. "As soon as they return, you can go."

Pat spat into the bushes at the side of the road. "We'll talk it over among ourselves, and we'll let you know. In the meantime, if you've got any more surprises, you'd better lay 'em on us right now, all right?"

"Nothing that I can think of." Alex didn't like the way this was developing. He wanted to make it clear to Pat Crowley and friends that he could be trusted. "Pat, what are you thinking?" he asked.

Crowley shook his head. "I don't know whether to believe you or not. You seem okay, but I never heard of anybody living through an infection before."

"I was the victim of a new kind of infection."

"So the old woman said." Pat narrowed his eyes. "But it's funny we've never heard of such a thing before."

"Neither had I up until a few days ago." Alex found himself tiring of this argument. "I sat at the side of a highway in Philadelphia through a long night, and I finally worked up enough craziness to drive the thing out of my body. That's all there is to it. You can believe it if you want to. I don't care."

Alex turned away to join the other guerrillas, without waiting to gauge Crowley's reaction. If these new people didn't trust him, there was little sense in trying to persuade them to fight alongside the guerrillas. It would be better to mount a smaller force that was strongly united.

"How did it go?" Jo asked as he approached her.

"I don't know. They're confused, and who can blame them? They've only known us for a few hours, and we tell them something that runs contrary to everything they know. How could we expect any other reaction?"

"Yeah, we should have thought of that."

Alex sighed and turned to the others. "The kids have had a few minutes' head start. Let's saddle up and get out of here."

The guerrillas piled into their vehicles and started up the engines. Grudgingly, Pat Crowley and his little group got into their cars, too. The convoy started across the marshes.

CHAPTER THIRTY

The soft mud showed the motorcycle's track clearly on the humped ribbon of road running through the meadowland. At every curve Alex feared that they would emerge into a vast mob of the infected, the wreckage of the Harley strewn into the rushes, the bloody bodies of Ronnie and Jack crawling with colloids.

But the track went on and on, and the narrow, muddy road made for slow going. Alex was grateful for the din of the engines, certain that the silence of the marshes would be extremely enervating.

From time to time a racoon or rabbit would dart out of their way, and birds frequently fluttered out of the yellow rushes. These creatures had not heard the roar of a motor for years, and they would not hear such a sound again once the convoy had passed—not for a very long time. Alex dared hope that it would not be forever.

The terrain became more hilly, and Pat pointed to the east. As they topped a rise, the skyline of New York came into view. Or what was left of the skyline, at least.

One of the World Trade Center towers lay broken on its side. Its mate was a shattered plinth standing over it in the afternoon light. The crumbling remnants of Manhattan ranged to the north; the Empire State Building and the Chrysler Building were both gone.

Pat Crowley, rifle slung over his shoulder, walked up to Alex and Jo.

"Where the hell are those kids?" Alex said.

Pat shook his head. "Jack can be impetuous," he said.

"Where does this road end?" Alex asked.

"It goes past the city, all the way to the Tappan Zee Bridge."

"Well, they should have turned back by now."

"Tell me about it," Pat said. He looked glumly at the

dry road here on this higher ground. There was no sign of the Harley-Davidson's tracks.

"Kids tend to get cocky," Jo said. "Maybe they wanted to see if they could get across the river."

"Jesus." Alex was growing more apprehensive by the moment.

"Maybe they had trouble with the bike," said Pat. "Or maybe they just decided to stop for awhile and take in the sights."

"Not Ronnie," Jo said. "She knows how serious this is."

"Oh, yeah?" Crowley said. "Then where is she? Maybe she's got one of these new-fangled infections you've been talking about."

"I doubt it," Jo said, annoyed.

"I'm sure they're all right," Alex said. But he knew that there was no sense in trying to put a good face on it. Something was definitely wrong. Crowley seemed to be blaming them for it.

"Well," Crowley said, "the way I see it is, we either wait here and sweat or go look for them."

"You're right," Alex said. "I think we should go after them, too, since we sent them out in the first place."

"The sooner we get over to New York, the better," Jo agreed. "But don't you think we better talk it over with the others before we do anything rash?"

"Of course."

Alex called the guerrillas, and Pat gathered his people, too. Alex put the question to them, and they were unanimous in their response. Riquelme summed it up: "We didn't come up here to admire the scenery. Let's go after them."

Samuel turned and raised his pipe-staff. "May the Lord bless you all," he intoned, "as ye journey to the valley of the shadow of death."

They were on the road again in seconds, bouncing on the dirt track toward the New Jersey turnpike. Their best guess was that Ronnie and Jack had gone into Manhattan. The bridges were all down, but the Lincoln Tunnel might have been open. It was possible that the kids were still on this side of the river, of course. But as the guerrillas approached the ramp leading onto the turnpike, the latter possibility seemed less plausible with every passing moment. Unless Ronnie and Jack were dead, they were now in New York City.

The asphalt, untended for these past thirty-six months, provided a bumpy ride, but they drove at the highest speeds they could, in spite of the discomfort. The lives of those two kids might very well depend on it.

There were no legible signs to guide them to the Lincoln Tunnel, but Alex remembered the way pretty clearly. He had driven to New York many times in the old days.

They followed a long, curving ramp around to the tunnel mouths. There were several dead cars blocking the way on the right side, so they took the other passage, intended for vehicles coming into New Jersey from Manhattan. There was little danger of facing oncoming traffic, Alex surmised.

Turning on the headlights, they went on into the darkness. They had only gone a few hundred yards before they came on the hulk of an old Cadillac blocking the way. Alex could see other cars behind it. They cut the engines, and he stood to shout back to the others, "We're going to have to walk from here."

They took all the ammunition they could carry, but the mortar and rockets, naplam canisters, and some of the other weapons were too heavy and cumbersome to manage. Fortunately, they still had the timber they had cut in New Jersey. They tied the bulkier ordnance to the birch logs and ten people hefted it like jungle bearers, while Riquelme strapped the flamethrower tank to his back and carried the nozzle in his hands. Three jeep batteries were brought along, too, in case they found functioning vehicles on the other side of the river. Gasoline was siphoned from the tanks, too.

They had had the foresight to bring lanterns with them, so there was some visibliity as they began to hike down the slope past the unmoving automobiles. Wet streaks stained the sides of the tunnel, and the floor gleamed with moisture in the lamplight.

The silence was broken only by the echoes of their boots scraping the asphalt as they went ever deeper under the river.

"I hope there's not too much water for us to get through," Alex said.

"Looks okay," said Jo.

"But as we get down toward the lowest point under the river, it might fill up."

Nobody said anything more about it. They would just have to keep moving and find out.

Once, Alex thought he saw something move. But it must have just been a rat. They were ankle deep in water now, still moving down a gradual incline. The sloshing of their feet was the only sound.

Again, something moved. But it wasn't in the shallow water. It was high up on the wall to the right. Alex shone his lamp up and caught the thing in the feeble rays.

It was a colloid.

"Holy shit!" someone's voice echoed.

The lamplight revealed other colloids, slithering along the walls. They seemed to be keeping their distance from the water, which made it fairly safe for the guerrillas. As Alex shone the light around, he saw a lot more of them crawling overhead, some of them even clinging to the tunnel ceiling.

Panicky voices came from behind Alex. He didn't want to start shooting in here if he could help it. After three years, there was no telling how much stress had been put on the tunnel by the enormous pressure of the Hudson's millions of tons of water. If this thing came crashing down on them, it would not only be the end of them, but quite possibly the end of the human race, too.

"Keep moving," he said. "They won't come down here. Not with all this water."

But Alex knew that the colloids could send the infected into the tunnel to bedevil them. If that happened, they were in a world of shit.

The water was almost up to their knees when Elvin spotted the Harley. It stood in the water on its kickstand, half of each wheel submerged in the black water.

"Ronnie," Alex called out, his voice reverberating through the cavernous tunnel. "Jack."

A girl answered from ahead. Alex couldn't tell what she was saying, but he was sure he recognized her voice.

"It's Ronnie," Jo said.

"Come on." Alex started splashing ahead rapidly, stepping as high as he could so that the water wouldn't slow him down. Jo was right beside him. Alex glanced over his shoulder and saw that Pat and a few of the Jersey people were behind them. Back further were Riquelme and a handful of the other guerrillas. The others lagged far behind, straining under the weight of the heavy weapons on their makeshift litter.

"Ronnie!" Alex cried. "Jack! We're coming."

"Alex!" Ronnie's voice was closer. "No!"

"Hold on!"

"Go back," Ronnie cried. "They've got us."

But it was too late. Alex held the lantern up high, and saw a phalanx of the infected blocking the way. Two of them gripped Ronnie's arms, and two others held onto Jack. The kids looked terrified.

Now the walls were thick with colloids, almost solid with them. They flowed like oil, parallel to the water's surface. But they would come no closer for fear of dissolution.

"Dad!" Jack cried. "Do something!"

Pat Crowley stepped forward and stared at the massed ranks of the infected. There must have been hundreds of them back there in the darkness. Strangely, Crowley did not seem to be afraid of them. He walked right up to them and said, "I'm sorry, son."

"Dad . . . ?"

None of the infected made a move toward Crowley. He turned and raised his rifle to his own head. Before anyone could even speak, he fired.

Half of Crowley's skull was blown away. His body sagged and slipped into the water with barely a ripple. He was still holding the rifle.

"*Dad!*" Jack screamed, as the rifle report echoed through the tunnel.

Perhaps only Alex and Jo realized what had happened, why Pat Crowley had just killed himself. But there was no time to explain to the others. The Ingram's safety was off in a fraction of a second. Alex blasted away at the infected. One of Ronnie's captors was hit in the head. Ronnie wrested herself free of the other one and splashed toward the guerrillas. The infected had loosened their grip on Jack, too. But now they were pulling him back even as he struggled to free himself.

Jo shot one of them in the chest, and Jack lunged forward past the floating body of his father.

"Riquelme!" Alex shouted, now that the kids were clear of the infected. "Burn 'em!"

Riquelme stepped up, holding the flamethrower's nozzle out in front of his fireplug body. As the infected began to stagger toward him, he unleashed a horizontal pillar of flame that seared the flesh off their shrieking faces.

A dozen of the guerrillas stood together now, shoulder to shoulder, firing methodically into the ranks of the infected. The bodies fell, blood darkening the water as Riquelme aimed the flamethrower at another clutch of the undead.

Calmly, Elvin handed a .38 revolver to Jack. Tears streaming down his face, the boy cocked the pistol and fired into the chaotic mob facing the guerrillas. He squeezed the trigger six times, and continued to squeeze it long after he was out of bullets.

Riquelme swept the flame across the infected's ranks. Black, oily smoke billowed off the flaming clothes and burning flesh of the enemy. None of them had enough presence of mind to sink into the water. They staggered about, shrieking horribly and flailing, while the glistening colloids gouted and squirmed on either side and above.

Slowly, the guerrillas advanced. Elvin, Polly, Riquelme, Jill, Irv, Dan, Claire, and Samuel, along with Alex, Jo, and the two kids, formed a solid front that moved steadily toward the enemy, blazing away with rifles, semiautomatics and pistols. The others backed them up, the New Jersey people locking and loading along with the guerrillas.

Dozens of bodies floated in the dark water. Dozens more howled in pain. Clouds of stinking smoke filled the cavernous space as the infected fell back against the onslaught.

CHAPTER THIRTY-ONE

They were at the tunnel's lowest point now. The carnage continued unabated, since the mindless infected did not know enough to run away. They tried to attack again and again, but each time their bodies fell in scores. There weren't very many of them left by the time the guerrillas slowly began to climb up the incline, the water up to their waists.

"Riquelme!" Alex shouted. "Take it easy with that flamethrower!"

Obediently, Riquelme shut the flamethrower down. Carried away in the heat of battle, he had forgotten that they would need the fuel later.

The few remaining infected were shot unceremoniously. The echoing thunder of gunfire ceased at last, and an eerie silence reigned in the tunnel, though Alex's ears rang for several minutes. He held the lantern high, pleased to see that the tunnel walls were no longer festooned with colloids. The fire had frightened them away, and they had left the infected to die for them.

"We whupped 'em pretty good," Elvin said in his flat voice, sounding as if he couldn't quite bring himself to believe it. "I thought we were finished, but we whupped 'em."

But along with the exhilaration was the knowledge that this was only the beginning. They had to find the neonate, and when they found it they had to destroy it. They were having enough trouble just getting across the river.

Jack Crowley leaned against the four-foot-high ledge on the right side of the tunnel, weeping. Alex put his hand on the kid's shoulder.

"Why did he do it?" Jack turned to him emotionally, his face wet with tears. He wanted to blame someone; it was in his voice. "Why did he kill himself?"

"He did it because he knew that he was infected," Alex said.

"No! He wasn't infected!" Jack screamed.

"Yeah, I'm afraid he was. It's a new kind of infection. They control your mind, and you don't even know it. He realized that he had sent you and Ronnie out to be captured. He killed himself so that the thing inside him couldn't do any more harm. He did it because he was trying to protect you and the rest of us."

This explanation of Pat's suicide calmed Jack. Alex couldn't be sure that it was true, but he believed that it might be. The only other explanation was that Pat had simply gone off his nut when he saw his son in the clutches of the infected. But he hadn't seemed the sort who would lose his cool like that.

"I'm sorry, Jack," Alex said. "But I think he saved your life by doing it. Maybe all our lives. The colloids were so surprised that it gave us those few seconds we needed."

Jack nodded. His father was dead, and there was nothing he could do about it. He had lived under combat conditions long enough to understand that bitter reality.

Ronnie joined them, looking very sad and concerned for Jack. "When we came into the tunnel they were waiting for us," she said. "They swarmed over us before we could do anything, and they dragged us down deeper into the tunnel. The colloids were just above, crawling around up on the ceiling as if they were pulling puppet strings. I thought they were gonna kill us, but they didn't. They just waited for you guys to show up."

"Yeah."

"But how did they know you'd come for us?" Ronnie asked. "How did they know you wouldn't just leave us in here with them?"

"They've analyzed enough human minds to know how we behave," Alex said. "Not always rationally, maybe, but somewhat predictably."

"Predictably in some cases, at least." It was Claire, wading toward them. "The colloids know we are here, and they must realize why we have come."

"Then we better get out of this tunnel before they

organize another bunch of the infected to attack us," said Alex.

The guerrillas were ready to move. They made their way up the eastern slope of the tunnel, seeing daylight after ten or fifteen minutes.

"Let's be careful going outside," Alex said. "They probably haven't had time to get organized yet, but let's not take any chances."

"I'll go on point with the flamethrower," Riquelme said. "If there's any trouble, I'll be able to get away by laying down some fire."

Nobody could argue with Riquelme's logic, and so he walked the last few hundred yards of the tunnel by himself. Alex watched him go until he became a tiny silhouette framed by the tunnel walls, while the guerrillas followed him at a safe distance. Then he was out of sight. Somebody sneezed, but other than that the tunnel was silent. They were out of the deep water now, though their toes were still submerged. Alex found himself shivering, soaked to the waist and exposed to the cold autumnal air. Up ahead there was no more water, only the wet asphalt that gleamed more and more brightly in the increasing clarity of the light from the world outside.

Footsteps echoed from ahead.

"Nobody move," Alex said.

They waited. The footfalls were closer, and the guerrillas were clearly nervous. Had Riquelme been ambushed? It was a sobering thought, the very real possibility of losing such a dependable soldier. Not only that, but another battle might exhaust their supply of ammunition before they reached their destination. And if this was not Riquelme returning to them, there would surely be another battle starting in the next few seconds. In spite of the damp cold, Alex was sweating profusely.

"Hey!" Riquelme, easily identifiable even in shadow because of the tank on his back, came into view.

"*All right!*" Ronnie said, laughing.

The others shared in her pleasure and relief to see Riquelme return unharmed. As they joined him, several people slapped him on the back.

"Come on," Riquelme said. "Wait till you see what's outside this tunnel."

They followed him up and out into the sunlight, blinking and gaping at the smashed buildings . . . and at something even more astonishing.

A rag-tag squad of gaunt people, some of them carrying guns, more of them carrying knives, and almost all of them carrying sticks and rocks, stood in a knot in front of the guerrillas.

"It's the New York resistance," Riquelme said.

They didn't look like much, but Alex reflected that the same might be said of his group of guerrillas.

"We're here to fight the colloids," he said. "Will you join us?"

A black woman, whose wild hair could not hide her exquisite features, stepped forward. "Whaddaya think we be doing all this time?"

"Well, we need your help."

She appraised the guerrillas, now emerging with the birch log litter. "Look like you're packing a lot of firepower."

"Yeah, you could say that."

The woman nodded. "You must have come looking for a fight, because this is where they at."

"That's right. We're here to stop them."

"We saw 'em march down into the tunnel, and none of 'em marched back out," a wild-eyed man said. "Did they go over to Jersey?"

A few of the New York guerrillas permitted themselves to laugh at this facetious question.

"No, they went to a far better place than New Jersey," Alex said.

More of them laughed at his reply.

"We'd like to send them all there," Jo said.

"Sounds good to me," the black woman said, sticking out her hand. "I'm Shina."

Alex shook her hand and introduced himself and Jo. "We come from Philadelphia."

"I hear the weather's nice down there this time of year," the wild-eyed man said, eliciting more laughs.

"Very tropical," Alex replied.

"So when do we get started?" Shina asked.

"The sooner the better," said Jo.

The sun was already setting over the ruins of Manhattan. "Tonight?" asked Shina.

"We have to find out where they're making their baby," Alex said.

"Baby!" several of the New York guerrillas chorused in surprise.

"That's right. They're making a new creature to rule the Earth when they're gone."

"Holy shit," an unwashed soul who could have been a man or a woman—or neither—croaked. Alex did not care to indulge in thinking about the reasons for the colloid's rejection of this person. An ally was an ally.

"They're making it out of the tissues of the people they've eaten," Alex said. "Out of themselves."

"What the fuck . . . ?" another of the New York guerrillas said. "How do you know this?"

"I found out the hard way," Alex said. He remembered the difficulty he had had with the New Jersey people, and said, "but there's no time to explain now. We have to get to this thing before it's too late."

"Are you with us?" Jo asked.

"I am," Shina assured her. "The rest of these dudes can make up their own minds."

"What do you say?" Alex asked them.

"I say all right," the androgynous creature said.

"Me, too," said a woman.

"What have we got to lose?" the wild-eyed man said.

There were seventeen of them in all, and every one of them was willing to go along. Alex was grateful for that; even if these people were poorly armed, they were survivors.

"Did you see the colloids come out of the tunnel?" he asked.

"Yeah," Shina said. "Like a river of shit with a mind of its own."

"Which way did they go?"

"South."

"Toward the waterfront," Alex said. "Of course."

CHAPTER THIRTY-TWO

Moving through the ruins of Manhattan was not always easy. Like Philadelphia, the city had been devastated by the ineptitude of the Army. Nobody in the White House, Congress, or the military had suspected that the colloid "virus" was really an invasion from space. SDI would have proven ineffectual, of course; no particle beam could have shot down mircroscopic viral cells, even if those in power had realized what was happening. The most heavily populated areas suffered rampant epidemics. Washington was no exception, and so the government had folded in a matter of months. The military had then taken over, declaring martial law and futilely attempting to wipe out the cities, which were perceived by military intelligence as the core—if not the cause—of the infestation.

As a result, the stone and concrete colossi of New York had fallen like dominos during the war. Alex suspected that the military might have destroyed the place years before if they had gotten their way, so polarized had the liberal northeast and the right wing become in the late twentieth century.

Whatever the military strategy had been, there was a lot more rubble to contend with than in Center City Philadelphia. At times it seemed like mountain climbing, as they scaled huge mounds made up of limestone chunks, twisted steel girders, and crushed automobiles. Their progress was slow, especially with the arsenal lashed to the log litter, and the darkness was soon upon the silent city streets.

"Think we'll reach South Ferry by dawn?" Alex asked Shina as he helped her down from a particularly large block. "Maybe we can take the subway tunnels."

"No, they're flooded. We'll have to go above ground.

When we get down toward the Village, things might not be so raggedy-ass."

"I hope you're right." It made sense, though. The buildings in Greenwich Village were not on the same cyclopean scale as those in midtown Manhattan, but who could guess what other obstacles they might encounter. After all, the colloids knew that the guerrillas were on the way.

"It might be wise to get some rest tonight," said Jo as she joined them.

"Can we risk it?" Alex said. "How can we know how close the colloids are to success? They might even have succeeded already."

"Well, if they have," Shina pointed out, "we can still kill the baby, can't we?"

"Maybe. We don't know. We're walking into this blind, you see."

"Then we've got as good a chance tomorrow as we have tonight."

"Maybe so."

"Unless you can prove otherwise," Jo said, "then we should go ahead and get some rest, like I said before."

Alex nodded. His sense of urgency prevented him from being enthusiastic, but he had to admit that they weren't likely to function very well in the morning, exhausted as they were. Still, the residue of colloid memory made him believe that they should not hesitate even for a moment. "I know you're right, Jo, but I still want to keep moving."

Jo looked at him, the moonlight reflecting in her beautiful eyes. She understood his fear at that moment; Alex was certain of it. Was their telepathic bond working even while they were not making love? Only time would tell, he supposed, but he liked to think that it might be so. "You understand why we have to keep going, don't you, Jo?" he said.

"Of course." She smiled at him, but he knew that she was frightened. They were fighting for something so large that none of them could really grasp it, not fully. The human race, who had cast them out, now relied on these few losers to take the world back from the invaders. The few skirmishes they had engaged in would be as nothing to this final battle, he sensed. Would it be a futile gesture? Or would they salvage their world for future generations? Alex had a headache from thinking about it, and his limbs were heavy with exhaustion. Nevertheless, he pressed on through the night, praying that they would reach the tip of the island in time to stop the colloids.

They *had* to.

The hard part was moving the boxes of ammunition, batteries, heavy weapons, and tanks of flammable fluids over the rubble. The people they had picked up in New Jersey and Manhattan made a great deal of difference; Alex was certain that the Philadelphia guerrillas would not have been able to carry the stuff half this far alone. He thanked God that they hadn't been forced to discard any of it. They would need every last round when push came to shove.

The moon rose high overhead as they struggled across the ruins of the city, Shina and her bunch showing Alex and the guerrillas the way. They were moving steadily toward South Ferry in spite of the constant obstacles; indeed, all of Manhattan seemed to conspire in an effort to prevent them from getting to their destination on time.

But Shina showed them some byways through the rubble that saved valuable time. She had moved around in the presence of the colloids without being captured or killed for three long years, and she seemed to know every last nook and cranny of the wrecked city. Alex had never been a religious man, but it almost made him believe in divine intervention. At least he could believe that they had all been very lucky in the past few hours—all except for poor Pat Crowley.

Alex glanced back at Jack, who walked next to Ronnie. The kid was still in a state of shock, but he was ready to avenge his father. Alex was convinced that Jack would fight like a demon when the time came. As for the other New Jersey people, well, they were still with the guerrillas. If any of them were infected, or any of the New York people, or his own people for that matter, things could go very badly. Sabotage would be a simple matter for someone working on the inside. There was no way of telling if anyone was infected. Alex had never suspected Pat; in fact, he had not even known that *he* was infected when the thing inside his brain led Tony Chang to his death.

If there were infected among the guerrillas' numbers, they might very well not know it themselves until it was time to do the dirty work. It was a chance that Alex and his people had to take.

He was prepared to shoot the first person who appeared to be out of line . . . no matter who it was.

As Shina had predicted, the going got a lot easier after they had traveled further south. By the time they reached 8th Street, they were walking on a more or less flat surface. In spite of the strewn detritus, there were clearly defined streets. Their progress became much swifter.

"Have you noticed that there isn't anything moving around here?" Jo said as they walked through the once quaint neighborhood. "I mean, we haven't even seen a rat."

Alex allowed himself a smile. "Thousands of colloids streamed through here a few hours ago. All the rats probably left town after that gooey stampede."

"Why haven't the colloids sent another army of infected to meet us?"

"My guess is that they're going to use them to protect the neonate," Alex said. "It's hard for them to stop us while we're on the march, and they haven't got enough infected people to put up an effective counter force. The best they can do is put as many of the infected between us and the neonate as they can manage, and hope that we don't get through."

"Yes," Claire said from behind them, "they didn't engage us in battle today for no reason. They want to make us use up our ammunition. They don't know how much we've got, but it probably exceeds their expectations."

"You mean they didn't expect us to get through the tunnel?" Alex said.

"Probably not, but now we're closing in on their breeding ground. They've got to do something to stop us. I think you're right. They'll doubtless put up hundreds of thousands of the infected as a shield."

"And give up all that food?" Shina asked.

"Yeah," Alex said. "They can't survive on what's left for more than a few weeks, a month at the outside. The neonate has to be created before the weather gets too cold. If they had developed the new infection earlier, their plan would have been foolproof. As it is, there's still a chance."

Shina looked at him suspiciously. "How the fuck do *you* know all this shit?"

"Did you hear what I said about the new infection?" Alex asked.

"Yeah."

"I had it."

"Shee-it."

Alex wasn't sure if she were expressing incredulity or belief. "Believe what you want, Shina, but that's what happened to me."

"And they just told you all about their plans while you were infected, right?"

"No, not exactly. But you learn some things just because of the colloid being inside your mind."

"It's true," Jo said.

"I guess you know because it happened to you, too. Ain't that right, honey?" Shina said sarcastically.

"That's right."

"I caught the virus from her," Alex explained. "We both have memories that the colloids didn't want anybody to know. It never occurred to them that we could free ourselves from the infection."

Shina looked from one to the other, and then at Claire.

"It's true," said Claire. "I was a witness to Jo's infection, and I was there when she recovered."

"Wow," Shina said.

"Yeah," Alex said. "Wow is right."

"They didn't eat 'em," said the androgynous creature, who Shina had called "Satch" a couple of times. "Why didn't the colloids eat 'em?"

"Because they wanted our brains in good shape," Alex explained. "Maybe as models for the baby's brains, or maybe so they could infiltrate. Maybe for both reasons."

Shina looked at Satch, and then glanced back at the others. "You telling me that any one of them could be a spy?"

"Any one of *us*," Alex corrected her. "*Any* one of us."

"Shee-it."

CHAPTER THIRTY-THREE

The darkness began to turn gray. Dawn was coming, and they were getting very near to South Ferry. It was time to stop and take stock of their weapons and ammunition, to make peace with themselves and their gods before they went into battle.

"The waterfront's only a few blocks away," Alex said. "I think we'll find what we're looking for there. If not, then we've come a long way for nothing. One man has died, and the rest of us are weary to our bones. The colloids might have left me with a false idea about all this, to throw us off, but I don't think so. I think we're closing in on their last hope to hold onto this planet, and I'm confident that other guerrillas are fighting back all over the world."

Alex was so tired that he was almost hallucinating, seeing shapes shifting in the ruins of the city. Somehow he kept going, though, a vision in his brain of the colloids dying, fading, vanishing from the earth. He knew the truth now; it had been buried deep inside him all the time, but his fatigue, combined with his sense of mission, brought it forth now that he needed it.

"They blew it," he said. "They almost did it, but they didn't develop the third stage soon enough. The trial infections didn't take. We all saw Pat Crowley take his own life rather than allow them to control his mind. That's the sort of courage they can't fight. They don't understand it, and they never will. That's why they're going to lose this war."

"Yeah!" Riquelme shouted, lifting his fist and shaking it at the lightening sky.

Seventy strong, they all lifted their clenched fists in solidarity and cried out for the downtrodden human race.

They were going to fight, and this time they did not intend to lose the battle, or the war.

Alex felt their courage reinvigorating him, filling him with renewed strength. He had never believed in destiny, but he was somehow certain that this was the moment he had been created for.

Locking and loading, the guerrillas prepared for battle. Alex no longer distinguished his own people from the New Jersey or New York people. They were the human race, united before this greatest of all threats; a threat not from within, as so many threats had been in the twentieth century, but from without. They had been humbled, enslaved, beaten into the mud, and now they would rise again.

Alex turned and led the guerrillas through the empty streets as the faint morning light grew ever brighter. Jo walked beside him, her .32 pistol in hand. Beside her was Riquelme, the flamethrower's nozzle in his hands as he walked proudly to battle. And beside him were Claire, and Samuel, and Jill, and Shina, and Ronnie, and Jack, and Dan, and all the others—the last best hope of the human race.

Alex had agonized through the night about the best method of attack, and he had been forced to conclude that there was nothing for it but to face the infected head on, to try to break through to the colloids' breeding ground. The guerrillas had learned that the infected were not really warriors, and, conversely, that they themselves were now seasoned veterans. Everything depended on how many of the enemy were left to send out against them. If the colloids had spread the infected too thin, the guerrillas might succeed.

They soon saw how many they were up against. In the gathering light, the infected were spread out all the way to the docks by the tens of thousands, as they had feared. There were at least as many colloids oozing irritably a safe distance from the waterfront. The guerrillas clung to the deep morning shadows of wrecked brownstones, moving stealthily. Alex raised his hand, signaling them to halt.

They retreated out of sight and earshot of the infected, to discuss possible strategies.

"I say we should hit 'em hard," said Riquelme, patting his trusty flamethrower. "Just burn a hole right through the middle of them."

"It might work," Claire agreed.

"If it is the Lord's wish," Samuel said.

"I don't know," Alex said. "It might be smarter to look around for some other means. There are just too goddamned many of them for a full frontal attack."

"He's right," said Shina, whose advice was welcomed by the others. "There might be a place where they ain't so thick, where we can get through and get a look at this baby you've been talking about."

"So what do we do?" asked Ronnie.

"Send out a scout to look around. There's gotta be a place where they're spread too thin."

"I think Shina's right," said Jo.

"Woman's intuition," Shina said, grinning at Jo. "Ain't that right, babe?"

Everyone laughed, breaking the tension for a moment. But the suspense seeped back into the air as surely as the morning mist.

"We'll send out two," said Alex. "One to the right and one to the left."

"I'll go," said Jack, eager to avenge his father's death.

"Not this time, son," Alex said. "You risked enough yesterday. This time I think I'll volunteer."

"Not spoken like an old Army man," said Riquelme, "but admirable, nonetheless."

"Well, we need to save you for the firefight."

"Firefight is right," said Ronnie, squeezing Jack's hand. The boy frowned in disappointment, but he didn't put up any argument. His father had apparently taught him to obey authority figures, a necessity in wartime.

"Who else is going to volunteer?" Claire asked.

"Jo is," said Alex.

"Oh, I am, am I?" Jo looked extremely dubious about Alex's assertion.

"You have to, Jo. You're the only one who has been infected."

"True, but so what?"

"Jo, there are millions of colloids just a few blocks

away. When you and I get close enough to them, their telepathic emanations are going to get through to us."

Jo's brow furrowed. "I was going to ask you how you know that, but a question like that would be a waste of time."

"Who knows what else might happen?" Alex said. "We've never been so close to so many colloids since we were infected. You *never* have been near thousands of them like I have. We've speculated on the possibility that their telepathy is enhanced by larger numbers of colloids. I remember how they seemed to scream when I shot them the night I met you. My mind was picking up their pain. If we're psychically receptive to them, maybe we can learn enough to second-guess them all the way to their breeding ground."

"You've been up too long, man," said Satch.

"No, I think it's possible," Claire said.

"Are you feeling any telepathic signals?" Alex said to Jo.

She looked a little frightened. "Maybe . . . I can't really be sure."

"I think you must be picking them up," Alex said. "I am. It's very faint, but it's definitely there."

Jo's eyes were furtive, frightened, but Alex took her by the hand.

"The infection can't hurt you, Jo," he said. "We drove it out of you once. And they aren't going to try it again. But you're sensitive to them now, just like I am. Can't you feel it?"

"Yes," she said. "God help me."

Alex put his arm around her. "This can help us win, Jo," he said. "This power they've accidentally left us with could make the difference between victory and defeat."

Jo nodded in understanding. She didn't like what was happening to her, but she had to accept it.

Now that he had become aware of the colloid's emanations, Alex read them more and more clearly. The guerrillas were indeed very close to the breeding ground, he sensed. The infected were under the colloids' control, of course, but very imprecisely. Once the virus matured, it became more and more communicative with the colloids, until it was a colloid itself. And then it was part of an enormous group mind, a psychic network that covered the entire planet.

"Do you want to take the Jersey side, Jo?" Alex asked.

She looked at him strangely. "You read my mind," she said, not realizing for a moment why the others were laughing. "But I guess that's the whole point, isn't it?"

"Exactly," Alex said. "Let's go."

Alex crouched as he made his way across an open area, and then hid behind a crumbling warehouse. He saw no indication that he had been spied by the infected, though he could see a few of them shambling about in the distance. He looked back toward the building where the guerrillas hid, and saw Riquelme watching him.

Alex felt, rather than saw, Jo making her way cautiously to the west. She worked her way toward the docks as she attempted to circle around the infected hordes.

Doing the same thing, Alex moved quickly from the shelter of one building to the next. Willing himself to stay in contact with Jo, he scurried a few blocks and then stopped to get his bearings.

He could smell salt on the breeze that was blowing away the mist. That meant that he couldn't have been more than a half mile from the ocean; perhaps he was even closer than that. Had he gone far enough east to avoid the infected?

If he climbed to the top of one of these piles of rubble, he might find it a good vantage point. In fact, there were a number of more or less intact buildings in the neighborhood. One of them might prove even more useful for reconnaissance. Looking for a high roof, he began to move furtively to the east again.

At last he found one with a fire escape. Climbing up and crawling across the roof, he made his way to the building's southern edge and peered out over the bay.

CHAPTER THIRTY-FOUR

The low-lying fog was burning away rapidly, revealing the dark mass of Staten Island and the wreckage of the Verazzano and Goethals bridges, as well as Governor's Island. Even Ellis Island was faintly visible. And just past it was Liberty Island, where the Statue of Liberty still stood. Colloids or not, Alex supposed, the Army had drawn the line at blasting the Lady—even if she did live in New York.

Closer in, along the rotting wharves lining New York Harbor, were the massed colloids and infected. Alex gasped involuntarily when he saw how many there were. Not tens of thousands, not hundreds of thousands, but surely millions. A black, viscous stream of agitated colloids roiled uneasily between the streets and the docks. Between the guerrillas and the colloids, the infected were so closely packed that he could easily believe that some of them were being crushed to death. Indeed, there were hundreds of lifeless figures lying on the broken asphalt near the docks. Many of them heaved with the feeding throes of their parasites, as the colloids rushed to finish consuming them before they rotted.

Reminded of Hitler's rallies, Alex watched a forest of mindless human bodies sway as they formed a barrier between their alien masters' breeding ground and the guerrillas.

But where, exactly, was the breeding ground? It occurred to him that perhaps "ground" was not the right word. But how could the colloids have bred the creature underwater? He thought about it and realized that an amphibious creature would be the fifth stage of colloid evolution on earth.

But that would come later, he knew. For now, a thing that walked on land was the colloids' aim. Why, then,

was Alex so certain that the breeding ground was somewhere beyond the waterfront, out in the harbor somewhere?

Alex tried to use his newfound telepathic gift to find
out. As he concentrated, he thought he saw something
move out there in the mist.

He focused his mind, for the moment forgetting everything, even Jo.

And he saw where the breeding ground was. Hundreds
of colloids were on Liberty Island, sliding around the
base of the Statue of Liberty! There were humans out
there, too—third stage infected.

It made sense now. They needed a lot of salt water, the
basic fluid that would compose most of the neonate's
body, just as it composed most of a human body. But the
colloids themselves couldn't deal with water, not even
saline water. So, to do the job for them, they manipulated human helpers with colloids in their brains. And the
guerrillas had once been naive enough to believe that the
third stage was simply a plan to infiltrate their ranks.

Alex's reception of the colloids' telepathic waves was
stronger up here on this roof than it had been on the
ground. Was it possible that the massed infected had
created a kind of interference to the transmission? That
might be another reason why the colloids had set them up
as a barrier between Liberty Island and Manhattan. For
surely they knew that Alex and Jo were receiving their
emanations.

Of course, Alex realized with a chill, that might also
mean that they knew where he and Jo were. And just
where *was* Jo now?

He shut his eyes, panicking to think that something had
happened while he had cut off contact with Jo. But she
was there, watching the masses of the infected from behind an old railway platform. He tried to talk to her with
his mind, but his thoughts were only a vague sensation to
her, as hers were to him. Nevertheless, she knew that
Alex was there with her.

As the sun slowly rose, its orange light gleamed on the
water. Alex tried to focus his thoughts on the activities of
the colloids out in the harbor, and he struggled to get
past the colloids and the milling zombies who protected
them.

Suddenly he felt an exultant rush that surprised him so much that he almost cried out. It came from Jo.

She had moved closer to the water, and had seen something that they needed desperately. A boat.

It wasn't much, just an old fireboat with rotting hoses coiled on its thirty-foot deck. Somehow the line that held it to the pier was still secured, and the fireboat had not been set adrift. Here was a way to get out to Liberty Island . . . if they could get past the infected. The brain damaged creatures were much less plentiful in Jo's vicinity, but there were still thousands of them only a few hundred feet from her hiding place, ominously crowding the broken streets.

Alex had little time to wonder at the clarity of Jo's vision, seen as it was through his own eyes. If they lived through this, there would be ample time to compare notes in the future. If they didn't live through it, then there might not be a future for anybody on the planet. With that in mind, Alex scrambled back to the fire escape and climbed down. In a few minutes he was back with the guerrillas.

"They're out on Liberty Island," he told them.

"How ironic," said Claire.

"It's far enough from the mainland that they feel safe," Alex said, "and I guess the water is probably a lot cleaner out there."

"Yes, the deeper waters are probably essential. Even after three years the water close to shore is still tainted with many toxins. The location of the breeding ground means that we have one thing to our advantage, though. There are only so many large population centers on earth situated on deep water harbors. If we win here today, we'll know where to look for the colloid breeding grounds from now on. Once we've managed to—"

"Hold thy tongue, woman," Samuel said. "This is the day for smiting our enemies, not talking."

Claire looked at Samuel with something between annoyance and amusement.

"Jo has found a boat for us," Alex said.

Everyone seemed a little confused, and Elvin asked in his flat way, "How do you know that? She's not back yet."

"Trust me," Alex said. "There's a roof a few blocks east that is a perfect place to set up the mortar." He quickly gave Irv Finney directions to the building. "You'll need a couple of people, Irv. Mavis and Judd, go with him."

The three of them got their weapons together and set off to the east. Irv had shown a knack for landing mortar rounds on target, or so Alex had been told by Riquelme, whose advice tended to be reliable.

"Let's get moving, then." Riquelme shouldered the flamethrower's fuel tank and stepped forward.

"Right." Alex started moving to the west, trying to focus his thoughts on Jo to stay put, assuring her that they would join her in just a few minutes.

It was very strange, tracing the streets that Jo had taken a short while before. Her memory was stronger than a feeling of *déjà vu;* Alex had actually been on these potholed streets with her, in a very real sense. At the time, he had hardly noticed how vivid her sensory emanations were, preoccupied as he was by his own mission. He hurried to her with such surefooted assurance that the others had a difficult time keeping up with him. The litter bearers, in fact, fell a good distance behind, so Alex paused to let them catch up.

Alex understood now that the infected would pay no attention to them until they came toward the docks. Once the guerrillas attempted to move toward Liberty Island, the neonate's guardians would try to stop the attack in their largely ineffectual way. Their sheer numbers were going to pose quite a problem, but Alex thought there was a chance that the guerrillas could break through to the fireboat.

He saw Jo, just ahead. She was crouching behind the platform waiting for them. Nobody else saw her for a few seconds, but of course Alex knew exactly where she was even before her image registered on the vision centers of his brain.

Their telepathic bond grew stronger all the time, and Jo turned knowingly toward him before she could possibly know he was there through the five human senses.

Her premature response was not lost on Claire Siegel.

"You are in communication with her, aren't you, Alex?" she asked.

"Yes."

"In New Jersey, you said that your telepathic ability was vanishing. Has the proximity of the colloids brought it back?"

"Yes, I think so." He left Dr. Siegel with that and sprinted toward Jo.

"Alex," she said. "I saw what you saw . . . "

"I know," he said, "but there's no time to talk about it now. We've got to get our hands on that fireboat."

"There are so many of the infected in our way," said Jo. "Do you think we can do it?"

"What choice do we have?"

CHAPTER THIRTY-FIVE

Alex watched the infected milling around, and tried to decide if the guerrillas' best bet was to go directly for the boat en masse, or for a raiding party to try to take it while the others set up a cross fire from cover. He discussed these alternatives with Jo.

"If we all go," she said, "then there won't be anybody left if we don't make it."

"So you think we shouldn't all get on the boat?"

"Right."

"Okay, but we're going to need enough people to fight the colloids *and* the infected once we get out on the island. What do you say we split the difference?"

"Well, that would leave us a chance if we don't succeed, all right."

"I've got a question," Claire said. "How are we going to get that boat started?"

"We've got those charged batteries, and we siphoned out the rest of the gasoline from the jeeps. We'll see if we can get the engine going. If we can't . . . then we can't. We'll have to think of something else."

Elvin, to the surprise of the Philadelphia guerrillas, and Dan Galouye each volunteered to carry a can of gasoline. The guerrillas had brought it along in case they found a vehicle on this side of the Hudson that would still run, but nobody had imagined that they would end up using it on a boat. Two other men, Clement and Stubbs, would each carry a battery. As Elvin and Galouye brought the sloshing cans forward, Alex began to pick those who would go with them if they could get the boat running.

He chose all of the original Philadelphia guerrillas, knowing that he could depend on them, and he chose Shina and Satch, who seemed as if they weren't afraid to fight. As he singled out those who were to go on the boat, he noticed Jack Crowley eagerly watching him.

Alex turned to Jack and Ronnie. "I want you two to stay here."

"No way," Jack said. "You gotta let me go with you."

Alex could not bear the thought of letting this boy die, not after what had happened to the kid's father. "We need cover when we try to take that boat," he said.

"You need to get the boat started, too," Jack said. "I can do that."

Alex didn't think that this was false bravado. There was such an expression of self-assurance and earnestness on Jack's youthful face that it seemed impractical to doubt him at this crucial juncture. "You're good with engines, huh?"

"Ask Ronnie."

"Yeah," Ronnie said. "The Harley conked out in Jersey, and Jack got it going somehow. I still don't know how he did it, but he convinced me that I shouldn't worry about it happening again. That's why I felt like we could keep on going to New York."

"Well, you should have come back as soon as he fixed the bike." In spite of his admonition, it seemed entirely likely to Alex that Jack knew a good deal more about engines than any of the adults among them. "That was a stupid thing to do."

"Sorry," Ronnie said meekly.

"Jack," Alex asked, "how long will it take you to know whether you can get that boat's motor going?"

"If I can just get a look at it for a few seconds, I'll have a pretty good idea if I can get it started."

"Okay, then the thing to do is to sneak you aboard so you can have a look at it, rather than risk everybody's lives."

"Right."

"Which means that we're going to need a diversion," Jo said.

"Hey," Alex protested, "who's the military strategist around here, me or you?"

"I've seen enough Rambo movies to figure it out," Jo said sarcastically.

"You like *Rambo*?" Jack said in amazement.

"Not really."

"It shouldn't be too difficult to draw the attention of those infected nearest the boat, not when Irv starts lobbing those mortar rounds. Jack and the other guys will board the fireboat, see if they can get the engine started and, if they can, pour in the gasoline. Once they give us the high sign, half of us will rush the boat while the other half cover us from a block away."

"And if they don't give us the high sign?" Ronnie asked, worry evident on her pretty face.

"If they start coming for you, Jack," Alex said, "dive in the harbor and swim for it. They won't follow you into the water, and once you've gotten away from where they're massed, I don't think you'll be in any danger from them."

"Your only danger will be from pneumonia at that point," Jo said sarcastically.

"Nevertheless, it might be your only way out. Don't hesitate to dive in, no matter how cold the water might be."

"Okay." Jack's jaw was set in grim determination. He intended to vindicate his father's memory today, one way or another.

"I'd like to go along," Harry, one of the men from New Jersey said. "Pat Crowley and me went back a long ways."

"You got it." Alex turned back to the others. "Let's do it," he said.

Everyone checked their firearms, took off the safeties, and followed Alex as he jogged out into the street. He ran straight for the nearest of the infected, shouting: "Here we come, you son of a bitches!"

He fired at one of them, seeing the creature's knees buckle as it fell back against its brethren. A few of the other guerrillas fired into the mob, too, wasting as little ammunition as possible while making sure that the infected knew they were being attacked by a sizable force.

At first the infected seemed confused. They moved in all directions at once, bumping into each other like Keystone Kops. Alex ran straight toward them and turned within a yard of the closest, thirty guerrillas following his path.

Like the pseudopod of a giant colloid, hundreds of the infected lunged clumsily toward them. They caught up with those at the rear of the column, but a few well placed gun shots extricated the guerrillas.

A mortar round whumped into the asphalt fifty yards to the east. Now Alex led the guerrillas away from the infected. As he ran, he glanced over his shoulder and saw that there was a spot near the fireboat where no more than ten or fifteen of the infected stood. Jack and Harry were running straight toward that soft spot in the colloids' defenses. Behind them were Elvin, Galouye, Clement, and Stubbs, straining under the weight of gasoline cans and car batteries. A second mortar round burst on the asphalt, this one only missing by a few yards.

Harry, a big man, bowled two of the infected over, and clubbed another with a .44 he was holding in his right hand. Galouye swung the gasoline can and smashed in an infected head with a resounding clang.

Jack shot a man who staggered toward him. Two others, lunging at him, tripped over the body and sprawled at the feet of their assailants.

The hundreds of infected who were reeling toward the guerrillas began to turn in all directions, confused by the sounds of combat coming from in front of them and behind them as the mortar rounds fell steadily, exploding in their ranks. Alex's heart swelled with hope that this actually might work.

And then a small figure dashed away from the guerrillas and toward the fireboat.

"Ronnie!" Jo shouted. "No!"

But it was too late. The kid was with Jack right in the middle of the action, almost before the words were out of Jo's mouth. Ronnie was able to catch up with Jack and the other guys easily, because they had been slowed down by the *mano a mano* fighting. Alex wanted to help them, but he didn't dare risk a shot at this distance. The kids and Harry were too close to the last few infected between them and the boat.

Jack shot one of the infected in the chest, and a huge meaty chunk flew out of the creature's back. The man, dead on his feet, spun and landed in the arms of one of his companions. The encumbered one howled in frustra-

THE PARASITE WAR 221

tion and fell backwards into the water, still holding onto
the corpse. The splash rained on some of the milling
infected who still stumbled about in confusion. But their
ranks were closing, more and more of them turning toward
the kids and Harry.

They weren't going to make it.

"There goes the fucking plan." The words might have
come out of Alex's mouth, but they didn't. He looked at
Jo, and she looked back at him. Without another word,
they sprinted toward the kids, bellowing at the top of
their lungs.

Alex fired the Ingram carefully, watching the infected
fall like sheaves of wheat each time he squeezed off a few
rounds. Jo fired only a couple of shots as they gained on
the kids, Elvin, and the other four. Jack and Ronnie disappeared behind a screen of diseased human flesh. Harry
went down, screaming, and disappeared almost immediately. Dozens of the infected were on top of him, tearing
at him with hands, nails, teeth.

Alex swept the Ingram across the mob, trying to save
Harry. But it was too late. Then Dan went down. Alex
saw the red gasoline can lying on the ground, a trail of
deeper red next to it. There wasn't much left of Dan, but
he could still hear Jack, Ronnie, Elvin, Stubbs, and Clement shouting imprecations at their enemies.

Jo and Alex were side by side, firing into the mob.
Bodies were falling everywhere, punctured by bullets.
But the infected kept coming.

Were the guerrillas following them? Alex didn't dare to
look back to see. He and Jo had their hands full, and now
he had fired enough rounds so that the Ingram was getting hot. He felt cold hands grabbing his arms and legs.
He didn't care. The madness overtook him as he killed
three more people. He heard Jo screaming with bloodlust,
as she slaughtered the infected by his side.

She screamed in his mind, too, sharing his mania, his
hatred, and his pain.

CHAPTER THIRTY-SIX

"We're with you, Alex!" It was Riquelme. He laid down a serpentine trail of fire, killing dozens of colloids.

Gun shots popped behind Alex and Jo, bullets whizzing past their ears as they reached the fireboat's wharf. Alex and Jo crouched at the same moment to afford the guerrillas better targets.

The infected were keeling over everywhere. The plan had failed, and the guerrillas understood that the only way to win now was to go for broke.

Alex couldn't see the kids anywhere. He could barely see the water on either side of the wharf. But he and Jo were standing on the rotting boards now, fighting their way through the remaining infected. Alex used his foot to shove one off the wharf and into the water.

He could hardly feel his own aching body anymore, and he knew that Jo shared his savage transcendence. They were unstoppable, more than human.

The body of Dan Galouye was at Alex's feet. He stooped to pick up the gasoline can while Jo covered him. Holding the Ingram in front of him he rose triumphantly, and they fought their way to the fireboat.

Ronnie stood on the fireboat's deck, firing at the infected. Jack was climbing into the engine hatch, while the batteries and gasoline cans were brought alongside. Jack was already starting to work on the engine. The kids were all right!

The fireboat listed as the guerrillas boarded it. A quick count told Alex that eight or ten had been lost in the fray. Twenty people were left to storm Liberty Island. But first they had to get the engine going.

The guerrillas ashore were shooting the advancing enemy like sitting ducks, as Jack poured one can of gasoline into the tank. Clement and Stubbs had set the batteries down and were firing at the infected. Elvin took the second can from Alex and lugged it over to Jack at the engine hatch. Alex tended to doubt that the kid could start it, unless he had some pretty good tricks up his sleeve. But it was the only chance they had, so they might just as well go down fighting on the boat.

Alex squeezed the Ingram's trigger and nothing happened. He reached in his kit for another clip. It was the last. From here on in, he had to make every shot count. Fortunately, the infected could only come at them a few at a time along the narrow wharf.

Alex saw Ronnie grappling with the heavy rope attaching the fireboat to a piling. It was as big around as her arm, and the weather of years had stuck it fast to the wood.

Alex signaled her to get out of the way, and shot the rope. At least now they would drift away. Perhaps they would float close enough to the island to get their licks in. There were two punts on the fireboat, so they could paddle to Liberty Island if necessary.

It was only when the boat had progressed backward a few yards and turned around that Alex realized the engine was running. The deafening din of gunfire and the screams of the dying had obscured its mechanical grumbling.

Jack was in the pilothouse, at the wheel. He backed the boat away from the wharf until he could turn the fireboat toward the open sea. Alex and Jo stood in the stern as the old rust bucket swung about. They watched the teeming infected diminish in size, still hearing shots from the guerrillas left on shore. Occasionally a body would fall into the water from one of the wharves as a mortar shell hit ground.

The guerrillas cheered wildly and embraced each other on the fireboat's deck. Alex felt exultation that they had gotten this far. He watched a rainbow slick of oil spread out among the whitecaps as they headed into the wind. He only hoped that the ship would make it out to Liberty Island, short distance that it was.

Alex knew that he and Jo were going to Liberty Island, even if they had to swim, and he sensed that the colloids knew it, too. The aliens had tried everything to stop him, and he was still on his feet. He could barely stand still now, anticipating this final battle. The mania had grabbed hold of him, and would not let go until it was played out—or until he was dead.

The water was choppy, so the guerrillas looked for handholds. Jo and Alex grasped the edge of the hose reel at the stern, the peeling paint flaking as they touched it. The firehoses looked as if they would crumble to the touch. The other guerrillas sat down on the deck or gripped the side bits. Elvin looked bilious, but he didn't lean over the side, as Alex expected. They hadn't eaten in nearly twenty-four hours, after all, so there was nothing in his stomach to disgorge.

The fireboat moved slowly to the south, leaving Manhattan behind. Alex was wired, his bipolar disorder wildly on the upswing. He couldn't remember when it had felt so good to be out of his mind.

Jo leaned against him, laying her head on his shoulder. He knew that the mania had passed from her, because he was able to cut her off from it. When the fighting started, he would not be able to stop it even if he wanted to. That was doubtless a good thing, though. Being crazy was all right in only one situation that he knew—war.

They were all kill crazy by now, of course, but the exultation on deck died down in spite of their madness. In a few minutes they would be on Liberty Island. Many of their comrades had died already, and many more would die before it was over.

But at least it would soon be over.

The salt air smelled so much fresher out here. The odor of the infected had mingled with the sea's scent on shore, but now the wind whipped in from the Atlantic and slapped them bracingly in the face. It was exhilarating. Alex felt as though he knew how tribal warriors had felt when they had gone out to fight. It was a good day to die.

In a matter of mere minutes they were within hailing distance of Liberty Island. They could see the gray gouts of the colloids slithering on the granite slabs in the very shadow of the Statue of Liberty.

On the south end of the tiny island, a squadron of the infected labored. Some of them were in rowboats, and others were actually in the water. These were clearly third stage colloid victims, now transformed into willing allies of the aliens.

Ringing the island were scores of the infected, these the same kind of mindless creatures the guerrillas had been fighting all morning.

As soon as they got close enough, the guerrillas would start picking them off. There was a pier on the west side of the island, where they could moor the fireboat once the odds were evened up a bit.

"Hold your fire until you've got a clear target," Alex shouted over the rumbling engines. He could feel the colloids' dread inside him. They had never dreamed that the guerrillas would get this far. If they had killed Alex when they had the chance, this could have never happened. At least that was what they believed. But Jo had been infected, too; she could have followed the scent as easily as Alex.

The colloids had miscalculated, and now they were threatened at this crucial and intimate moment. They would do everything in their power to protect the neonate, to succeed in their plan of domination and conquest.

The fireboat drew closer to the island, and Alex raised the Ingram. All of the guerrillas waited, as the infected lined up on shore like sitting ducks.

Alex fired a burst, and watched with satisfaction as an infected woman was jerked off her feet and slammed onto the granite. Another spun and sprawled over her. The rest of the guerrillas followed suit, shots popping from bow to stern, and the infected were falling all over the north end of the island.

Jack steered the fireboat around toward the pier, while the guerrillas continued their fusillade. The bloodlust was growing in them, as if Alex's mania was contagious.

More of the infected were shambling toward them from the other side of the island. But gunfire brought down most of the newcomers before they were even close to the pier. The acrid smell of burnt gunpowder combined with the sea air in a heady mix.

Alex mowed down three more of the infected as the pier seemed to grow larger and larger. They were coming in fast, the moorings only a few feet away now. And then Alex saw that they were moving *too* fast.

They were going to collide with the pier.

"Hang on!" he shouted, uncertain if anybody besides Jo could hear him.

CHAPTER THIRTY-SEVEN

The fireboat's prow crunched into the pier with an ear splitting sound of splintering wood. Screams came from all over the boat as people were thrown overboard or slammed against bulkheads. The davit swung around like a giant's arm, but fortunately it didn't strike anybody.

Alex and Jo managed to hang onto the rotting hoses, which cushioned them from the shock somewhat. The prow crumpled, but the fireboat stayed afloat. Not for long, but perhaps long enough.

The pier had been cleared of the infected, a few of whom were crushed under the immense weight of the thirty-foot vessel. The others were tossed into the ocean to drown while their colloid masters dissolved in the salt water. There were hundreds more advancing, but they hesitated to go out onto the broken pier. Perhaps seeing the fate of the others had given the colloids controlling them pause.

The guerrillas who had managed to stay aboard the fireboat were sprawled all over the deck, many of them dazed and flailing down among the scuppers.

The engine was silent, and Alex couldn't see Jack and Ronnie up in the pilothouse. He hoped that they were all right, but there was no time to find out.

The boat was hung up on the remains of the pier, floundering at an angle. Alex and Jo tried to make their way to the bow, but they slipped on the canted deck, sliding down the port side. They got up and crept along the bulkhead while the other guerrillas began to get on their feet and follow them.

Alex was at the prow, Jo right behind him. He leaped off the fireboat and onto the rotting wood, the Ingram at the ready.

"Let's kick ass!" he bawled.

He did not wait to see if anyone was with him. He was certain that Jo was, and that was all that mattered. The Ingram was part of him; he squeezed off rounds as easily as he might point a finger, without thinking about it at all. The enemy fell as soon he looked at them, the 9mm slugs tearing through their blue-blotched, diseased bodies.

Their screams were like music, the battle cries of the guerrillas a counterpoint to the slaughter. The infected were falling everywhere, but their reinforcements kept coming, slowly closing in as their comrades died.

Still, the guerrillas continued to cut a swath toward the Statue of Liberty. Jo was firing her .32 methodically, falling to one knee to reload from time to time.

Suddenly the Ingram stopped firing. Alex squeezed the trigger again and again, but nothing happened. He was out of ammunition. He turned it around, seizing the hot barrel in his hands, and swung it like a baseball bat even as it singed the skin on the palms.

The stock banged against the head of an oncoming infected with a satisfying, jarring impact. Then he swung it backhand, stopping cold another one who was rushing toward Jo.

The little band of guerrillas moved steadily, if slowly, towards the base of the statue. But a fearful scream made Alex look over his shoulder just in time to see Elvin pulled away from the band of guerrillas by dozens of clutching hands. Several shots were fired at Elvin's captors, but he was swallowed up by the mass of the infected, and there was no going back for him.

The guerrillas were surrounded. The only way out was to fight their way through to the end. But the gunfire was less frequent now, as more of the guerrillas ran out of bullets. Others were plucked from the crowd by the surging infected, including the shrieking Satch.

Huddling together, the remaining guerrillas moved ahead as if they were one. At their center was Riquelme and the flamethrower. They had to get him close enough to stop the colloids, and they could not afford to waste what little fuel was left.

From behind them came the cry of a familiar voice. Alex turned to see Claire in the grip of four infected, then five, then seven, then ten.

"Claire!" he and Jo screamed simultaneously.

But she was beyond their help. Samuel flailed at them with his pipe, but to no avail. She was gone in an instant. Screaming in rage and pain, Samuel leaped into the heaving mass of the infected and vanished along with her.

Alex did not need to catch a glimpse of Jo's anguished face to know how she felt. Her rage and sorrow coursed through his own mind and body.

But they were almost to their goal now, and the infected's ranks were thinning. Many of them slipped in the blood of their fellow creatures as they continued to attack the guerrillas.

Alex and Jo reached the base of the statue. Now the enemy could only attack from the guerrillas' right rear flank. With their backs protected, the guerrillas turned and fought until the last of the infected were lying dead and wounded on the ground.

There was no time to celebrate the obliteration of this last obstacle, however. It appeared to Alex that fewer than ten guerrillas were still alive, perhaps only six or eight. But he couldn't stop to count them now.

He ran to the corner of the statue's pedestal, the other guerrillas right behind him. Turning the corner, he saw for the first time what had lurked in his conscious mind since his infection. He hesitated long enough for the others to catch up, and then the little group stood together for a moment, gazing in horror at what the colloids had wrought.

CHAPTER THIRTY-EIGHT

The thing stood twelve feet high if it was an inch. Its gigantic hands gripped the metal guard rail, naked sinews and pulsing veins clearly visible through its gray, translucent skin. Massive bones showed through the flesh, muscles flexing and stretching grotesquely. Its head was its most offensive feature, a misshapen skull bearing a hideous caricature of a human face, grinning skeletally and dripping with slime. The creature did not seem fully formed, though it appeared to be climbing up from the foaming sea.

But no, it was poised there, half of it in the water and half out. The colloids were crawling over its hands and arms and onto the mutating torso. Below were third-stage infected, some in rowboats and some treading water, as they kneaded the living colloids into the shape of a giant human body, sculptors working with human tissue instead of clay.

In his worst nightmares, Alex had never imagined anything so monstrous. And though he had known of the neonate for days, he had seen it only through the colloids' projections. There had been moments when he had questioned whether he could kill the newborn creature, but now he knew that there was only one thing to do.

"Burn it!" he shouted.

The colloids did not intend to give it up so easily, however. They gushed in pinkish-gray streams across the granite, prepared to defend their hybrid child with the fierce passion of a mother's love.

Riquelme calmly stepped forward with the flamethrower. He didn't see the colloid until it was too late. It crawled up his pants leg.

He tried to shake it loose, dancing wildly as he shrieked.

But more colloids were slurping toward him. His foot struck one and he slipped.

They were all over him, sucking the tissue off his bones. But Alex ran toward his friend in spite of the danger.

"No, Alex!" Riquelme screamed. "Stay back!"

Alex knew that there was nothing he could do for Riquelme, but he had to get the flamethrower. They didn't have a prayer without it.

Somehow, even while he was dying, Riquelme managed to roll onto his stomach and tear the tank's straps from his shoulders. While his very flesh was dissolving, he tossed the flamethrower toward the guerrillas.

Alex didn't stop to pick up the tank. He pointed the nozzle toward his friend's shuddering body and let fly a stream of fire that mercifully finished Riquelme off.

The colloids' inhuman wailing reverberated inside Alex's head, but he found that he enjoyed the sensation of their telepathic suffering. He watched with pleasure as the rippling gouts of colloidal tissue behind the body retreated, quivering gelatinous forms flowing toward the neonate.

And Alex knew that the colloids might escape if they could all join flesh on the gigantic baby. He knew that the neonate's skin would congeal and it would swim away toward Manhattan, where it would seek succor among the hundreds of thousands of infected lining the waterfront.

But Alex also knew that it was too soon for it to escape. The skin of the neonate's torso and upper extremities had not cohered, and the living tissue that was uncovered would dissolve in the salt water.

The colloids must have known that it was fruitless, too, but they flowed away from the flames and onto the inchoate body of the newborn monster. There were too many, though, and as the colloids swarmed up and down the neonate's gargantuan body, its shape became ever more distorted. Its chest grew unnaturally on first one side and then the other. One arm swelled to gigantic proportions, and a shoulder ballooned alarmingly.

The monster's face rippled and bulged. Its strange, vacant blue eyes showed no emotion as the volume of its body increased and shifted. Alex could not pity it; it was an abomination.

Despite the danger, the newborn began to climb awkwardly down the granite face. One of the rowboats was drawing up, and the neonate attempted to board it.

Shina aimed at the boat and shot some holes in it, along with the man rowing it. The guerrillas opened fire on the half dozen other boats manned by third-stage infected, making short work of them all. The third-stage infected swimmers were shot, too.

But there were still hundreds of colloids swarming over the island. Now Alex sensed that the aliens knew there was no escape for them. The best they could do was save their creation. Once again, they rushed the guerrillas.

Alex let them have it with the flamethrower, watching with satisfaction as black smoke poured out of their boiling remains. He swept the flame across the other colloids, their horrid cries echoing inside his skull like the wailing of damned souls in hell. They backed away from him, but there was nowhere for them to go—the neonate could not stand any more weight on its newly formed bones, they could not go into the water, and the finite space of the island afforded them no place to hide.

Alex advanced slowly, sweeping fire from one side to the other, making sure that he cooked every last one of the colloids. When he was through, the island was completely cloaked in the most fetid smoke imaginable. What had been living creatures were nothing more than bubbling bits of black ooze.

They were all dead, all except for the horror they had spawned here on Liberty Island.

Alex turned the flamethrower toward the neonate. It stared back at him without understanding. It seemed to know nothing, as if the colloids had not given it a brain. Perhaps it was only that, like its creators, it did not possess emotions that corresponded to those of humans.

Alex didn't care. The monster had to die. He pointed the flamethrower at it. He squeezed the trigger.

"Nighty-night, snookums," he said.

Nothing happened.

Shaking the flamethrower, he tried to fire it again.

Again, nothing happened. The battery would no longer strike a spark.

"No!" he screamed.

The colloids, squirming on the limbs of the neonate, were pleased. Flesh and bone displaced itself, writhing happily at this unexpected turn of events.

"Jesus Christ!" Alex howled. "How could we come this far and have this happen?"

"It's all right," Shina shouted to him. "We'll just shoot the fucking thing."

"No, we can't kill it that way," said Jo. "And once its skin coheres, the water won't be able to stop it, either."

The neonate, who had been staring at Alex from eye level, began to climb back up onto the granite. It clambered awkwardly over the guard rail and stood towering over them.

Alex could see skin forming over the featureless crotch, slowly working its way up. The human hands of the third-stage infected could no longer shape the flesh, and so the monster would never be the perfect prototype that the colloids had wanted, but it was still alive.

It reeled toward them through the drifting smoke. The last few guerrillas had no choice but to fall back. Alex stood there cursing at the monster, but Jo and Shina tugged at his arms, pulled him away from danger.

"Back to the boat," Jo said. "It can't get off the island yet. Maybe we can think of some way to stop it."

As they backed away, Alex took one last look at the hated travesty of humanity. Its transforming features seemed to smirk at him, as if it somehow understood that its assailants had failed. But perhaps it was only the wriggling, unformed flesh that made it seem to express so human an emotion.

They retreated onto the decaying planks of the pier and boarded the fireboat once again.

"The kids," Alex said as soon as they hit the deck. "They were in the pilothouse." He climbed up and flung open the pilothouse hatch. There, sitting in a corner with Jack's head on her lap, was Ronnie.

"He hit his head when we crashed," Ronnie said. She wiped at a bloody cut on Jack's forehead.

"I'm all right," Jack said weakly.

"They're all dead," Alex said. "The only thing living on the island now is the neonate."

"Why didn't you kill it?" Jack asked.

"Because bullets don't seem to do the job, and the goddamn flamethrower's out of whack."

"What about that can Dick Philips was carrying?" Ronnie asked. "Wasn't there something in those?"

"Can?"

"Yeah, shaped like the gas tank on my Harley, only with bumps on each end."

"Of course! A napalm canister!" Alex was on his way out of the pilothouse as soon as the words were out of his mouth. He leaped down to the deck and fell on his ass, but got up and started looking for the canister.

Had Dick Philips carried it onto the island? Alex glanced at the piles of bodies and the black, smoking remains of the colloids—and saw nothing that looked like a canister of napalm B.

At that moment the neonate lurched around the side of the statue's pedestal, making a loud, strangled cry as it stumbled toward the fireboat. Its sudden appearance was bad enough, but as Alex looked into its face he saw something that had not been there before.

The colloids had activated all the centers of its semi-human brain now, and their intelligence shone in the monster's blue eyes. The neonate would soon receive and absorb the telepathic knowledge of millions, perhaps billions of colloids.

But not yet. It was still transmogrifying, shapeshifting before Alex's very eyes as it reeled drunkenly about the island, making its clumsy way toward the fireboat.

Where was that canister? Alex dashed around the deck, the surviving guerrillas staring at him, doubtless wondering why he was taking exercise while the monster was coming closer. Only Jo knew what he was doing.

"The napalm!" she cried. "Does anybody know what happened to it?"

Polly pointed toward the neonate. Alex stopped and looked, seeing the monster crush corpses beneath its dripping feet. There, directly in its path, was a metal canister.

CHAPTER THIRTY-NINE

The slimy death's-head face of the neonate showed a glimmer of understanding. It looked down at the canister, hesitating for just a few seconds.

Alex leaped onto the pier, feeling the wood giving way under his bootheels. He scrambled for shore as the beams collapsed. The rotting wood tumbled into the frothy salt water, but he was a step ahead of the collapsing pier.

Now he was sprinting toward the canister, the neonate jerkily coming toward him. Its huge strides should have got it there first, but Alex's more practiced movements evened up the race. In a dead heat, the gap shortened to thirty, twenty-five, twenty yards. The guerrillas shouted encouragement somewhere far behind him.

The neonate, hunched and horribly determined, stretched its oozing fingers toward the canister as it came within ten yards of its goal. But Alex was close now, so close that he feared that man and monster would reach their mutual destination at the same instant. The madness welled up in him, threatening to blow him apart if he didn't get there first.

He dived and rolled the last twelve feet, and came up like a fullback in the end zone. Holding the heavy canister, he scrabbled to his feet and tried to run, but something held him back.

The monster had him, one of its gigantic, oozing hands on his shoulder and the other closing around his waist. Alex struggled, but he could not free himself. The neonate lifted him high into the air, as easily as if Alex were the newborn and it the adult.

No matter how much he squirmed and kicked, Alex was powerless in its awesome grip. It held him in one hand and lifted him up to its eye level. Its crawling features split in a demonic grin, long sticky strands stretch-

ing across its spade-like teeth, as it expressed the delight
of all the colloids feeding its awakening brain. Their
nemesis was in their grasp, literally.

Alex had only one option. He must drop the canister
and burn both the neonate and himself. He had no desire
to become a martyr through an act of self-immolation,
but it was the only way. Surely it would be quicker than
what was in store for him otherwise. If the detonator
worked, the canister of napalm B—magnesium casing
and all—would go up, consuming him and the monster
almost instantly.

A loud pop sounded over the creature's gurgling voice,
as its head whipped back. For a moment Alex thought
that he had dropped the canister.

But now he saw that the monster's right eye had been
shot out. Viscous, black glop issued from the socket as it
howled in anguish. Alex could see its vocal chords working, like the strings of a violin. Its fingers convulsed,
almost crushing him, and then relaxed.

Alex fell to the hard granite, his body cushioning the
canister. In spite of the mania, he was overcome with
pain. He felt as if his back were broken, and he didn't
seem to be able move his legs. He stared straight up into
the face of the wailing monster. Its huge hands covered
its face as it howled like a hurricane. It scooped up the
black goo running from its exploded eyeball and stuffed it
back into the socket.

As Alex watched, the eye began to reshape itself.

Dazed, he felt hands on him again. But these were not
the neonate's; they were human hands. They helped him
to his feet, and he saw that they belonged to Jo.

"Hurry, Alex," she said, "inside the statue."

He was barely able to walk, but with Jo's help he
began to limp toward the immense pedestal. The monster, preoccupied with restoring its damaged eye, did not
follow them. It didn't even seem to notice that they were
gone.

A metal door at the base of the statue was ajar. Jo
guided Alex toward it, and they somehow made it inside.

"Gotta close it," Jo said.

Still holding the canister, Alex put his shoulder against

it, and so did Jo. The rusted door didn't budge at first, but then it groaned and moved a fraction of an inch.

The monster cackled triumphantly, its eye completely healed. It cast about, looking for Jo and Alex. Instead, it saw Stubbs, who had just climbed up onto the pier. He glanced at the monster fearfully, and turned to try to get to the fireboat. But the demolished pier seemed too much for him, and he hesitated. At that moment the neonate lurched and stretched out a hand, scooping him up like a steam shovel.

Stubbs screamed and kicked, but the monster held him fast. Then, as casually as a child might pluck the petals of a daisy, it pulled off his right arm. Wailing as the blood sprayed out of the empty socket, Stubbs flailed with his left arm. But the neonate caught that one, too, and jerked it off with ease.

"Jesus Christ!" Alex said as he strained at the sheet metal door.

The neonate tired of Stubbs's pathetic cries, and, grasping him by the torso, wrenched him in two. Casting down the bloody halves, it turned its attention back to the search for Alex and Jo. As they nudged the door an inch or two further, the sound attracted it, and it turned toward them.

Letting out a terrifying roar, it advanced. Alex and Jo redoubled their efforts to shut the door, but the salt air had done a good job of locking it in place. Still, they moved it by increments as the creature stalked steadily toward the Statue of Liberty. The sweat stood on Alex's brow as he strained. But the monster was looming larger and larger through the opening. With a tremendous effort, they closed it a few more inches. But it was still far from shut.

The neonate was at the door now. It pounded on the metal, each blow slamming the door back with a resounding clang. Its free hand reached inside, dripping sausage fingers groping for them.

"Hey, you ugly motherfucker! Over here!"

The pounding stopped as the neonate turned to see who was shouting at it. Shina stood perhaps fifty feet away, pistol pointed at the hideous creature. She fired, the bullet missing as it spanged against the metal door.

The report echoed loudly through the interior of the copper statue.

Angered, the neonate forgot about Alex and Jo. It lumbered toward Shina, a liquid growling erupting from its malformed throat.

"Yoo hoo!"

Confused, the creature turned toward Ronnie, who taunted it from fifty yards across the way. It looked from one to the other, as both women fired at it.

Alex and Jo glanced at each other, put their shoulder to the door, and shut it with one terrific effort. The monster's pounding had knocked some of the rust off the hinges, actually making it easier for them. There was a heavy bolt on the door, which they easily shot into place.

"Got to get up to the top," Alex said. He knew that Shina and Ronnie would not be able to distract it for long. He had to drop the napalm from a sufficient height so that he and Jo wouldn't be cooked, and that meant that they had to go all the way up to the statue's crown.

"I'll take the canister," Jo said.

Alex shook his head, though she already knew his thoughts. It was too heavy for her. He would have to carry it up it spite of his pain. Holding it like a baby, he started up the stairs.

Already, the pounding at the door had resumed. The neonate had figured out the ruse and was ignoring its tormentors. It wanted Alex, and it wanted him now. The force of its blows began to dent the door. It worked on the weakened spot until the top of the door began to bend inward. A shaft of light penetrated the gloom as the opening became larger and larger.

Alex struggled up the stairs, gasping under the weight of the canister despite Jo's help. Each step was an agony, but he kept going. It was no longer mania that gave him strength, but the knowledge of what was at stake.

The neonate was out of their sight now, but the shriek of twisting metal echoed through the statue's interior. It would be inside in minutes.

Alex tried to climb the stairs more rapidly. The pain was too intense, though, and he almost blacked out. If he dropped the canister now he would kill Jo—and the neonate would live. He had to keep going.

They were inside the statue's head now, the concave imprint of Liberty's face looming large. But they had to go higher. The openings in the crown were what they needed.

But Alex couldn't go on. Even with the sound of the crumpling sheet metal door floating up from the statue's base, he couldn't do it. He fell back against the railing, dripping with sweat.

"You've got to go on, Alex," Jo said, tugging at his arm. "I can't do it. It's too heavy. You've got to keep going."

Alex nodded, his ragged breathing too labored for him to speak. He pushed himself away from the railing with one foot and staggered upward the last few steps.

Jo helped him to one of the openings in the front of the crown. Alex leaned out and peered down. Far below, he could see the impossibly huge creature bending back the sheet metal furiously, trying to get inside. It had been unable to smash the door in because of the heavy bolt, so it would crumple the sheet metal, pull it out, and toss it away. It was only seconds from doing just that when Alex dropped the napalm B.

The canister tumbled end over end, diminishing in size as it went. It hit the granite and erupted in a fiery torrent that engulfed everything around it. Flames cascaded up the front of the statue like a blazing waterfall in reverse.

The neonate hissed and staggered across the granite slabs, bathed in a gel of inflamed polystyrene, benzine, and gasoline, burning at over fifteen hundred degrees Fahrenheit. The creature turned in circles, arms outstretched, blindly trying to find its way to the water. Its screaming was the most nightmarish sound Alex had ever heard. At last it fell to its knees and toppled over, cinders flying from its quaking limbs.

It shuddered for several minutes, and then was still. The flames gradually died down and only the blackened bones, thick as steel girders, smoldered in the morning sun.

CHAPTER FORTY

Six survivors returned in the fireboat's punts, Jack manning the oars of the one in which Jo and Alex rode. Shina, Polly, and Ronnie were in the other. Alex stared back at Liberty Island, watching the smoking black hump. He almost expected the neonate to resurrect itself and come after them. Logically, he knew that it was impossible, of course, but he was well past caring about logic at that moment.

The choppy water made the little craft bob around a bit, but he didn't care about that, either. Jo held him tight as they neared the docks of Manhattan.

The infected at South Ferry had dispersed, and the waterfront was deserted now except for the guerrillas who stood on a wharf waiting for the survivors to return. Rowboats passed the punts, sent out to bring back the dazed guerrillas on the floundering fireboat, as well as any survivors who were still in the water. As the two punts approached the wharf, a line was thrown down. Jack caught it and secured it to a piling.

Alex had to be helped onto the wharf. He was sure that he hadn't suffered any broken bones, though he considered that a miracle.

There was no cheering, in spite of their victory. Too many of their comrades had died on Liberty Island for them to celebrate today. A few of the guerrillas who had stayed ashore had been killed in skirmishing, too.

A little knot of twenty-eight people gazed silently out at the smoke rising from Liberty Island, as Shina rowed the other punt to the wharf. A moment later, she and Ronnie stood in silence with Jo, Alex, and the rest of the guerrillas.

At last Shina spoke, saying, "It's too cold to stand here all day. Besides, we got us some hunting to do."

Most of them murmured in agreement, and turned away from the harbor. Jack hesitated, waiting to see if Alex would need more help.

"It's all right, son," Alex said. "You and Ronnie go ahead."

That left only Jo, who embraced Alex fiercely. "We won," she said.

"Yeah," Alex agreed, tears in his eyes. "We won."

The sun was high over the ocean as they turned to join the others. For the rest of their lives, Alex and Jo would share one another's thoughts, and this knowledge consoled them after all that they had lost.

The guerrillas had already come such a long way, but it was only the beginning. There was hope now, at least . . . and perhaps something more than hope. Through the horror of recent days, a glimpse of eternity had been revealed to Alex and Jo, a vision of the stars. They had reason to believe that once the human race regained its birthright, there would be no limit to what men and women could achieve.

They walked back through the ruins of the city, tired but eager to rebuild their world.